Meet ~~cute~~ Disaster

THE DEMPSEY SISTERS

D.E. Haggerty

Also By D.E. Haggerty

My Forever Love
Forever For You
Just For Forever
Stay For Forever
Only Forever
Meet Not
Meet Dare
Meet Hate
Bragg's Truth
Bragg's Love
Perfect Bragg
Bragg's Match
Bragg's Christmas
How to Date a Rockstar
How to Love a Rockstar
How to Fall For a Rockstar
How to Be a Rockstar's Girlfriend
How to Catch a Rockstar
A Hero for Hailey
A Protector for Phoebe

A Soldier for Suzie
A Fox for Faith
A Christmas for Chrissie
A Valentine for Valerie
A Love for Lexi
About Face
At Arm's Length
Hands Off
Knee Deep
Molly's Misadventures

Chapter 1

Disaster – the meaning of my life

AN ELDERLY WOMAN WEARING a bright pink t-shirt with the words *Gossip Gal Party Helper* printed on it marches my way and halts smack dab in front of me.

"You're next," she declares and the group of elderly ladies with her – all wearing matching bright pink t-shirts – nod at her declaration.

Next? For what? She can't possibly be talking to me. I have no idea who this woman is. I look behind me but no one's there except my sisters, Cassandra and Elizabeth. None of the other attendees at this petting zoo engagement party – yep, you read those words correctly – are around.

"E-e-excuse me?" I pause and take a deep breath to stop my stuttering. "Who are you?"

She gestures toward the group of women standing with her. "We're the women who are going to make all your wishes come true."

All my wishes? Can she rid me of my shyness? Can she erase all the mistakes I've made over the past two years? Trust me. I made some doozies.

"Are you a genie? I don't see your bottle." Elizabeth pretends to search the ground for a bottle.

"We're not genies," says another woman. "We're the best dang matchmakers the town of Winter Falls has ever seen."

Winter Falls put the Q in quirky. Its claim to fame is being the first carbon neutral town in the world, but it should be famous for being crazy pants. Don't believe me? They had an honest to goodness pagan festival for Midsummer's Day. If goats running around Main Street isn't proof enough, there was a limbo contest, too. It was awesome.

I would love to live here, instead of being stuck in a house with two of my sisters who think bickering is a national sport. It's not. What it is, is annoying. Sigh. Maybe someday I'll be brave enough to move out on my own again.

"I have a list of possible matches here for Gabrielle."

For me? I don't know who this woman is. How could she possibly have a list for me? How does she even know my name?

"Matches?" Cassandra asks. "As in love?" She feigns gagging as if saying the word love is poisonous.

"What other kind of matches are there?" the woman asks.

"Better you than me," Cassandra claims as she rubs her knuckles over my head. Ah, the time-honored tradition of the noogie. Don't you just freaking hate it?

"Leave her alone." Elizabeth shoves Cassandra off of me.

Sisters. Can't live with them, not willing to do the prison time for their disappearance. And sister number three isn't even here today.

"I wish Olivia was here," I say.

Olivia is the 'missing' sister. She's not missing as in no one knows where she is, although she is the queen of 'hey, guess where I am?'-middle of the night phone calls. No, she's missing as in she didn't re-locate to Colorado from Saint Louis with Cassandra, Elizabeth, and me when we followed our brother, Beckett, here after he landed the CEO position at *Clean Mountain Environment.*

Cassandra rolls her eyes. "Why, Gabrielle? So, she can ruin Beckett's day?"

It's technically not Beckett's day. The petting zoo engagement party – yeah, I never thought I'd say those words either – is to celebrate a friend's engagement, but my brother stole the show when he did this grand gesture to get his girlfriend Lilac back. It was super romantic.

I frown at Cassandra. She never has a nice word to say about Olivia. Does my oldest sister have problems? Yes, she does. But who doesn't? They need to cut her some slack.

"She doesn't ruin things on purpose."

Cassandra snorts. "And you're not naïve," she says before she pats the top of my head like I'm a child and walks off.

Elizabeth wraps her arm around my shoulder. "Don't listen to her. She's just jealous of Beckett and Lilac."

She's lying. Cassandra isn't jealous of anyone or anything. Why would she be? She does what she wants, when she wants and has no interest in a long-term relationship.

No, Cassandra is doing what she always does – making me feel like an idiot because I'm the youngest sister and she knows

I won't call her out in public. Being shy sucks ninety-five percent of the time.

"The older sisters are going to be a challenge," one of the elderly women says and I startle. I'd kind of forgotten they were standing here in front of us.

"Which is why we're beginning with the young one," another woman answers her. "Are you ready to listen to us, Gabrielle?"

Am I ready? Um, no. But I'm not the sort of person who can be assertive and walk away from people the way Cassandra did. I nod.

"First off, Phoenix."

At the name Phoenix, my pulse quickens and my belly dips. The goat farmer is gorgeous with a capital G. He has thick brown hair I want to run my hands through to discover whether it's as soft as it appears, light brown eyes always sparkling with humor, and a square jaw with two dimples on his right cheek. Dimples I want to explore with my tongue. Like I said – gorgeous.

But his looks aren't the best thing about Phoenix. No, his best character trait is how gentle he is with his animals. Trust me, I know. One of his goats, Pan, decided to eat my skirt at the pagan festival, but Phoenix didn't berate the animal. He gently but firmly removed the goat's teeth from the material.

Afterwards, he grinned up at me with his dimples showing as he apologized for his goat's behavior and – bam! – my crush was born. It's possible I even did some research about goat farming, although you'll never hear me admit to such out loud. No way.

"Phoenix doesn't want to be matched," I tell the group.

I might have accidentally overheard his brother say Phoenix is terrified of being matched. What? Eavesdropping isn't a crime. It's not my fault people forget about the shy girl.

I didn't understand the comment at the time. Matched? Who uses a matchmaker anymore? Apparently, I should have paid better attention. In my defense, who would think there's an honest to goodness group of women running around matchmaking the people in their town?

"Which is why we should match him first."

"He should know better than to think he can tell us what to do."

While the women bicker amongst themselves, Elizabeth pushes me behind her. "Go," she whispers. "Escape. I'll hold them off." I don't hesitate to rush off before the ladies realize I'm fleeing.

I glance at the different enclosures with various animals – including fennec foxes and llamas – but my feet carry me to the fenced in area where the goats are. I wonder if Pan is here, although I don't know how I'd recognize her. All goats kind of look the same to me.

I'm not fooling myself. I know I'm hoping to catch a glimpse of Phoenix while I'm here. There's no harm in looking.

I open the gate and step into the grassy area. A goat immediately rushes to me and bleats before chomping down on my skirt. This has to be Pan. At least, I hope not all of Phoenix's goats enjoy eating my skirts.

"And here I thought I wouldn't recognize you. How are you, Pan?"

I pet her for a few seconds before I decide I better free my skirt or I'll end up walking home in my panties. Gosh, no. I can embarrass myself just fine without walking around in my undies, thank you very much.

I tug on the fabric, but the goat isn't relinquishing her hold.

"Come on, Pan. Let go. You don't want me to go home naked, do you?"

Guessing by the way the goat continues to munch on my skirt, she isn't moved by my pleas. I scan the enclosure for anyone who can help and spot Phoenix. I pause to watch as he stalks through the grass. He's wearing a white t-shirt molded to his chest and a pair of faded jeans. His butt was made for wearing those jeans. It fills out the worn fabric to perfection.

Pan tugs on my skirt and I come out of my Phoenix-induced stupor. Oh right, I need help before a goat eats my skirt.

"Phoenix," I holler, but he doesn't hear me.

Shoot. I search the area but no one else is in the vicinity as most of the crowd has now migrated to the picnic tables near the barbeque. I contemplate my options. Stand here and wait until Pan has had her fill of my skirt or drag her across the field to Phoenix? Not much of a choice.

"We're going for a walk, Pan," I say as I start across the field.

I hope the goat will let go of my skirt as we proceed, but she has no problem munching away on my skirt and walking at the same time. Figures.

"Hey," I yell as I approach Phoenix, but he still doesn't hear me as he rounds the pen out of my sight.

"Hi, Lyric," Phoenix says, and I stop. I don't want to intrude.

"Hey, little brother."

I grunt. What is it with older siblings constantly reminding their younger siblings how they're the oldest? We already know the birth order. We don't need to be told we're the baby constantly.

"What's up?"

"Not much. Have you seen Beckett's sisters? They're a pretty bunch."

My eyes widen and I creep closer to make sure I don't miss a word of what they're saying. Yes, I'm officially eavesdropping. Although, in my defense, they're standing outside, which technically makes it overhearing and not eavesdropping.

"What are you? A member of the gossip gals matchmakers now?"

"Nah. But the youngest one, Gabrielle, seems to have a crush on you."

I wince. How does Lyric know? I didn't think I was being obvious.

"Gabrielle's nice." I cringe. Nice is a death knoll. No one wants a nice girl. "But I'm not interested in a relationship right now."

Dang. I should have known. I finally meet a man who I'm interested in, and he doesn't want a relationship. Figures.

"You need to get over her." Her? Who's her?

Phoenix growls. "I'm over her."

"Which is why you're running scared when a nice girl's interested."

"Gabrielle's soft. She could never handle life on the farm anyway."

I slam a hand over my mouth before anyone can hear me gasp. Soft? If nice is bad, soft is worse. Much worse.

"Your loss."

Footsteps approach. Shoot. Shoot. What do I do? I try to flee, but Pan is still latched onto my skirt.

"Stop it!" I yank at my skirt. It rips, but I manage to pull it out of the goat's maw.

I don't pause to check how bad the tear is. In a contest between a ripped skirt and a man realizing I overheard him tell his brother I'm soft and nice, a ripped skirt wins every dang time. I bolt across the field as fast as my short legs will take me.

"Gabrielle!" Phoenix cries my name.

Shoot. Shoot. Shoot. Does he know I was eavesdropping? I feel my face heat until it's the color of an overripe tomato. There's no way I'm turning around now.

I'm such an idiot. Why would I think Phoenix could ever want me? I know better. I'm worthless as a girlfriend.

Chapter 2

Home Sweet Home – a place where unwanted visitors drop in without invitation

I SET THE BOX down on my new bed, in my new bedroom, in my new apartment and smile. It happened. My dream came true. I have a place of my own for the first time since moving to Colorado. Don't get me wrong. I love my sisters, but no twenty-eight-year-old wants to live with her sisters if she can help it. Especially when one of those sisters thinks it's her job to 'help you break out of your shell'. No thanks.

Besides, living in Winter Falls is going to be interesting. The town of 1,001 people is the very definition of eccentric. Don't believe me? Cars are banned in town. Seriously. Or I guess I should say cars with gas-turbine engines are banned. Told ya. Eccentric.

Lucky for me I own an electric car since my brother, Beckett, jumped on the green train after he was made CEO of an environmental engineering company.

"I don't like this."

Speaking of my brother.

"Don't like what?" I ask. As if I don't know.

"

His girlfriend, Lilac, follows him into the room. "What's wrong with this apartment? It's perfectly adequate for a person living on her own."

Oh boy. Living on my own is exactly the problem.

Beckett wraps an arm around me and hauls me near. "Don't you want to stay in White Bridge with us?"

I push him away or, rather, I try. Beckett's six-foot-tall to my measly five-foot-two. He also works out whereas my idea of exercise is speed walking to the café when there's a sale on hot chocolate. Pushing him is equivalent to trying to move a freight train – impossible.

I huff. I want to tell him he's not my dad and he can't choose where I live, but the words would be cruel since Beckett raised me and my three sisters after our parents passed away. I'm grateful he did as we would have ended up separated in foster care otherwise, but he needs to accept we're adults now and stop trying to control our lives.

"Do you want to live with two of your sisters?"

He ruffles my hair. "Do I get to choose which two?"

"Me!" Cassandra declares as she enters the room. "Obviously, he wants to live with me."

"But I don't have any trellises for you to climb down from."

She shrugs. "No biggie. I don't need to sneak out anymore."

Cassandra was the queen of sneaking out when we were growing up. Poor Beckett didn't know what to do with her. Although, her antics couldn't compare to Olivia's. She was brought back home by the police more times than I can count.

Not me. I was the good girl. Beckett had enough baloney to deal with considering my two oldest sisters thought rules were for 'sissies'. I wasn't going to add to his problems.

Beckett groans. "You girls gave me gray hair."

"Gray hair is hot on older men. Don't you think, Lilac?" Elizabeth says as she too joins us in my bedroom.

Lilac's brow wrinkles. "Are you trying to make Beckett appear attractive to me? You do know I moved in with him already."

And I thank the stars in heaven for it. Lilac moving in with Beckett is how I ended up with this place since it's her old apartment. She has six months left on her lease and asked if I wanted to live in her apartment for the remaining time. For once, I didn't ask whether Elizabeth or Cassandra wanted the opportunity first. No, I snatched it up with both hands.

"Hellooo!" someone shouts.

"Maybe the welcome wagon has arrived," Elizabeth says before bounding away.

I follow her to the front door where the elderly women I met at the engagement party last week are standing in the open doorway. Today they're wearing hot pink t-shirts with the words *Welcome Wagon* on them. They must have a fondness for hot pink.

"Yep." Elizabeth nods. "It's the welcome wagon."

"Time for introductions," one woman says as they march into my apartment. I have to scooch out of the way before she runs me over.

"I'm Sage. I'm the leader of the group." She indicates the woman next to her. "This is Petal. You can go to her for all your sexy candle needs as she owns *Sensual Scents.*"

Sexy candle needs? What is she talking about? I don't get a chance to ask before she continues with the introductions.

"And this is Feather. If you have any questions about sexy books, she's your woman. She also owns the ice cream store, *Feather's Frozen Delights.* Clove is standing next to her. She owns *Clove's Coffee Corner.* And, finally, Cayenne. She manages *Earth Bliss,* the yoga studio."

I should probably be writing this down. I'll never remember all of their names.

"H-h-ow can I help you?"

Ugh! I hate it when I stutter, but they're making me nervous – barging into my house and making themselves comfortable. Do I offer them drinks or kick them out? Who am I kidding? I'd never kick anyone out.

"We're here to discuss your potential matches," Sage announces with a wide smile on her face.

Potential matches? The flush from my stutter disappears and the blood drains from my face. Surely, they don't think they're going to matchmake me? I know they said they're the best matchmakers in town, but don't I need to agree to be matched before they begin?

"Uh oh. I know pink symbolizes love and kindness. I didn't realize it also symbolized busybody." Elizabeth's eyes widen when she realizes what she said and she slaps a hand over her mouth.

Cassandra hip checks her. "Ignore her. She's prone to saying awkward shit when she's nervous."

"No worries, dear." Petal pats Elizabeth's hand. "We actually prefer the term busybody."

"But then we realized gossip gal has a certain ring to it," Cayenne adds. "Don't you think?"

When everyone fixes their attention on me, I force a smile. "Yes?"

"Now." Sage removes a notebook from her oversized bag. "I've got the list ready for you, Gabrielle." She sits on the sofa and pats the spot next to her. "Perhaps you should sit down for this."

I eye the door opening. I wish I were the kind of person who could run away or tell these women to get out of my home, but I'm not.

Cassandra notices where I'm looking and slams the door shut before smirking at me. Dang it! The woman is such a pot stirrer. I'd never actually say those words to her face, but I can certainly think them. And maybe fantasize I actually said them later on today when I replay this conversation in my mind over and over again.

Sage slaps the spot next to her. "Sit, Gabrielle."

My body obeys without my permission, and I end up with my toosh planted on the couch.

"I already told you Phoenix is our first choice. But, if you prefer, I have more names."

She raises an eyebrow at me, and I shrug since I don't trust my mouth to speak without stuttering.

"The other possibilities are River, Peace, or Cedar."

"You're being ridiculous," Lilac says as she enters the living room. Her hair is a mess, and her lips are swollen. "Cedar doesn't even live in Winter Falls."

"Did you have a quickie on Gabrielle's bed?" Cassandra raises her hand as if to high-five Lilac. When Lilac merely frowns at her hand, Feather slaps it.

"This is better than reading those sexy romance books," Feather says with a grin on her face.

Someone, please shoot me now. My brother and his girlfriend had sex on my bed while I was in the other room with five elderly ladies who want to find me a boyfriend. Could my life get any more embarrassing?

"We don't need the list. Gabrielle has already chosen a man." Elizabeth winks at me.

I bury my face in my hands. Ask and thy shall receive.

"Well, who is it?" Sage asks.

"Phoenix," Cassandra and Elizabeth respond in unison.

This is why I need a place of my own. I never said a word to my sisters about my crush on Phoenix but somehow they sussed it out. Maybe if I'm not around them all the time, I can have a semblance of privacy.

"This is going to be our biggest challenge yet."

I peek between my fingers to figure out who spoke. It's Petal of the sexy candles, although I've yet to puzzle out what sexy candles are. I don't think I want to know.

Beckett grunts. "You are not matchmaking my sister with a goat farmer."

"Hey!" I drop my hands from my face to glare at him. "What's wrong with a goat farmer?"

"Besides him not wanting to be matched?" Oh yeah. Beckett was there when Lyric told everyone Phoenix didn't want to be matched. He turns to Lilac. "Do you know why?"

She frowns. "I believe I do know, but I'm unsure whether I'm at liberty to tell you."

There's no need for her to break whatever promise she made. I know why Phoenix doesn't want to be matched. He's still in love with *her*. Whoever *her* is. He doesn't want me anyway. I'm too 'nice' and 'soft'.

"It's okay, Lilac. I don't need to know." Or rather, I'd prefer not to hear anyone say Phoenix is in love with another woman in front of me ever again.

"But I do," Cassandra insists. "I want all the dirty details."

Lilac frowns. "Details can't be dirty."

Lilac has a tendency to interpret everything literally. It annoys the hell out of Cassandra, but I think it's amusing. To be honest, if it annoys Cassandra, it amuses me. Although, I'm not finding anything amusing about this conversation.

Sage slams her notebook shut and stands. "It appears we have work to do."

She struts out of the apartment with a wave and the rest of the group file after her.

"What just happened?" I ask as I stare at the door they left through.

"I believe you've been officially accepted into Winter Falls," Lilac says.

My eyes widen. "I have?"

"You may want to stay out of the way of the gossip gals, though. They can be quite meddlesome."

"I think they're awesome."

I roll my eyes at Cassandra. She would think they're awesome. I wouldn't be surprised if she asks to join their ranks. She may think love is for suckers, but my sister lives to meddle in other people's lives. Or maybe she sticks to meddling in her sisters' lives?

In any event, I'm taking Lilac's advice and staying out of the way of the gossip gals. They're scarier than Cassandra when she's on the warpath.

Chapter 3

Fantasy – imagining something you really, really want but think you can't have because you're an idiot who's living in the past

PHOENIX

No matter how many times I enter *Electric Vibes,* I'm always surprised by the hippie vibe the bar has, although nothing hippie should come as a surprise to me considering I grew up in Winter Falls.

After all, the town was founded by hippies. And my parents, although not original founders in Winter Falls, embrace all things hippie. It's how I ended up with an organic goat farm after they retired since I took over the farm.

"Hey, Phoenix, where are your goats?" Lennon asks.

Lennon owns *Electric Vibes.* His real name isn't Lennon. He changed it because his hero is John Lennon. He also tries to emulate his hero by copying the Beatles' appearance of shoulder-length hair, round glasses, and shaggy beard.

"At the farm where they belong."

My brother, Lyric, arrives and claps me on the back. He's wearing a shit-eating grin. His fiancé, Aspen, must be nearby. Since the two of them reunited, they've turned into horny teenagers. I'm happy for them, but he could make some effort not to throw his sexcapades in my face.

"River already got us our first pitcher."

He nods to where our brother is sitting. Naturally, he isn't alone. He never is. There's a bevy of women surrounding the booth vying for his attention. I swear all he has to do is snap his fingers and women come running.

"Ladies, these are my brothers Lyric and Phoenix."

Lyric holds up his hands as he sits down. "Not available."

At his words, the women swivel their attention my way. "Not interested," I grunt as I sit across from Lyric.

River whispers to the woman nearest to him and she nods before leading the rest of the women away. I frown at his antics. It's a good thing Winter Falls pulls in an abundance of tourists. Otherwise, my brother would have caused a riot amongst the local women by now.

"Thanks for leaving all the ladies to me." He smirks as he stretches his arms along the back of the booth.

"Whatever," I mumble as I pour myself a beer.

"I don't need to ask how Lyric is doing," he remarks.

Lyric grins. "Nope."

"The wedding is a little over a month away. You ready to tie yourself down to one woman?"

Lyric glares at River. "Don't put your inability to commit on me. I know how it feels to have the love of a good woman."

I had the love of a good woman once upon a time, but she couldn't handle my life as a farmer. I warned her it would be hard work. She said she didn't mind. But she sure as hell did mind when she couldn't go shopping with her girlfriends every day in town. What the hell kind of shopping is there to do in Winter Falls anyway?

"How's it hanging?"

I groan at the question from Forest. He owns the local pet shop, *Unleashed.* He also thinks wearing pants is equivalent to torture.

River chuckles. "I don't know, Forest. How is it hanging?"

Forest grunts. "All bunched up now. Damn tourists. Lilac said I had to wear pants or go home." He pulls at the crotch of his pants. "This shit is uncomfortable."

Lyric frowns. "What's uncomfortable is watching you play with your crotch."

Forest raises his hands in surrender. "Oh no. The po-po is in the house."

Lyric rolls his eyes. He's the chief of police in Winter Falls and the locals love to give him hell about his job despite having elected him to the position.

"I'm off duty. If you have any problems, you need to phone Peace."

He's talking out of his ass. He's never 'off duty' unless Aspen has him in her grips – literally.

Lyric's face lights up. "Hey, Sunshine." Speaking of Aspen. He tags her waist and pulls her onto his lap before kissing her. I glance away. I have no interest in watching my brother make out with his fiancé.

My gaze lands on a woman with long blonde hair in a booth across the room. My pulse quickens when I realize Gabrielle is here. She twists her head to the side, and I'm treated to her beautiful face. Light green eyes I want to drown in, high cheekbones, and a slightly pointed nose and chin.

She's sitting now, but I know she's a tiny thing. The top of her head barely reaches my chin when she's standing, which means she'd fit perfectly in my arms. I shove those thoughts out of my mind. No. She wouldn't fit perfectly. I've learned my lesson about women. I'm better off talking to my goats.

River elbows me. "Go talk to her."

I force my gaze away from Gabrielle. "Talk to who?"

"Don't play the stupid game with me. I know you were giving Gabrielle googly eyes."

"What the hell are googly eyes?"

"You should join us," Aspen says from her spot on Lyric's lap.

"I thought we were having a guy's night out."

She snorts at my response. "You're at the one-and-only bar in Winter Falls. Did you think you could get away with sitting by yourself in the corner?"

Actually, yes, I did. Otherwise, I would have stayed home with my goats.

I stand. "I should probably get back to the farm."

Aspen springs to her feet and grabs my hand. "You should probably let your hair down once in a while."

While River pushes me from behind, Aspen drags me across the room toward the table where Gabrielle is sitting with her sisters. Since Gabrielle's brother, Beckett, is together with Aspen's sister, Lilac, everyone knows each other. Of course, in a small town like Winter Falls, everyone knows everyone anyway.

River brings a chair over, but I get shoved into the booth next to Gabrielle. I glance over at her. Her hair is shielding her face. I want to gather those silky strands together in my fist and pull until her neck is exposed to me. I clear my throat and shift my legs as my pants suddenly tighten.

Bloody hell. I shouldn't be thinking those types of thoughts about Gabrielle. She's entirely too nice and innocent for the likes of me. She wouldn't last a day on the farm.

"Hi, Phoenix," she murmurs, and I want to hear her gasp my name in her soft voice after I've kissed her silly.

Crap. I need to get the hell out of here. The woman has a crush on me. I can't encourage her. No matter how much I might want to, it's a bad idea. I slide to the side, but River blocks my exit. He winks at me, and I snarl at him.

"I'm Cassandra. Gabrielle's big sister." The smile drops from her face, and she narrows her eyes on me. "And gatekeeper."

Gabrielle huffs as her cheeks darken. "You are no one's gatekeeper," she mumbles in a soft voice.

"Yeah," says the other woman in the booth. "You can't guard the gate when you're always sneaking out of it." She waves to me. "I'm Elizabeth by the way."

"We should get a pitcher of margaritas."

No sooner are the words out of Aspen's mouth than Lennon is setting a pitcher of strawberry margaritas down on the table.

"It's been a bit boring around here since your sister got knocked up. Have at it."

Lyric groans. "Boring is good."

"Mr. John Q. Law, aka Mr. Boring himself, strikes again," Lennon grumbles before marching off.

Aspen giggles. "I guess Lennon forgot about how you and your brothers enjoy skinny dipping in the falls."

Gabrielle's eyes widen. "You skinny dip? As in swim without any clothes?"

I wiggle my eyebrows. "Without any clothes is the definition of skinny dipping."

I didn't think it was possible, but her cheeks darken further. The blush travels down her cheeks to her neck. I want to follow the pink skin to discover where her blush ends.

Damn it. No. Gabrielle is soft. She'd be eaten up at the farm.

"When does this happen? I need to make a note in my calendar." Cassandra whips out her phone.

Elizabeth knocks it out of her hands. "You are not going to play peeping Tom."

"Don't worry. I won't be playing. It'll be real." Her eyes sweep over me and my brothers, and she licks her lips.

Aspen growls at her. "No one sees my fiancé naked except me."

"No worries. He has two scrumptious brothers I can feast my eyes on."

Gabrielle grunts, but she doesn't say anything. Disappointment fills me. No. I refuse to be disappointed. I need to stop with these fantasies. Gabrielle will never be mine.

"What else do you do for fun around here in this Podunk town?"

At Cassandra's question, the music screeches to a stop, and quiet descends on the bar. Podunk and Winter Falls do not belong in the same sentence. There's nothing dull or insignificant about this town.

"I believe Ms. Cassandra of the big city of Saint Louis has thrown down," Forest announces from the small stage.

"Holy crappola, do you have listening devices planted all over the bar?" Cassandra claps and squeals. "Awesome. How does this throw down work?"

She jumps to her feet and throws her arms in the air. "I accept your challenge."

"Please say the challenge is someone hogtying and gagging her," Gabrielle mutters, and I burst out laughing.

River stands. "I'm in."

Cassandra rushes off and River chases her. Elizabeth frowns at them. I hope she doesn't want my brother, because to say the man is a player is a vast understatement.

Lyric grunts. "I guess I better go make sure they don't burn down the town."

"I wouldn't worry about fire. Cassandra's afraid of it. I would worry more about her breaking into the brewery and trying to drink her weight in beer," Gabrielle says.

"Wouldn't be the first time!" Gabrielle and Elizabeth chant in unison.

Huh. Did I misjudge her? Is Gabrielle stronger than she appears?

Nah. It's wishful thinking. I know better. No woman can handle living out on the farm with me no matter how gorgeous and sweet she is. I've learned my lesson already.

Chapter 4

Family — people who drive you crazy but who you are obligated to love anyway

"YOU'RE HERE," CASSANDRA SAYS instead of greeting me when I enter Lilac and Beckett's house.

"Of course, I'm here. Where else would I be? It's a family dinner. Did you expect me to bail on you?"

"Can't I be excited by a visit from my sister who moved far, far away?"

I roll my eyes. "I moved to Winter Falls from White Bridge. It's a thirty-minute drive. Stop being melodramatic."

"I'm not being dramatic."

Elizabeth snorts from behind her. "When aren't you being dramatic?"

The two begin to bicker about the definition of dramatic. I want no part of their arguments and go in search of Lilac. I find her in the kitchen.

"How can I help?"

"You can phone your brother and tell him to come home immediately."

My eyes widen. I've never heard Lilac sound frustrated before. Normally, she's the definition of calm, and I can't help but wonder whether she has emotions.

"What's wrong?"

She huffs. "Friday nights are supposed to be family dinner nights. Beckett is required to be here as he's part of the family."

"Since when are Fridays family dinner night?"

"Since Lilac joined the family and decided we needed a family get together ritual," Elizabeth answers from behind me.

"Fine by me. One less night for me to cook." Cassandra raises her hands in victory.

Elizabeth shoves her. "You never cook anyway."

"Maybe not, but you give me a guilt trip every time it's 'my' turn to cook and I don't."

This is why I jumped at the chance to move to Winter Falls. Sharing a home with my two sisters who live to argue with each other was getting on my last nerve, especially since I work from home.

My decision to move had nothing to do with the proximity of the apartment to Phoenix's farm. Nothing at all. Now to tell myself those same words another gazillion times and maybe I'll actually believe them.

"Let me phone Beckett," I say and retrieve my phone from my purse.

I unlock it and notice yet another message from *him. Why are you hiding from me?* Ugh! Why can't he let me be? It's been over a year since I left. Let me go already.

My phone beeps with another message. *I will find you.*

"Who is it?"

I peer up from my screen to discover Lilac, Elizabeth, and Cassandra staring at me. I duck my chin to allow my hair to cover my face.

"No one," I mumble.

"Don't lie to us!" Cassandra shouts.

"I'm not lying," I lie.

"Yes, you are. You're displaying several indicators of lying. You're averting your gaze, your hair is hanging down hiding your face from view, and you're fidgeting," Lilac says.

Did I mention in addition to Lilac not displaying emotions she's a walking, talking encyclopedia?

"Lying is bad," she continues.

She also doesn't believe in lying. Not even tiny white lies to make someone feel better.

"Maybe it's none of our business," Elizabeth suggests, and I want to throw my arms around her and hug her for giving me an out.

"Bah! Everything about Gabrielle is our business," Cassandra claims. The meddlesome sister strikes again.

Oh, how I wish I was one of those people who could tell my sister where to shove it. Or, at the very least, march out of this house without looking back. But I'm not.

I don't enjoy making waves or causing trouble. I don't want anyone to be upset. I want everyone to get along and be happy. It's not too much to ask, is it?

"Gabrielle is entitled to her privacy," Lilac says.

I told you I approved of my brother's choice of this woman. Now, to get them married off before she realizes how overprotective and overbearing Beckett can be.

Cassandra grunts. "You really don't know how this sister thing works."

"I have four sisters. I believe I am fully acquainted with how the dynamics of the family relationship work."

Lilac's four sisters – Aspen, Ellery, Juniper, and Ashlyn – are even crazier than my three, which is saying A Lot.

Ashlyn is the youngest. She's definitely a wild child. She's also married to former NFL quarterback, Rowan Hansley. Aspen is the oldest. She's engaged to Phoenix's brother, Lyric. After her is Ellery who owns *The Inn on Main*. She's engaged to Cole and has an adorable baby girl, Willow. Lilac is next and then there's Juniper. Juniper manages the *Wildlife Refuge* outside of town and is engaged to Maverick Langston. Yes, *the* Maverick Langston – everyone's favorite rom-com hero.

"She's got you there," Elizabeth sings.

Cassandra crosses her arms over her chest. "Agree to disagree."

"You can't agree to disagree. It's an utterly ridiculous saying."

Cassandra ignores Lilac. "We need to know what's going on with Gabrielle to avoid another Olivia situation."

"Uh oh. She pulled the Olivia card."

"What are you talking about? Olivia and I have nothing in common." I realize how harsh my words sound and backpedal. "I don't mean to say there's anything wrong with our oldest sister, but I am not her. Have you seen me being brought home by the police? No, you haven't. I've never even been in the backseat of a police car."

"You aren't missing much," Cassandra mumbles before raising her voice. "I don't mean Olivia being a troublemaker. You'd need a complete personality change to become her."

"Please tell me you realize a personality change isn't possible."

Cassandra shoves her palm in Lilac's face before continuing, "I mean Olivia's break from the family."

"You think I would break from the family?" She must be joking. This family is the only thing I've got.

Elizabeth wraps an arm around my shoulders. "I know you wouldn't break from this family."

Cassandra plants her fists on her hips. "What about the six months before we moved when she hardly talked to us and skipped all the family gatherings, huh?"

Shame washes over me. Why did I let Patrick isolate me from my family? How did I let him?

Elizabeth tightens her arm. "I hate – seriously hate – to agree with Cassandra but she's not wrong in this instance."

I sigh. I might as well give in. I can't win when Elizabeth and Cassandra team up.

"Fine. The text was from my ex-boyfriend."

"Charles?"

Charles was the last man I introduced to my family. I never introduced them to Patrick. At least, I wasn't a complete idiot where he was concerned. Of course, Patrick calling my family a bunch of orphans he didn't care to meet didn't hurt either.

"No, Patrick."

"Who's Patrick?"

"You had a boyfriend we didn't know about?" Cassandra's eyes couldn't get any wider. "I don't know if I should be proud or appalled."

"It wasn't serious," I claim.

"Is she lying again?" Elizabeth asks Lilac.

I speak before Lilac can call me out for lying once again. "It wasn't serious on my side. Patrick on the other hand…" I shrug as I let my words trail off.

"And he's unhappy you moved away?" Cassandra guesses.

"Mm-hum."

It's not a lie if you make a noncommittal sound, right? Because there's a chance I told Patrick I needed to meet with a client in Chicago before hightailing my butt to Colorado with my family.

"Does he eat pineapple?" Lilac asks.

My brow wrinkles. What a bizarre question. "Um…"

"In my experience, there are two types of people. Those who eat pineapple on their pizza and those who think pineapple on their pizza is disgusting and refuse to eat the pizza even after the pineapple has been removed."

"Okay?" I'm unsure where she's going with this.

"I can send this Patrick Hawaiian pizza with pineapple on it in the middle of the night for weeks. I can even arrange for him to pay for it."

Cassandra's mouth gapes open. "Oh, my word. I think I'm in love. And here I thought glitter bombs were the ultimate revenge."

"Patrick loves pineapple."

Lilac purses her lips together. "Never mind."

"But he hates mushrooms. He won't even touch a pizza if mushrooms have been on it."

She smirks. "Excellent."

"Can you really ensure he has to pay for the pizza himself?" I ask. Cassandra's not the only one in awe of our future sister-in-law.

"Naturally. It's not difficult."

Cassandra claps her hands together as if she's praying and bats her eyelashes at Lilac. "You have to teach me. Can you imagine the revenge pranks I could play?"

Elizabeth groans. "I don't think we have enough money for bail if you learn how to hack."

"Please, I'd never get caught."

"You don't even know how to hack yet and you're already claiming you're invincible."

"I didn't say invincible, but Lilac can teach me how to cover my tracks."

Lilac bites her lip. "I don't think Beckett would approve of me teaching you any of my tricks."

Cassandra bats her eyelashes. "He doesn't have to know."

"I don't lie."

"But—"

"No, before you say omitting the truth isn't a lie, let me stop you there. It is a lie."

Cassandra opens her mouth to argue with her once again, but the door opens and Beckett shouts, "I'm home," before she gets the chance.

"It's about time," Lilac mumbles before shuffling down the hallway to greet him.

"We'll keep this amongst ourselves for now," Cassandra says as if she's doing me a big favor.

I wish. She's not doing me a favor. She's keeping the information from our big brother because she wants to spring it on him at some unsuspecting moment how she knew something before he did.

Whatever. As long as I don't have to talk about my jerk of an ex-boyfriend with my brother, I can go along with her.

Chapter 5

Embarrass — the moment a bunch of old biddies tell everyone and their dog about your 'no longer much of a secret' crush

PHOENIX

"Hey, bro, nice of you to join us."

I glare at Lyric. He knows damn well and good I don't want to be here, but River suckered me into coming to the town's monthly business meeting. I usually avoid the hell out of these meetings as everyone spends more time gossiping than conducting business.

I don't give a crap what the latest gossip is. I believe in 'live and let live'. Apparently, I'm in the minority as the majority of the residents of Winter Falls enjoy gossiping almost as much as they love sticking their noses in other people's business.

"I'm going to kick River's ass," I grumble.

Lyric slaps my back. "He can't help it he had a tourist group today."

I snort. Sure, he could. River always has a tourist group since it's his job as a tour guide.

Unfortunately for me, River has several other jobs on top of giving green tours of Winter Falls to tourists. He's a volunteer firefighter and police deputy when needed. He's also the town secretary and takes minutes at these meetings. And yet, here I am prepared to fill in for him.

"You really should learn not to play poker with him."

I snarl at the humor in my brother's voice. What I need to learn is not to use an IOU as a chip. I won't be forgetting my wallet again.

"I don't think I should be here."

At the sound of Gabrielle's voice, I turn to find Ashlyn, the current mayor of Winter Falls, dragging her into the town hall.

"You shouldn't mess with the mayor," Ashlyn says.

At Ashlyn's announcement, Gabrielle comes to a halt. "You're the mayor?"

"And the best damn mayor Winter Falls ever saw."

"I think I need to see some proof," Gabrielle mumbles.

"Dream girl," Rowan, Ashlyn's husband, growls, "will you stop dragging the poor girl around?"

He snatches his wife's hand away from Gabrielle.

"But I didn't usher her to her seat yet."

"I'm fine," Gabrielle says, but when she scans the room for a place to sit all of the seats are suddenly filled with purses or bags or coats. She begins backing up toward the door. "Maybe I should leave."

"There's a seat right there, missy," Sage yells and indicates the chair next to me.

I rub a hand down my face. I should have seen this coming. It's a setup. No wonder every chair in the room was suddenly occupied. Those damn gossip gals.

River doesn't have a tour. He's probably sitting at home enjoying his free time. He better thank his lucky stars he's not on the gossip gals' hit list. I'm getting my name scratched off the list as soon as I can.

I stand to glare at Sage. "I'm not one of your experiments."

"Experiment?" She places her hand over her chest. "Would I ever?"

Yeah, she would but arguing with her is the same as talking to a brick wall – a complete waste of time.

"I shouldn't be here. I'm not a business owner anyway," Gabrielle mutters.

"Really? I guess someone else owns *Gabrielle Go Viral*," Ashlyn says loud enough for everyone in the room to hear.

Gabrielle's cheeks darken and she ducks her chin. "H–h–ow did you know?"

Ashlyn indicates her sister, Lilac, who's sitting in the front row with her other sisters Aspen, Ellery, and Juniper. The West daughters should come with a warning label – Caution: Will sell your secrets for a pitcher of margaritas.

They wave to Gabrielle, and Juniper lifts her beer bottle. "Welcome to the chaos."

"They have beer at the monthly meeting?"

"And snacks." I indicate the back of the room where Lennon has set up a stand selling beer and popcorn.

"Sit down, Gabrielle." Ashlyn points to the chair next to me, and Gabrielle drops into it. The smell of cinnamon and apple wafts toward me and I clench my jaw to prevent my moan from escaping. Nothing smells better than apple with cinnamon.

Bang. Bang. Bang. Ashlyn pounds the gavel on the table. "Let's bring this meeting to order."

I open my notebook and write down the time.

"What are you doing?"

I frown at Gabrielle's question. "Apparently, I'm playing secretary today."

"Playing secretary? Who's usually the town secretary?"

"My asshole brother."

"Phoenix Apollo Alston, don't speak about your brother with such language."

I sigh. "Yes, Mom."

Is it wrong to wish my parents would go on another year-long voyage to 'discover' themselves? Their year in Bali was cut short when Lyric and Aspen got back together after a decade-long misunderstanding.

Their trip was inspired by Mom reading *Eat, Pray, Love.* Maybe I should buy her *Zen and the Art of Motorcycle Main-tenance.* Dad has always wanted to buy a motorcycle.

"Your mother is here?" Gabrielle's gaze darts around the room until she notices my mom waving at her. Her eyes widen and she tucks her chin to her chest.

"The first order of business is the upcoming Lammas festi-val." Ashlyn motions toward Lilac. "You want to bring every-one up to speed, Ms. Keeps Her Eyes on the Money All the Time?"

"Why is Ashlyn calling on Lilac?" Gabrielle whispers.

"She's the town comptroller."

"Is there anything Lilac can't do?" she mumbles as she watches Lilac stand and march to the front of the room.

"Boo! Boring!" The gossip gals in the back heckle her.

Lilac bristles. "There's nothing boring about ensuring one of our many annual festivals makes money for the town. We depend on the proceeds for maintaining the streets, the school—"

"But we're rich now," Feather interjects.

"No," Lilac insists. "Almost all of the proceeds from the treasure—"

"The missing loot!" Ashlyn corrects.

Lilac's nostrils flare but she perseveres. "Have been allocated for the community center."

"What are they talking about?" Gabrielle asks.

"It's a long story, but basically Ashlyn and Aspen recovered the money a bank robber had hidden in Winter Falls over sixty years ago."

She gasps. "You're kidding."

"Nope. They dug the money up themselves."

"This town is awesome."

Is she serious? I study her face for any signs of deception, but she's smiling and her eyes are sparkling. She's even bouncing in her seat a bit. Maybe Gabrielle is worth taking a chance on after all.

"Aren't you supposed to be writing all of this down?" she asks when she notices I'm not taking notes.

"I think the meeting notes are supposed to be limited to actual town business."

"I guess your mom scolding you for swearing isn't included." She giggles.

I let the sound of her laughter wash over me. What I wouldn't do to hear the sound in my house every day. But it's an illusion. She wouldn't last a day at the farm. Hell, she barely moved to Winter Falls a few weeks ago. There's no telling if she has any staying power yet.

"As I was saying." Lilac tries to bring a semblance of order to the meeting. "We need to ensure we aren't overspending in the lead-up to the Lammas festival."

"No one wants to talk about the Lammas festival," Sage yells.

The door slams shut, and Old Man Mercury enters. A hush falls on the crowd as he limps to the front row on his cane.

"I want to talk about the Lammas festival," he claims before starting to lower himself into a chair. Gabrielle rushes to help him sit down. He bats at her hands. "I don't need any help."

She nods but remains next to him until he's safely seated. She smiles at him, and he grunts before she returns to the chair next to mine.

"Who is he?"

Before I can answer, Aspen greets him, "Hi, Mercury."

He frowns at her before motioning for Ashlyn to proceed.

"Old Man Mercury," I lean close to whisper my answer to Gabrielle. I immediately regret the action when the scent of apples and cinnamon hit me.

"He's one of the original town founders." He's also a grumpy old man whose house is haunted, but he has exceptional hearing, so I don't add those traits to my explanation.

"No more of your interruptions," he orders the gossip gals.

"Don't be a fuddy duddy, Mercury," Sage says.

"Yeah, Mercury," Feather agrees, "we have to continue our matchmaking or the whole town will die out."

"The town would have died out long ago without us already. Who do you think made sure the West sisters were all matched up with local men, so they'll have their babies here and won't move away from town?" Petal asks.

Juniper raises her hand. "My man isn't local."

"You don't count, honey. Everyone knows you'd never leave the animals out at your *Wildlife Refuge*."

"What about me?" Lilac asks. "Do I count? My partner isn't local either."

Clove snorts. "She's funny. As if she'd abandon our town any sooner than the animal obsessed one would."

Mercury bangs his cane on the floor. "I said no more interruptions."

"We have to interrupt. We can hardly pair Gabrielle and Phoenix up if we're mute, now can we?"

At Sage's words, Gabrielle gasps.

"I'm not... I mean... I don't..."

She fans her hands in front of her face, but it doesn't help to dispel the bright color now painting her cheeks.

"Don't worry about it. It's just the gossip gals. No one listens to them," I lie in an attempt to soothe her.

"Yes, they do," Sage claims, "and we listen to the townspeople, which is how we know Gabrielle is the best pick for you since she already likes you."

Gabrielle squeals and jumps to her feet. Her eyes are wild as she glances around the room. Her mouth gapes open, but no words come out. She slams it shut again before sprinting out of the room.

I close my notebook and stand. "You should be ashamed of yourselves."

"We didn't—"

"No!" I interrupt. "I'm talking for a change."

Sage snaps her mouth shut.

"You embarrassed her. Gabrielle is a brand new resident in town. Since when do we embarrass new members of the town? We should be welcoming her with open arms. But no. Your group," I point my finger at Sage, Feather, Cayenne, Clove, and Petal, "mortified her. I'm ashamed of the lot of you."

I bend down and retrieve Gabrielle's purse before stalking out of the room.

Chapter 6

Trouble – the moment you realize your crush is more than just a little crush

I RUSH OUT OF the town meeting into the hallway and hurry for the doors. I lift up my— Shoot. Dang. Gosh. And Darn. I forgot my purse.

I start for the door to the meeting room but stop a few feet away. Nope. I'm not going back in there. Not when I was a complete ninny and ran out not two minutes ago.

But who can blame me? Those gossip gals are terrifying. It's bad enough I have a crush – an unrequited crush no less – on Phoenix, but now everyone knows! Including Phoenix.

I feel my cheeks heat with the idea of him knowing how I feel about him. I mean he probably figured it out before. What with me turning into an awkward high school girl whenever he's around, not to mention Lyric spilling the beans about my crush, but it's different *knowing* he knows.

I pace the hallway as I contemplate what to do. If I could pick a lock, I'd be gone. Forget about my stupid purse.

What a great way to begin my life in Winter Falls. I will forever be known as the jumpy girl who got embarrassed and ran away from a meeting.

This is exactly what happened my freshman year of high school. Well, not exactly. No one told the entire school about my crush on Jeremy – the star of the high school soccer team – but I may have sat down on a piece of chocolate during lunch break. Needless to say, the stupid thing melted and before I knew it, it appeared as if I'd pooped my pants.

Trust me. Poopy pants is not a nickname anyone wants to have. Even my scary protector big brother Beckett couldn't get the kids to stop calling me the name. Lucky for me – but extremely unlucky for her – another freshman peed her pants while climbing the rope in gym and my days as poopy pants were over.

Ugh. I bury my face in my hands. My life is one long tale of embarrassing episode after embarrassing episode.

The door to the meeting room creaks open and I scan the area for somewhere to hide – I have zero desire to talk to anyone right now – but there's nowhere to go. I'm standing in a hallway with a staircase. But wait. There! It's a small alcove halfway down the stairs.

I hunch my shoulders and make myself as small as possible. Footsteps click on the tile floor as someone walks along the hallway. I wait, but no one else exits the meeting room. Is the meeting not over yet? Why is someone out in the hallway if the meeting isn't over?

The footsteps draw nearer, and I dip my chin until my hair is covering my face.

"Gabrielle?"

Gosh darn it! Of all the people in Winter Falls, it has to be *him*?

"I can see you."

I'm not falling for his trap. Cassandra used to cheat at hide-and-seek all the time when we were growing up. She'd say she could see me and stupid me I'd step away from my hiding spot so she would indeed see me. Never again.

A pair of scuffed brown working boots appear at my feet. A hand brushes my hair out of my face and tucks it behind my ear. At the feel of Phoenix's hand on my hair, I shiver. I want to know how it feels to have his hands thread through my hair and massage my neck as his mouth devours mine. I do a full body quake at the vision those thoughts bring forth.

"I'm sorry."

Wait. What? Why is Phoenix apologizing?

"For what?" I croak. I clear my throat and try again. "For what?"

He chuckles, and I lift my gaze until our eyes meet. His smile causes the two dimples on his right cheek to make an appearance. My tongue longs to explore those ridges.

"For how my entire hometown acted. I'm sorry they embarrassed you."

At the reminder of why we're standing in this little alcove on the stairs, my face warms. With my light skin, I probably resemble a tomato.

"It's not your fault," I mumble.

"They should have never said the things they did."

You mean things like how I've got a crush on you? I think but don't say.

"It's okay."

A muscle twitches in his jaw and I'm unsure which attribute is more attractive – his dimples or his appearance as my defender.

"It's not okay."

"It is," I insist. "If I can survive being poopy pants in high school, I think I can survive everyone in town knowing I have a crush on you."

My eyes widen when I realize what I've said, and I slam a hand over my mouth. Phoenix peels my fingers away from my mouth and cradles my hand in his. My heart stammers in my chest at the feel of him holding my hand. Wow. If the mere holding of my hand makes my heart stammer, what would it feel like if he touched my chest or my—

I cut those thoughts off before I begin to pant and jump him. I mean, I don't think I'd jump him – I'm not the jumping a man kind of girl – but it's Phoenix, my normal reactions don't count here.

"There's nothing wrong with a little crush."

I'm thinking there's nothing little about my crush. In fact, the word 'crush' isn't big enough to encompass how I feel about this man who's doing his best to be gentle with my feelings.

And then I remember. He wasn't gentle when he didn't know I was around.

"I know I'm too nice and too soft for you." The words are out of my mouth before I can stop them.

He growls. "Who told you?"

You, I think but do I dare say it was him to his face? I bite my bottom lip and stare at the floor as I contemplate my answer.

His free hand moves to cradle my face. He uses his hold to lift my chin until I'm forced to meet his gaze.

"Who told you?"

"You did."

I gasp at my revelation. The hand holding mine spasms. "What?"

"Do we have to talk about this?" I whine the question.

"I think we do, Gabby."

Gabby? No one calls me Gabby. Probably because I'm the furthest thing from being a gabby person there is in this world. Me, chatty? Not hardly.

"Can't we pretend tonight never happened?"

"I prefer not to pretend."

Of course, he doesn't. He's freaking perfect. He has no reason to pretend. Unlike me. I pretend I'm not shy and embarrassing all the time. Sometimes I even pretend I'm doing karaoke in front of a crowd. Snort. Never gonna happen.

I stare into his eyes and the sincerity and determination are plain to see. Darn it all.

"You're not going to give in, are you?"

He smirks. "I never give in."

"I overheard you tell Lyric I'm nice and too soft to live on the farm," I blurt out before I can stop myself.

Phoenix swears under his breath for a good thirty seconds. I'm serious. I timed him. Not with a stopwatch – where would I get one of those? – but I can count Mississippily as good as any second grader.

His hand on my cheek rubs gently against my skin and it's all I can do to not close my eyes and lean into it.

"I'm sorry. It's nothing personal."

Not personal? Being condemned as soft felt awful personal.

"Lyric was pushing me, and I said the first thing I could think of to get him off my back."

My nose twitches as I consider his answer. I don't think he's telling the truth, but do I push him on it? Gosh no. I don't want this conversation to last any longer than it already has.

I force myself to meet his gaze. "I understand."

Big fat lie. Seriously, Lilac would lose her mind with the amount of lying happening in this stairwell at the moment.

"Thank you, Gabby."

At the sound of him using his nickname for me in a soft voice, I don't feel bad for lying. Not if he's going to gaze at me with soft eyes and squeeze my hand.

"Nothing to thank me for. It was all a misunderstanding."

And then I get a brilliant idea. "I'll forget all about what you said if you agree to forget about my my…" Dang it! You can say the word, Gabrielle. "…my feelings for you."

He grins. "You have yourself a deal."

"I should go." Before I give in to temptation and test how his grin tastes.

I manage to force myself away from him and descend two steps down the stairs. His hand tugs me back. Oops! How did I forget he was holding my hand?

"Did you forget something?"

To kiss you good-bye? What am I thinking? He's not asking to kiss me good-bye.

He holds up my purse. "This perhaps?"

"My purse," I shout, proving I'm a complete nincompoop, before I grab it.

This time when I rush down the stairs, he lets me go. Why wouldn't he? He doesn't want me. I may have said I believe him, but we both know he thinks I'm too nice and soft for him. So much for me forgetting about what he said. Although I knew the chance of me forgetting was pretty much zilch.

An ache blossoms in my chest at those thoughts but I ignore it as I rush down Main Street on my way home where I can hide from everyone and everything.

Chapter 7

Unrequited – a fancy word for describing when the man you want doesn't want you back

"You know," Cassandra says as she practically skips down Main Street. "The last time I came to a pagan festival in Winter Falls I was declared queen of the town."

Elizabeth shoves her. "You were not. No one was bowing down to you."

"But they should have."

Elizabeth grunts. "Me and my stupid mouth. I meant there are no queens in America. We're a democracy, not a monarchy."

"No take-backs. The good people of Winter Falls should bow down to me, so sayeth my sister."

Elizabeth sighs. "What is this festival about anyway?"

Why did I guilt trip my two sisters into coming to this festival with me today is the question I should be answering. Oh right. I know the answer to that question. I'm the town embarrassment and too scared to come to the festival by myself.

"It's Lammas. It's a day to celebrate the importance of the harvest according to Google." Google's my guide because I didn't stick around the business meeting to learn more about the festival.

"How do we celebrate a harvest?" Cassandra asks as she scans the area. "Do we have to kill all the adults to ensure a good corn harvest?"

I shiver at her reminder of the movie *Children of the Corn.* She tricked me into watching it when I was ten. I haven't looked at a cornfield the same since.

"Can we start with you? Since you're an adult and all. Supposedly," Elizabeth mutters the last word, but Cassandra hears her.

"I am an adult."

I roll my eyes so hard I'm afraid they're going to get stuck. Cassandra an adult? Not hardly.

"Gabrielle!"

I scan the area and discover Lilac's youngest sister, Ashlyn, waving at me. She's standing behind a booth in front of the bakery, *Bake Me Happy.* Awesome name. Baked goods always make me happy.

"What are you doing?" I ask as I examine the muffins, cupcakes, and mini pies.

She beams. "Helping my baby daddy out with his bakery."

Rowan growls next to her. "Stop referring to me as your baby daddy."

She flutters her eyelashes at him as she rubs her obviously pregnant belly. "Are you not the baby's father?"

His head falls back, and he stares up at the sky as if searching for answers. Poor him. I know from experience he won't find any up there.

"Do you have any sea salt caramel and chocolate cupcakes?" I ask before they can get into a squabble about her calling him baby daddy.

I haven't known Ashlyn long, but you don't need to be a genius to figure out arguing with her is futile with a capital F.

"Try this," Rowan says and hands me a mini-cupcake.

I pop the entire treat into my mouth at once and moan. "Will you marry me?"

When I realize what I've blurted out, I shrink away, but Ashlyn isn't offended. She threads her arm through his. "Sorry. He's all mine and I'm not letting him go. It was way too much work catching him."

"Dream girl," he chastises but there's a smile on his face.

"I'll have two of whatever heavenly delight I just tasted was." When Ashlyn hands me the bag, I ask, "How much?"

"No charge for members of the family."

"We're not technically family."

She shrugs. "Close enough. My sister is marrying your brother."

Although her sister, Lilac, and my brother, Beckett, aren't engaged yet, I expect them to announce their engagement any day now. I caught Beckett researching engagement rings the other day.

"Does this mean all of your sisters are my sisters now?" Cassandra asks.

I don't know why Cassandra sounds excited. Ashlyn and her sisters – Aspen, Ellery, Lilac, and Juniper – put the crazy in crazy pants, although Ellery and Lilac appear somewhat normal.

"Of course!"

Elizabeth moans. "Great. More sisters I have to deal with. Herding cats would be easier."

"Tell me about it," Ashlyn mumbles.

"P-lease," Ellery says as she joins us with her baby, Willow, in her arms. "You don't herd cats. You throw them in the wind and laugh as chaos erupts."

Ashlyn grins. "Nothing wrong with a bit of chaos."

Ellery rubs her baby's back. "I can't wait until your baby is born."

Ashlyn rubs her swollen belly. "Me either. Me either."

More customers arrive and we shuffle out of the way. Ellery grasps my elbow. "I'm sorry about the meeting."

"What meeting? What are you talking about?" Cassandra asks.

Ellery's nose wrinkles. "Sorry. I thought they knew."

"Knew what?" Cassandra is like a dog with a bone.

"I tripped and fell down at the town business meeting." I blurt my lie out and hope she believes me.

Elizabeth snorts. "Better you than me."

"You don't fall all the time," I claim.

Another lie. I'm racking up the lies lately, but this one doesn't count. White lies to make a person feel better aren't lies. I don't care what Lilac says about the matter.

"Sure. And I didn't have to start wearing shorts underneath my skirts in high school because I kept flashing everyone every time I fell either."

"You're a trendsetter. All those mini-skirts have attached shorts nowadays."

"I need to go. My guests are waving me over." Ellery mouths *sorry* to me before leaving.

"What should we do now?" Cassandra asks as she twirls around in a circle. "I'm seeing lots of booths with stuff to buy or eat, but I'm not hungry and I'm not in the mood to shop."

"Let's keep walking. There's a big crowd up ahead."

We make our way down Main Street until we reach the town square. It's not a long journey. Winter Falls isn't a big town by anyone's imagination. Coming from Saint Louis, I'm experiencing cultural shock. But in a good way. Knowing all the residents in town is nice. Except for when everyone knows you have a crush on a certain goat farmer. I could do without *that* particular aspect of small town living.

"Holy batman! Is that a loaf of bread? I've never seen anything this big in my life." Elizabeth indicates the giant loaf of bread in the town square.

"Oh darling," River says. At the sight of him swaggering toward us wearing a fireman uniform, I have to fan myself. This man should not be living in a small town in Colorado. He should be strutting down a runway in Paris or Milan. "I can show you something big."

Elizabeth rolls her eyes. "What are you wearing? Is it dress up in the outfit of the person you want to be when you grow up day?"

Judging by the smirk on his face, Phoenix's brother isn't bothered by the snarky comment. "I'm a volunteer fireman. I put out fires of all kinds." He winks in case it isn't clear what kind of fires he's referring to.

Cassandra wiggles her eyebrows. "You can put out my fire anytime you want."

Elizabeth's shoulders fall at Cassandra's flirtatious remark to River. Huh. Is Elizabeth crushing on River? Talk about a disaster waiting to happen. River is a player in ALL CAPS. He's not intending to settle down any more than his brother Phoenix.

Baa.

Speaking of Phoenix. "Hey, Gabrielle," he greets, and I pretend my heart doesn't burn at hearing him use my given name.

"Hey," I practically whisper. Ugh! Why can't I be one of those girls who bats her eyelashes and flips her hair? I'm not. I'm the girl who covers her face with her hair. Such a loser.

"You doing okay after the meeting?"

My face flames at his question. Doesn't he realize I don't want to talk about it? And I certainly don't want my sisters knowing what happened. In fact, it's kind of amazing they don't already know.

"Geez, Gabrielle. You must have fallen pretty hard if everyone's worried about you," Cassandra remarks.

"Fallen?"

"You know. I fell." I plead with my eyes for him to go along with the story.

He clears his throat. "Yeah. You didn't hurt your knee too bad, did you?"

The air whooshes out of my lungs. Phew. His goat butts my hand and I scratch underneath her chin.

"Is this Pan?" I ask; eager to change the subject to anything in the world but the stupid meeting.

"Yeah. She wouldn't let me leave the farm without me bringing her with."

"She's such a good girl."

"Depends on how you define good girl," he mutters.

River rolls his eyes. "My brother the dorky farmer."

Phoenix shoves him. "Nothing wrong with farming. Or did you forget you grew up on a farm, too?"

River leans back as he pulls on the suspenders of his uniform. "And now here I am all grown up," he says and winks at Elizabeth who blushes in response.

Pan bleats before jerking on her leash and darting off. Phoenix holds on as she barges into a group of tourists. River notices all of the tourists are women and smirks.

"Duty calls, ladies." He swaggers off.

Cassandra crosses her arms over her chest. "You two are hopeless."

"What do you mean?" Elizabeth asks.

"You have to ask?" She points to me. "In love with a man she can't have." She points at Elizabeth. "In love with a man she can't have."

"Hey!" Elizabeth protests. "I admit he's pretty to look at, but I'm not in love."

I don't say anything, because I'm afraid Cassandra's right. I am in love with a man I can't have. Or, at the very least, falling in love with a man I can't have. I don't know what's scarier. Being in love with a man who will never return my feelings or Cassandra being right. Both scenarios scare the living daylights out of me.

Chapter 8

Railroad – when everyone decides they know what's best for you. Spoiler alert – they don't

"I'm home now," I say to Beckett over the phone as I open the door to my apartment building. He's such a worry wart.

"Are you in your apartment?"

I roll my eyes. "You do realize I now live in Winter Falls."

"Small towns can have crime."

I snort. "A crime in Winter Falls is when you use a plastic poop bag instead of a biological paper one."

I'm not making stuff up. The owner of the pet store, *Unleashed,* was handing out paper poop bags at the Lammas festival. I explained to Forest I don't own a pet, but he insisted I keep a few 'just in case'. In case of what?

"You should still be careful."

"I know, Mr. Overprotective."

I enter my hallway and notice something in front of my door. I check the other apartments but no one else has a package in front of their door. I must have gotten a delivery. Since I work from home, it's not unusual for me to receive packages.

When I step closer, I realize it's not a package. It's a bundle of flowers. My heart rate increases as I kneel to pick them up. Did Phoenix send me flowers?

I open the envelope and read. *Found you.* No. No. No. He didn't. I gasp.

"What's going on?"

I'm too busy trying not to hyperventilate to answer.

"Gabrielle, answer me or I'm coming over there. Right. Now."

"I'm fine," I claim but I'm wheezing as I say the words.

"You don't sound fine. I'm getting in my car now."

"No!" The last thing I need is for Beckett to learn about Patrick. He already treats me like a child. He'll have me locked up in my bedroom if he learns what a naïve fool I was.

"Is there someone in your apartment?"

"I haven't unlocked my door yet," I admit before I can think better of it.

"Go to the neighbor's. I'll be there in twenty minutes."

"It's a thirty-minute drive. Besides, there's no one in my apartment."

Patrick isn't waiting for me in my home. He was never physically violent with me. This bouquet of flowers is merely a threat and a reminder. I'm unworthy.

"Do not open your door."

I hear him switch his car on. Dang it. I don't want Beckett here. He won't understand. He'll make me feel stupid for falling for Patrick's charms. I am stupid for falling for his charms, but I don't need anyone rubbing my mistakes in.

"It's fine," I say.

I stare at my apartment door. I can be brave. I can enter my own apartment without anyone holding my hand. My hand trembles as I unlock the door, but I manage it. I throw the door open and shout, "Hello!" because everyone knows scary people run when you shout a greeting at them.

"Who are you talking to?" Beckett asks.

Oops. I forgot I still have my phone to my ear.

I scan the living room. Nothing seems out of place. The book I was reading before I left for the festival this morning is laying on the sofa, and my empty cup of coffee is on the end table. I sniff as I continue further into the apartment. It doesn't smell as if anyone's been in here since I left either.

"There's no one here," I tell my brother. "I'm perfectly safe."

"I told you not to go into your apartment," he growls.

I don't bother reminding him he isn't my keeper. He didn't listen the first million times I told him, why would he listen now?

"Go home," I try instead.

"We'll be there in fifteen minutes."

We? Who's with him?

"Shut and lock your door. We're coming."

Again with the we. I don't get a chance to ask who's with him before he hangs up. Rude.

I shut and lock my door. Not because he asked me, but because I'm a single woman living alone and I'm not stupid. Or, at least, I'm not always stupid.

I drop my bag and phone by the door before rushing to pick up my things. I'm not a slob, but I work at home and since this is a one-bedroom apartment, the kitchen table has turned into my office. I pile all my notes and papers together. There. Good enough.

A mere ten minutes pass before there's a knock on the door.

"It's me. Let me in," Beckett yells through the door.

"It's us, he means."

Great. Cassandra is here, too. Elizabeth won't be far behind.

I open the door to discover Beckett holding the bouquet of flowers. Dang it. I must have forgot them on my doorstep.

"Who sent these?" he asks as he barges inside with Cassandra, Elizabeth, and Lilac hot on his heels.

"Hi, Beckett. I'm fine. How are you?"

"Don't be cute with me." He waves the bouquet in the air. "Someone sent you flowers with a creepy message. Who was it?"

"Is it a creepy message?" Lilac asks, and Beckett glares at her. She holds up her hands in surrender. "The message said 'found you'. You might be taking the words out of context."

I mouth *thank you* to her and she smiles at me. Beckett's gaze ping pongs between the two of us.

"What's going on?"

This is when I wish I knew how to bat my eyelashes and act coquettish. Unfortunately, I didn't get the flirtatious gene. I tuck my chin in and let my hair hang in front of my face.

"No! No more hiding from me. Haven't you hidden enough from me for the past two years?"

"Year and a half," Cassandra corrects.

"What?" Beckett explodes. "Do all of you know what's going on?"

He scans the room and I duck my head. Elizabeth hums and averts her gaze. Lilac frowns at the floor. Cassandra beams up at him.

"Explain," he demands.

"It's Patrick," Cassandra says, and I gasp. I can't believe she betrayed me this way.

Elizabeth sidles close to me and pats my back. "Sorry, but you knew she'd tell the minute she could lord it over big brother."

"Who's Patrick?"

"Gabrielle's ex-boyfriend."

"You only recently learned about him. Don't act as if you met him because you didn't," Elizabeth chimes in.

"And you." Beckett points at Lilac. "I thought you didn't lie."

She plants her hands on her hips. "Don't you dare tell me I don't lie when you insisted I lie when we first started dating."

I've never heard Lilac angry before. She's always even keeled. Dang it. I can't let her and Beckett get into a fight because of me. They had enough problems getting to where they are in their relationship. I won't let my stupid problems cause issues for them.

"Don't be mad at her. I asked her not to tell you."

"Tell me what?"

I cringe at Beckett's angry tone. Elizabeth wraps an arm around my shoulders. "Go ahead. Tell him," she whispers.

"There's not much to tell. Patrick is my ex-boyfriend. He's not happy I moved away. End of story."

"Why is he sending you flowers saying found you?"

"Because he found me." At his growl, I hurry to elaborate. "I didn't tell Patrick where I was going when we left Saint Louis. I wanted a clean break from him."

There. I don't sound too much like a ninny, do I?

"You can't live here on your own," Beckett declares.

"What? Why not?"

"Because this Patrick asshole knows where you live."

"Maybe, but it's not as if he's here in Winter Falls."

"It's true," Lilac speaks up. "It'd be the talk of the town if there was a new resident."

Beckett cocks his eyebrow. "And what about if he's hanging around as a tourist during this Lamma festival."

"Lammas," Lilac corrects.

"My point stands."

She sighs. "I concede you may have a point."

Wait! What? Lilac's conceding. This can't mean good things for me.

"Pack your stuff. You're moving in with us."

I retreat a step. No way am I living with my brother and his girlfriend. First of all, ew. I already caught them in the middle of an extremely steamy make-out session – body parts were exposed for gosh sakes – once. I don't fancy entering the kitchen to— Nope. I don't want to think about it.

But worse of all? Beckett would suffocate me. Oh, he wouldn't mean to. He'd think he was being protective. Until I woke up at the age of fifty and realized I was an old cat lady.

"I think she should stay in Winter Falls," Cassandra says. Judging by the smirk on her face she has some trick up her sleeve.

"She can't stay here alone," Beckett insists.

"I didn't say she should stay here alone. I'm thinking she should stay on a farm outside of town."

I groan and cover my face with my hands. She didn't. She seriously didn't throw me under the bus.

"What farm?" Beckett walks right into her trap.

"Phoenix's farm."

Lilac taps her chin. "It's not a bad idea. The farm is isolated. They'd spot any strangers approaching. Plus, Phoenix knows how to fight."

Phoenix knows how to fight? I file the information away for consideration later. Right now, I need to get this train derailed.

"You can't decide I'm going to live with some random dude."

"He isn't some random dude. It's Phoenix."

The man who doesn't want me. Why the hell would he agree to me living with him?

"He isn't even here."

Lilac retrieves her phone from her purse. "I'll phone him. I'm certain he'll agree to help out. It's the Winter Falls way."

Chapter 9

Torture – when the woman you want but can't have is living in your house

PHOENIX

I can't believe Lilac conned me into doing this. But she said, 'it's the Winter Falls way', and I knew I couldn't refuse her. Damn her.

Having the woman, I desire but can't have, in my house is going to test my control, but not in a fun way like when I'm bringing a woman pleasure and holding off my own. No, it's going to be sheer torture with Gabrielle in my house.

At least, I managed to convince the rest of her family to go home and not follow us to the farmhouse. I don't need an audience to witness my torture.

I swing the door open. "Home, sweet home."

Gabrielle gasps and her eyes widen as she studies her surroundings.

"Holy cow, it's gorgeous."

I think it is. Women, however, usually disagree. On the right-hand side is a large dining area with a typical farmhouse kitchen. There are green Shaker cabinets on two walls with a large window over the farmhouse sink. The table is made from the wood leftover after I tore down the old barn. The chairs are mismatched as I haven't gotten around to replacing them yet.

Straight in front of us is the living room. On the left wall is a large fireplace I use to heat the house in the winter. Surrounding the fireplace is a sectional couch. There's none of that girly crap like throw pillows and blankets.

Gabrielle ignores the kitchen and the living room to approach the window seat on the far wall. She kneels on it while staring out of the window.

"This is the perfect place to read."

I imagine her laying on the seat reading while I'm watching football on television. I shove those thoughts from my mind. Gabrielle isn't here permanently. She's merely staying here while she deals with some asshole ex-boyfriend.

"Although," she begins again and tears my thoughts away from punching her ex in the face, "I don't know how much reading I'd get done with this view."

She motions out of the window to the foothills in the distance. I snort. She'd get tired of staring out the window soon enough. Women always do.

"Do you want the five-dollar tour?"

She glances over her shoulder at me and smiles. I have to lock my knees to stop myself from going to her and hauling her into my arms before molding my lips to hers.

"You sure it's not the fifty-dollar tour? Because this place is the shit." She squeaks and covers her mouth with her hand. "Sorry. I didn't mean to swear."

She's cute. Does she seriously think I give the first shit about her swearing? Obviously, I don't.

"It's fine." I motion toward the kitchen. "This is the kitchen."

She bounces up from the window seat and skips to the kitchen. She caresses the butcher block countertop and I'm suddenly jealous of a countertop.

"It's gorgeous. I love the black and white Spanish tiles. They match perfectly with the green cabinets."

I remove my ball cap and run a hand through my hair. "I don't know about those tiles being Spanish. I bought them at the DIY store in White Bridge."

She giggles. "Whatever their name is, they're gorgeous."

I indicate the living room. "This is the living room."

When she plops down on the sofa, she falls backward, and her legs fly into the air as the cushions swallow her. "Eek!"

I rush to her and grab her hand to help pull her out. She ends up plastered to me and I breathe in her cinnamon and apple scent. I want to bury my face in her hair while I slide into her. My cock twitches at the thought.

I try to push her away, but she looks up at me with a huge smile on her face. "Thanks. I didn't realize your couch was a carnivore eager to eat me up."

I groan. The couch isn't the only thing eager to eat her. I clear my throat and step away before I decide throwing her over my shoulder and taking her to my bedroom to live out all my carnal fantasies with her is the best idea I've ever had.

"There's an office through here." I lead her to the room past the staircase and open the door.

Her mouth gapes open as she spins around the space. "Wow. If I had an office like this, I'd never get any work done."

My heart warms at her words. I rebuilt this room myself, and I'm proud of how it turned out. I added built-in bookshelves on two walls and stained the wood to match the hardwood floor. My desk, an antique my dad used when he farmed this land, is centered in the room with a view of the farm out of the two walls of windows.

"What kind of work do you do?"

She bites her bottom lip and studies the floor. Her movements serve to make me more curious than I already was. Fuck me. I want to learn everything there is to know about this woman.

"You don't have to tell me if it's embarrassing."

Her eyes widen. "Embarrassing? What kind of work would be embarrassing? It's not as if I'm an online call girl."

She clamps both hands over her mouth. "I'm not," she mumbles through her hands. "I'm not."

I chuckle as I peel her hands away from her face. "I didn't think you were."

"I'm a social media manager."

"A social media manager?" I don't know what a social media manager is or why she wouldn't want to tell me.

Her eyes scrunch up and her chin falls to her chest. "No one believes me when I say I'm a social media manager," she mumbles.

I use my index finger to lift her chin up. "Hey now. I didn't say I don't believe you. I'm not clear what a social media manager does, is all. I limit my social media to Facebook, and I wouldn't bother with it at all except the town of Winter Falls has a page and residents are expected to keep up with it."

"Oh." She clears her throat and I drop my hand before I decide to cradle her face with it. "Basically, I manage the social media accounts for other businesses. I create content and post it for them, respond to comments, etcetera, etcetera."

"Why don't people believe you when you say you're a social media manager?"

She rolls her eyes. "Because I'm shy."

"You're not being shy right now with me." Although she is painfully shy at times, at this moment, she's being talkative.

She puffs out a breath of air and averts her gaze. "Because you make me feel safe," she mumbles.

I heard her perfectly the first time, but I ask her to repeat herself anyway, "What did you say?"

She throws her arms in the air. "You make me feel safe." She hurries out of the room. "What's upstairs?"

I don't bother hiding my grin as I follow her to the second floor. Keeping my hands off Gabrielle while she's living in my house may be torture, but it's also going to be fun.

"Which bedroom should I stay in?" she asks as she peers through the doors of the three bedrooms.

"The master."

"No way. I'm not kicking you out of your bed."

"You're not kicking me. Your feet aren't even moving."

She feigns kicking, and I chuckle. She's barely taller than five feet. What does she think her little kick is going to do to me?

"The master has an attached bathroom." Which means there's zero chance of me catching her walking down the hallway in nothing but a towel.

My mind latches onto the idea and runs with it. I imagine Gabrielle walking down the hallway with her hair hanging down her back and her hands clamped onto a towel barely long enough to cover her ass. She sashays as she walks, and the towel gapes open in the front just enough for me to glimpse a tantalizing strip of her bare skin.

I groan as my cock hardens and lengthens. I imagine reaching forward and whipping the towel off of her, exposing her naked body to me.

"Are you okay?" Gabrielle asks.

I slam the door on my fantasies. Nothing can come of them. No woman wants to live on a farm long-term, remember? Especially not one who grew up outside the town of Winter Falls.

"Fine. Let me show you the master."

I motion to the last door on the right.

"I don't want to put you out."

"Wait until you see the bathroom before you decide."

"The bathroom?" She rushes down the hallway and through the bedroom to the attached bathroom.

"Holy guacamole! You have a soaking tub!"

She rushes to the tub and climbs in, clothes and all.

"I think you're supposed to undress before you get in there." My cock hears the word undress and twitches. I turn away, so I can attempt to squeeze it into control.

"I think I need a swimming suit since this tub is big enough to swim in." She feigns swimming the breaststroke. "I didn't expect a goat farmer to have a huge bathtub."

I frown. I thought building this luxurious bathroom would convince her to stay. It didn't. Nothing I did changed her mind. The brand-new kitchen wasn't 'modern' enough. The living room sofa was too 'comfortable'. How the hell can a sofa be too comfortable?

"I'm sorry," Gabrielle whispers from directly in front of me. She must have climbed out of the bath while my mind wandered.

"Why are you sorry?"

She dips her chin, and her hair covers her face. Damn it. Shy girl is back.

"I didn't mean to upset you."

I allow myself to tuck her hair behind her ear but drop my hand before it can wander elsewhere. "You didn't upset me."

"You seem upset."

She's not wrong but, "It has nothing to do with you."

She winces and I realize I'm an asshole. Here I am thinking about another woman when the woman I want is right in front of me. No, asshole. You can't have her, remember? She won't stay.

"Don't forget, Gabby. You're safe with me." Hopefully, *from me* as well.

Chapter 10

*Eager – when you can't wait to dig into someone else's business and
cause trouble for them*

"Good morning." I wave to Petal as I stroll down Main Street.

"Make sure you stop by today," she hollers. "The new batch
of mood-enhancing candles is ready."

Mood-enhancing candles? I don't want to know what she's
talking about.

"I'm going to work at *Clove's Coffee Shop*," I tell her in the
hope she'll back off at my words.

"Tomorrow then," she says before rounding a corner.

Maybe getting no work done at Phoenix's place is better
than going in town? I thought working at the farmhouse
would be great, but I couldn't help myself from staring outside
the entire time. When I realized it was ten o'clock and I hadn't
posted a single update on social media, I decided I needed to
get out of there.

I smile as I continue down Main Street. Winter Falls resi-
dents may be crazy pants but the town itself is beyond adorable.
Main Street is full of locally owned and quirky stores. I pass
Bohemian Treasures, a jewelry store full of items 'carefully crafted

by the owner'. On the opposite side of the street is *Naked Falls Brewing*. I'd love to go there for dinner sometime. Craft beers are yummy.

There's a construction site between the jewelry store and *Bake Me Happy*. I believe this is where the community center is being built. A man in a hardhat waves at me, and I duck my chin and scurry across the street.

My mouth gapes open when I find myself standing in front of *Bertie's Recording Studio*. I've heard of this place. I have several indie bands as clients and a few of them have actually recorded albums here, but I didn't know the studio was in Winter Falls. How cool.

I force my feet to move again before someone thinks I'm some super fan stalker person. Next to the studio is *Eden's Garden*. I breathe deeply as the smell of lavender hits me.

Past the flower store is the town square. In the middle of the square is a small grassy park with a gazebo. On one side of the square are the courthouse and police station. The other side is the library. I could work in the library and not a café, but I need a shot of caffeine.

I cross the square and open the door to the coffee shop. Clove grins at me from behind the counter.

"Look what the cat dragged in."

I smile and order a large cappuccino. When she hands me the drink, I ask, "Do you have Wi-Fi?"

I try to pull my drink from her hands, but her grip tightens. "Do I have Wi-Fi?"

I'm confused. Does she not know what Wi-Fi is?

"You young whippersnappers are always asking about Wi-Fi."

I've never been referred to as a whippersnapper before. I'm not certain I know what one is, to be honest.

I swallow and force words out of my mouth, "Um, I need to work?"

I cringe when the words come out sounding like a question. Forget whippersnapper. I'm a total ninny.

"I don't understand all this working on computers and the line."

The line? "Do you mean online?"

"Online. The line. What's the difference?"

My nose scrunches up. "Nothing?"

Maybe I should have gone to work in the library.

"Does the library have Wi-Fi?"

"Gabrielle Grace Dempsey," Clove huffs.

"How do you know my middle name?"

She smirks. "We gossip gals know everything."

The bell over the door rings and Old Man Mercury enters. "She means they snooped in the public records." He glares at Clove. "You should know better."

Clove finally releases my coffee allowing me to step away from the counter, which I don't hesitate to do.

"Hi, Mr. Mercury." See? I can be brave. I'm not always a ninny.

He grunts at me. "It's Mercury. No mister."

"Oookay."

"Stop scaring the poor girl, Mercury," Clove scolds. "You old curmudgeon."

"I'm not bad tempered."

I beg to differ, but I won't be telling him he's a grumpasaurus out loud. Not me. But I can handle him. I'm used to grumpy dinosaurs after all. My brother was one until he met Lilac. Although, he can still be a grumpity grump on occasion. Such as when he's being Mr. Big Brother Protector.

"Please, if you're not bad tempered, I'm the Queen of Timbuktu."

"Timbuktu doesn't have a queen. It's a city in Mali," I mumble.

"What did you say?" Mercury barks and I jump.

Clove snaps a towel at him. "I told you to stop scaring her."

"I-I-I'm not scared." And I'm not stuttering either. Liar. Liar. Pants on fire.

"How are we going to convince her to stay in Winter Falls with Phoenix if you keep scaring the pants off of her?"

My eyes widen and I retreat a few steps. With Phoenix? Don't they know the man doesn't want a woman? Least of all me.

"You women and your infernal matchmaking. You're ruining this town."

"We are not! We're giving this town a new generation. If it weren't for us, the town would die out."

"Behave or I'll tell Sirius what you're up to."

She smirks and her eyes light up with excitement. "Are you going to tell him I've been a bad girl?"

Is Sirius her husband? Is she referring to her love life? I cringe. I don't need to hear the details of Clove's love life. Don't get me wrong. Good for her. Go, Clove! But I don't want any details. Time to sneak out of here.

I'm nearly at the exit when Clove asks, "Where do you think you're going, missy?"

I scan the area in the hope she's speaking to someone else, but the place is deserted except for Mercury. Where are all the tourists who were here this past weekend when you need them?

"Don't pretend you don't know I'm talking to you."

But I'm good at pretending. I can pretend all day long. I can pretend I'm not an idiot girl who fell for the wrong boy. I can pretend I don't have a monster-sized crush on Phoenix. See what I mean? Master of pretending right here.

I glance over my shoulder at Clove, and she gestures toward the wall. "The Wi-Fi code is there."

Dang. I need to be more observant. Patrick was always telling me not to live with my head in the cloud all the time. I frown. Patrick. What is he up to? Why is he sending me flowers? Why does he care? He said I'm useless. How can he possibly want a 'useless' woman back?

"Thanks," I whisper before scurrying to the table in the corner furthest from the counter.

When the phone rings and snags Clove's attention, I release the breath I was holding and pull my laptop out of my bag to get to work. I'm logging into the Wi-Fi when I realize she's talking extremely loud and knocking on the counter. I glance over at her.

"And I'm asking you what do you need her address for?"

Geez. Does she always talk this loud? I should have gone to the library. I could survive one morning of working without coffee even if it's Monday. And what's with the knocking?

"I'm telling you. We don't have anyone by that name in Winter Falls."

Good thing I stuffed my headphones in my work bag. I dig them out, but when I place them on my head, Clove snaps her fingers to get my attention and mouths *no*. What? Does she have some weird rule about wearing headphones in her café?

"Don't call me stupid, young man. I know who lives in my town and I know Gabrielle Dempsey is not one of the residents."

My heart stalls at hearing my name. Don't tell me Patrick is phoning everyone in town trying to find me since I'm no longer in the apartment he did find? What is wrong with him?

"If she's your girlfriend, you should have her phone number and know where she lives."

She snorts.

"I sincerely doubt *your girlfriend* lost her phone and forgot to give you the new number. Good day."

She hangs up the phone and lifts a brow at me.

"Is there something you need to tell me?"

"And me?" Sage asks as she rushes inside.

"I'll get Lyric," Mercury declares.

"There's no need to involve the Chief of Police," I claim.

He flicks a hand to indicate he heard me but continues on his way to the police station.

"Now, missy." Sage crosses her arms over her chest. "What kind of trouble are you in?"

I can't hold her gaze, but I do manage to speak without stuttering. "I'm not in trouble."

Clove snorts. "Which is why some man claiming to be your boyfriend phoned here searching for you this morning."

I fiddle with the tablecloth. "I don't have a boyfriend."

"Then, who's Patrick?"

My mouth opens but before I can figure out what lie to tell Sage and Clove, the rest of the gossip gal gang rushes into the café. Cayenne, Feather, and Petal are practically rubbing their hands together in anticipation.

"I can't wait to get started," Cayenne says and proves me right.

"Hold up." Lyric strolls into the room and glares at the women. "This is a police matter, not a gossip gal matter."

Sage rolls her eyes. "I bet it's both."

Chapter 11

Nosy – when a bunch of old ladies decide they have a right to know all of your secrets

THE CAFÉ IS SOON crowded with all of the gossip gals in attendance as well as Lyric, Beckett, Lilac, River, and my sisters. At least, Phoenix isn't here to witness my shame. Phew.

"Shouldn't you be working?"

"Yes, we should," Lilac answers, "but family emergencies have priority over work."

I gulp. "Emergency?"

"How else would you refer to your ex-boyfriend sending you flowers? And then, after you re-locate, trying to find your new location?"

Embarrassing because now everyone knows what a loser I am.

Beckett stares down at me. "It's time."

"T-t-time for what?" Whatever it is isn't going to be good.

"For you to come clean about this Patrick guy." Yep. It's not good.

"I don't know what you mean," I tell the floor.

"She's lying," Cassandra announces to the entire room full of people. Geez. Maybe there's someone in town who didn't hear her.

"Of course, she is, but I believe this is one of those situations where you don't allude to a person's inability to tell the truth," Lilac says.

Beckett kneels in front of me and grasps my hands. "Please, Gabrielle. Tell us what he did. Did he…," A muscle in his jaw spasms as he growls his question. "Did he hit you?"

My hands spasm in his. "He never hit me," I whisper.

Gosh. Does he think I'd put up with a man hitting me?

"What did she say?" Clove shouts her question.

"She said he never hit her," Cassandra shouts back.

I feel my face heat at how loud they are. Couldn't they at least keep their voices down? This situation is embarrassing enough as it is.

"Abuse doesn't necessarily encompass physical attacks," Lilac says.

"Thank you, Ms. Encyclopedia." I can practically hear Elizabeth roll her eyes.

Beckett ignores everyone around him. He releases my hand to lift my chin until I'm forced to look him in the eye.

"What did he do?"

I contemplate how I can answer without coming off as a complete moron. Patrick may not have hit me, but I still shouldn't have put up with what he did do. I should have dumped him long before I snuck out of Saint Louis and moved to Colorado.

"No one here will judge you."

I'm pretty sure everyone here is already judging me.

"I'm not judging you," Elizabeth says and begins to raise her hand, but instead of lifting her hand into the air, she smacks River in the face.

"Ow. Woman, pay attention to where you're throwing your hands."

"I'm not throwing my hands. It's not my fault I didn't notice you standing next to me."

"Didn't notice me?" River's brow wrinkles in disbelief. "I'm over six-foot tall. How could you not notice me?"

She pats his arm. "Now, now, River. There's no reason to get your panties in a twist because I didn't immediately start panting like a bitch in heat the second you entered the room."

River coughs. "A bitch in heat?"

She freezes when she realizes what she said. "I didn't…I mean… Let's concentrate on Gabrielle's problems, shall we?"

At her words, everyone in the room returns their attention to me. I promptly drop my chin and stare at the floor.

"What did he do?" Beckett repeats his earlier question.

Silence falls on the room as everyone waits for my response. A response I have yet to formulate. How do I explain what Patrick did? How he slowly isolated me from my friends and family? How he made me feel worthless? How he destroyed my self-confidence? How I let it all happen?

Lilac clears her throat. "I believe we don't need all of the details to understand what's happening here."

I want to throw my arms around her in thanks. I won't, because I'm not the type of person who spontaneously hugs others, but I want to.

Lyric kneels next to Beckett. "I agree with Lilac. We don't need the details, but I do need—"

"Ahem!" Sage clears her throat. "Are you sure we don't need the details for the police report?"

My eyes widen. Police report? What kind of police report? My breathing speeds up until I can't catch my breath.

Beckett rubs my back. "Breathe. Deep breaths in. Slow breaths out."

I stare into his eyes as I do as he says. After a few minutes, my breathing returns to normal.

"Police report?" I squeak.

Lyric smiles at me and my breathing hitches for a different reason. The family resemblance to Phoenix is obvious when he smiles.

"There isn't going to be a police report. Don't you worry."

"But how can we run him out of town if there isn't a police report?" Sage asks.

"Don't we need a restraining order?" Clove asks.

"I don't need no damn restraining order to run a scoundrel out of my town," Mercury declares.

Dang it. I forgot Mercury was here.

"We don't need to run him out of town." I glance up at Cassandra and notice she's grinning. Uh oh. She's up to no good. "There's a better way to get rid of Patrick."

"We don't condone violence in Winter Falls," Petal tells her.

"Who said anything about violence?" Cassandra asks. Uh oh. She's using the innocent me voice. Spoiler alert: Nothing innocent is ever said when she uses that voice.

"Killing someone is considered violent," Lilac explains.

Cassandra winks at her. "I never said I was going to kill Patrick."

"I wouldn't mind getting a few licks in myself," Beckett grumbles.

I hold up my hands. "No, no, no. You can't get in trouble for me. I'm not worth it."

He growls and snatches my hands to squeeze them. "You, Gabrielle Grace Dempsey, are my baby sister and are worth everything."

"Agreed." Elizabeth nods and crosses her arms over her chest.

"Oof." River grunts.

"What now?"

"You elbowed me."

She frowns at him. "You don't need to stand this close to me."

Cassandra huffs. "Doesn't anyone want to hear my idea?"

I don't, but I've learned to keep my opinion to myself when it comes to my older sister. She loves a good argument. Her words, not mine. There are no good arguments in my opinion.

"This is going to be good," Elizabeth mutters.

"Phoenix and Gabrielle should pretend to be a couple," Cassandra says before bowing as if we should applaud her.

The door slams shut. "What the hell is going on here?"

Awesome. Simply awesome. As if this day isn't mortifying enough, Phoenix has arrived to witness my shame. Go me.

"I love this idea. It'll be the same as the book we read a few months ago. What was the title again? *The Dummy Engagement*. No. That wasn't it." Feather taps her chin. "I'll think of it. Give me a minute."

Sage scowls. "I don't like it."

Cayenne chuckles. "The only reason you don't like the idea is because you didn't think of it."

Sage frowns and crosses her arms over her chest.

Petal rubs her hands together. "This is excellent. Those mood-enhancing candles are going to come in handy after all."

"What the hell are you talking about?" Phoenix's voice is loud enough to silence the gossip gals who are frankly beginning to scare me.

I thought they were joking when they said they were the matchmakers of Winter Falls. Lilac made it sound as if they were all talk but no action. She misled me.

"Here's the skinny," Cassandra answers. "Gabrielle's asshole of an ex-boyfriend phoned here searching for her. Apparently, he figured out she's no longer at her apartment."

Phoenix growls but she waves away his concern. "Don't worry. He never hit her."

I groan and bury my face in my hands. Is she going to tell the world my secrets?

"What the hell did he do to her?"

Do they have to talk about me as if I'm not here? I'm right here.

"She won't tell, but it doesn't matter."

Phoenix's nostrils flare. "Doesn't matter? Of course, it matters."

He glances over at me, and our eyes meet. His are full of concern. Concern. Not pity. My stomach warms and I want to reach for him, but then I remember – he doesn't want me.

"You can ask her later." Cassandra dismisses his question with a wave of her hand. "In the meantime, I have the perfect solution."

"You want us to pretend to be a couple."

He sounds disgusted with the idea. My stomach sours. What else did I expect? He doesn't want a relationship and definitely not with me.

"It's not a bad idea."

I gasp at Lilac's comment. If Ms. Cool, Calm, and Collected thinks it's a good idea, I have no chance of stopping this disaster from happening.

"They're already living together." Living together? I wish. Roommates is a more accurate description. "It won't require much more to convince Patrick they're involved."

Beckett stands next to his girlfriend. "But do you think Patrick will leave her alone if she's involved with another man?"

"P-p-patrick's several states away. There's no reason to put on a show for him."

"I disagree. He phoned here this morning trying to find you," Clove reminds me.

"He phoned here?" I nod in answer to Phoenix's question, although I'm pretty sure it's a rhetorical one since Cassandra already told him Patrick called the café.

"Fine." He scowls. "I'll pretend to date Gabrielle until the asshat stops bothering her."

Chapter 12

Rule – an agreement you make with the woman who you're fake dating that you don't have a chance in hell of not breaking

PHOENIX

As soon as I agree to this farce, noise erupts in the café as everyone talks at once. I glance over at Gabrielle. Her hair is hanging in her face again while her shoulders bunch up as she tries to retreat into herself. I need to get her out of here.

I march to her and hold out my hand. My heart warms when she doesn't hesitate to grab hold of me. She trusts me. The feeling makes me feel ten-foot tall despite not having earned her trust.

I lead her toward the door, but Cassandra steps in front of me and halts our progress.

"Where are you going?"

"Home," I grunt and try scooting around her. She blocks me again.

"But we need to discuss the details of how this is going to work."

"Stop being nosy." Elizabeth shoves Cassandra. *Go,* she mouths to me.

Thankfully, no one else tries to stop us, because my patience is gone. When I received a message from Clove telling me to get my butt to her coffee shop because Gabrielle needed me, I nearly lost my mind.

The message was already fifteen minutes old when I read it since I don't carry my phone with me at all times – a mistake I'll be rectifying from here on out. I rushed to the café to discover Gabrielle being interrogated by damn near the entire town.

We reach my truck and I help Gabrielle in before hurrying to the driver's side and getting the hell out of town.

"I thought cars were banned in Winter Falls."

"I have a permanent dispensation since you can hardly haul hay and manure in a golf cart."

She giggles and I can breathe for the first time since I read the text message from Clove. She's okay. And if she's not, she will be.

"What were you doing in town anyway? The whole idea of you staying with me was to keep you out of harm's way."

She turns away to stare out the window. Shit. I need to be more gentle with her. She's not strong.

She clears her throat. "I couldn't concentrate at the farm."

I knew it. Women don't want to live on the farm. They never stay.

"I keep getting distracted by how beautiful the view is outside of the windows."

Wait. She wasn't bored?

"And I wanted a cappuccino."

I should have known. A fancy coffee she can't get out on the farm. The farm is never fancy enough.

"Although, I should have gone to the library. Clove is a chatterbox."

Yeah, well, everyone's a chatterbox next to Gabrielle. Although, she never has a problem chatting with me. Because she trusts me. I rub a hand over my chest when it begins to ache. Damn it. Why can't I be the man she needs?

We arrive home. *No, not her home*, I remind myself. I'm doing a hell of a lot of reminding myself these days.

I escort her into the house and straight into my office.

"You can work in here from now on."

"But this is your office, and it was your dad's office. I can't intrude on tradition."

"You're not intruding." I insist as I gather the documents on the desk and make a stack of them. I set the stack down on an empty shelf in the bookcase. "Is this enough room for you to work?"

Although the papers are gone, my desktop computer occupies nearly half of the desk.

"I don't need much space." She lifts up her bag. "As long as I have room for my laptop, I'm golden."

I motion to the desk. "Have at it." I march toward the door. "I need to get back to work."

"Um…"

I spin around. "What is it?"

Her cheeks darken. "Shouldn't we… uh… talk about this fake dating thing?"

How the hell did I allow the town to talk me into this? Gabrielle and I pretending to date is the most ludicrous idea Winter Falls has come up with yet. But when I heard her asshat ex-boyfriend rang the café searching for her, I couldn't open my mouth and agree fast enough. I want – no need – Gabrielle safe.

But I never considered her side of this. Is she not okay with pretending to be my girlfriend?

"You didn't respond when I agreed to the fake relationship. Do you have a problem with pretending to date me?"

She waves away my concern. "It's fine. Totally unnecessary but fine."

I disagree. If her ex is snooping around Winter Falls, it won't be long before he ends up here. But there's no sense scaring her. She's safe with me.

"Good. What did you want to talk about?"

"Um… what are the rules?"

I chuckle. "Rules? Do you usually have rules when you date someone?"

"I don't usually 'pretend' to date a man." She uses air quotes. She's fucking adorable.

"Okay. What rules do you want us to have in place?"

"Do we hold hands? Do we kiss?"

There's nothing I'd enjoy more than getting my lips on hers. As for holding hands, I've never been a man who cared much for it, but with Gabrielle, I'd be willing to give it a try.

"I mean, I know our relationship isn't real." Her words bring me out of a fantasy of fisting her golden hair while taking her lips.

"No kissing but we can hold hands in public," I grunt out like an idiot caveman.

Her shoulders fall and I realize how my words must sound to her. She has no fucking clue how hard it is for me to keep my hands off of her. She won't stay, I remind myself. I'm turning into a broken record at this point, but the reminder is necessary.

I open my mouth to explain – how I have no clue – but she speaks before I get the chance.

"And we need a story."

"A story?"

"How we met, our first date. You know … our back story."

"We met when my goat decided to eat your skirt."

"Okay, our meet cute is decided." She giggles. I have no idea what the hell a meet cute is, but if it makes her giggle, I'm all for it.

"How did you ask me out?"

"Easy. I asked you out right then and there." Which is what I wanted to do when my goat, Pan, latched onto Gabrielle's skirt months ago.

"And where did we go on our first date?" Her cheeks darken and I reckon it's taking all of her courage to have this discussion, but she's doing it. Huh. Maybe she's braver than I give her credit for.

"Easy. The brewery."

"Naked Falls Brewing? The brewery next to the recording studio?" At my nod, she grins. "I bet they have some great IPAs."

"You drink beer?"

"I do now."

I raise an eyebrow and she explains. "I thought I didn't enjoy the taste of alcohol." She gazes out of the window, and I wonder what her asshat ex said about her drinking to cause her to have such an injured expression on her face.

I fist my hands before I can reach out to her.

"But now you do like it?" I prompt.

She shakes her head and whatever memory haunting it off of her. "Yeah. Lilac introduced me to IPAs and the rest as they say is history."

A woman after my own tastes. And one full of surprises. I didn't expect quiet, shy Gabrielle to be a beer drinker, but I'm beginning to realize she's only shy and quiet when surrounded by a bunch of people she doesn't know. Or when people confront her about something she doesn't want to talk about.

"I have some in the refrigerator you can try tonight."

"I can't wait. What time should I have dinner ready?"

"You're a guest here. You don't have to make me dinner to earn your keep." I don't want her thinking she has to be my maid and cook.

"I enjoy cooking after a long day of working." She notices the time on the clock on the wall and cringes. "Maybe not such a long day today, though."

"I'll make you a deal. You cook tonight and I'll take you out to the brewery tomorrow. Tuesday is two for one IPAs from six to seven."

"You have a deal, mister! Plus, us going out on a 'date' will sell this whole fake dating thing better."

I blow out a puff of air. I don't like the idea of this date being anything but real, but I'm happy to pretend to be dating her or be her fake boyfriend or whatever it is I've signed up for if it keeps her safe.

This whole plan has the added benefit of keeping the gossip gals off my back. I know they've decided I'm the next Winter Falls resident they're going to match. They're shit out of luck. There's not a woman out there for me.

I'm not an idiot. I know they think this fake relationship will become real. They're wrong. Gabrielle is a city girl. Soon enough she'll be missing the bright lights.

I glance over at her. No matter how much I might wish her to be the woman to stay, I know better. If Tina who grew up on a farm wouldn't stay, why would Gabrielle?

Chapter 13

Smelly – what happens when you land in a pile of shit. Literally.

"Stop staring outside, Gabrielle," I admonish myself.

And, yes, I'm talking out loud to myself in an empty room in an empty house. I can't help it. It's now 10 a.m. and I've done nothing but stare out the window all morning. I haven't gotten a single item on my to-do list crossed off yet.

This farm is everything I've ever dreamed of but didn't know I wanted. I know I sound crazy, but it's hard to explain. The minute I stepped foot inside the house I felt peace settle over me. As if the house didn't bring enough peace, I can gaze outside at the green pastures and foothills in the distance for more peace.

Don't get me wrong. I haven't yearned to live on a farm all my life. I was perfectly happy living in Saint Louis. It's where I was born and lived with my parents until their unfortunate early deaths. I went to high school and college there. All my friends live there, although – to be honest – most of those so-called friends didn't stick around after Patrick.

I know, I know. I'm the one who stopped returning their calls, who didn't want to meet up for drinks, who didn't reach out to them anymore. But I wasn't ever exactly what anyone would refer to as a social butterfly. Besides, I only dated Patrick for six months, although it felt longer – much, much longer. They couldn't stick with me through a six-month blackout?

My laptop dings with a message and I force my gaze away from outside and back on my computer. I'm digging into my work when I hear a loud curse.

"Pan, knock it off!"

I glance out the window to discover Phoenix strolling across the nearest pasture. Pan is bleating and running in circles around him. He bats her away, but she's determined. She buts him in his behind, and he slips and falls.

"Damn it, Pan!"

I burst out laughing at his predicament, but when he doesn't immediately stand up the laughter dies in my throat. Oh no. Is he hurt? I rush from the room to the backdoor where I shove my feet into a pair of galoshes. I open the door and hurry across the porch and fly down the stairs.

"Are you okay?" I yell as I sprint across the field to where Phoenix is still laying in the mud.

He stands and dusts the front of his jeans off. "I'm fine."

I sniff. What's that smell? I step closer to him and sniff again.

"Did you…?" I giggle before I can complete my question. I cough and try again. "Did you fall in poop?"

He glares down at the ground where he fell. I follow his gaze. Sure enough. It's a big pile of goat poop.

"I'm going to kill Pan and put her in a stew."

I throw my arms around the goat's neck. "It's not her fault you fell into a pile of poop." I can barely get the words out as laughter bubbles out of me.

He steps toward me. "I'll show you how it feels to fall into a pile of shit."

"No! No!" I shove the goat in front of me. "Save me, Pan!"

He pushes Pan out of the way and saunters toward me. "What? You don't think I smell good? Don't I smell sexy?"

I hold out my palms and back away. "Maybe if I were a female goat, you'd smell good."

"The does get off on the smell of urine, not shit."

Wait! He's serious? I was joking. "What?" My goat farming for dummies book didn't say anything about does enjoying the scent of urine.

"Billy goats – let's say pee – all over themselves to attract the does."

Let's say pee? Does he mean something other than pee?

"Do you have any Billy goats?"

He cocks an eyebrow. "If you think the smell of shit all over me is nasty, never meet a Billy goat."

"Why don't—"

My question is cut off by Juniper yelling, "Bark Twain! Indiana Bones! Come back here, you two."

What in the world is Lilac's sister doing all the way out here? "Does Juniper live out here?"

"The Wildlife Refuge she manages is next door."

His definition of 'next door' must be different than mine since farmland stretches for miles and miles in front of me. I hear dogs barking and scan the area for sight of them.

"You don't have a dog, do you?"

He sighs. "Nope. But I bet Juniper's dogs are in my pasture again. Damn hole in the fence."

The barking grows louder until I spot two dogs racing toward us. When they near, Phoenix moves to stand in front of me. He whistles and the dogs immediately screech to a halt.

I peek around him. "Who do we have here?"

I kneel down and reach out my hand to let them sniff. "Who's a good boy?" They both bark in response. "I amend my statement. Both of you are good boys."

"Good boys, my ass," Juniper grumbles as she arrives. She bends over at the waist to catch her breath.

The dogs roll onto their backs and I scratch their bellies.

"I told you they'd be at the farmhouse."

I peer up at the new arrival and my mouth drops open. Maverick Langston as I live and breathe. Juniper's engaged to the movie star. I've met him a few times before but never when we weren't in a big group. Up close and personal I can understand why women scream and run after him because he is gorgeous. Not as hot as Phoenix but definitely an eleven on a scale of ten.

I realize I'm staring at the famous man with my mouth gaping open and drop my gaze before he realizes I'm a total dweeb.

Phoenix moves slightly to block my view of Maverick. What's he doing? Maverick isn't a threat to me. I don't think Patrick is either – not anymore anyway – but you try convincing this town otherwise. Geez. Talk about bull-headed.

I peer around Phoenix's legs and Maverick winks down at me. Phoenix growls and moves to block my view again. What's wrong with him?

I slap his leg. "What are you doing? Are you trying to hide the poopy stains on your pants, because I gotta tell you the stain isn't nearly as bad as the smell." I wave a hand in front of my face as if to dissipate the stench.

Maverick bursts out laughing before throwing his arm over Juniper's shoulder and hauling her near. "Priceless. This one." He hugs Juniper closer. "Has come home more times than I can count covered in shit. And then there was the skunk incident."

Juniper rolls her eyes. "The skunk wouldn't have sprayed me if you hadn't gone tromping through the bushes and scared him."

"Best mistake I ever made." He glances down at her with heat in his eyes.

Is skunk a metaphor for sex? People in Winter Falls are difficult to understand sometimes.

Juniper clears her throat and elbows Maverick. "We're not alone," she whispers to him. Yep. Skunk has something to do with sex.

Maverick clears his throat. "I heard you're in a spot of trouble."

Spot of trouble? He knows what's going on? I forget all about being enamored with the famous person at discovering he knows my secrets. "Is nothing private in this town?"

"Ha!" Juniper barks out a laugh. "You haven't lived in Winter Falls long enough if you think the word private exists in this town."

"Ain't that the truth," Phoenix mutters.

"Besides," Maverick adds, "we can't keep our eyes out for this Patrick guy if we don't know how he looks."

"Wait!" I start to stand but my foot ends up in the pile of poop Phoenix fell in and I slide forward. Before I can face plant into the mess, Phoenix grabs me under the arms and sets me on my feet.

"Not as funny when you're the one covered in shit, now is it?"

I ignore him. I have bigger issues than goat excrement to deal with.

"How do you know what Patrick looks like? I didn't show anyone pictures."

Juniper hums and glances away. She might as well have screamed *you don't want to know.*

I'm seething now. I wouldn't be surprised if smoke is coming out of my ears. "What did you do?"

She lifts up her hands. "It wasn't me."

I plant my hands on my hips. I suck at staring someone down, but there's no time like the present to get some practice in.

"Lilac went through all of his social media profiles and downloaded a few pictures for us," Maverick explains.

"Us? Who's us?"

Juniper's nose wrinkles. "The town of Winter Falls."

My face falls forward until my hair forms a curtain across it. Great. Just great. Everyone in the entire town knows what an idiot I am. Some clean slate this is turning out to be.

"Hey now." Phoenix pinches my chin and lifts my head until my eyes meet his. "There is nothing to be embarrassed about."

Easy for him to say. He's probably never done an embarrassing thing in his life.

"He's the one in the wrong. Not you."

But I'm the dummy who let him control me for such a long-time.

"It's … I'm …You know…"

I can't manage to get my thoughts in a row let alone form sentences to explain them. Escape. Yes, escape. That's what I should do. I throw my hands in the air and twirl around on my heel before stomping toward the house.

I make it exactly two steps before I slip. My right foot flies forward and I bat my arms in the air in a useless attempt to remain standing. I haven't got a chance. I slide to my ass and use my hands to brace my fall.

When I glance down, I realize my hands are covered in mud. No, not mud. Guessing by the smell I fell in poop. Awesome, Gabrielle.

And that's how I ended up on my ass in a pile of poop in a goat pasture next to a farmhouse owned by my fake boyfriend.

Chapter 14

Bet – an excuse to stick your nose in someone else's business

PHOENIX

I pace the living room as I wait for Gabrielle to come down the stairs. Will she come down the stairs? She ran away after falling in the pasture and I haven't seen her since, although she did message me to say she was okay and merely busy with work.

We're supposed to be going on our 'date' tonight, but I'm not convinced she won't hide in her room all night. I run my hand through my hair as I glance toward the second floor. What do I do? Do I knock on her door? Do I let her stew in her embarrassment or do I encourage her to come out?

Knock it off, Phoenix. Gabrielle isn't your girlfriend. It isn't your job to comfort her.

A door squeaks open and heels click on the hardwood floor in the hallway. Huh. Maybe she isn't cowering in her bedroom while reliving flashbacks of her embarrassment. Maybe she's made of sterner stuff than I thought.

Gabrielle appears at the top of the stairs, and the breath whooshes out of me at the sight of her standing there in a short summer dress. Holy crap. The top is tight and showcases her perky tits. I'm suddenly jealous of the material hugging her body.

She smiles and waves before descending the stairs.

"Aren't you going to be cold?" Yes, those are the words my dumbass mouth utters upon seeing how gorgeous she is.

She holds up a sweater. "I'll be fine."

I motion toward the door. "After you."

After she passes me, I place my hand on her back to escort her out of the house. I immediately feel the heat of her skin against mine and realize I made a mistake. Now my hand is itching to travel from her back to encircle her waist before pulling her flush to my body.

I clear my throat and speak before my body overrules my brain. "Are you hungry?"

"I'm starved. After I showered this morning because, you know, I had goat shit all over me…" She giggles and I allow the sound of her happiness to wash over me. It's a sound I want to hear every day for the rest of my life.

"I got to work and a client had an 'emergency'." She uses air quotes and rolls her eyes making it clear she didn't think much of this so-called emergency. "I put off lunch, but before I knew it my alarm went off letting me know it was time to get ready."

"You set an alarm?"

"Duh. It's two for one IPAs from six to seven. Of course, I set an alarm."

I usher her into the cab of my truck. "I better get you to the brewery then."

Once we're on the road, she asks, "Are you allowed to drive your truck when you're not doing farm stuff?"

Farm stuff? She's fucking adorable.

I shrug. "Probably not, but I don't want you getting cold riding in the golf cart."

I glance over at her shoulders exposed from her dress and I can't help wondering if her skin is as soft as it appears. Will she melt for me if I touch her? Or will she push me away after watching me fall into goat shit earlier today?

I shake my head. Gabby isn't Tina, I remind myself.

When we enter *Naked Falls Brewing* five minutes later, her eyes widen as she scans the area. The restaurant is pretty cool. It has an industrial vibe with brick walls and exposed ductwork painted a matte black. The building used to house the local newspaper, but after the newspaper went bankrupt, it sat vacant for years.

When the owners of the brewing company showed up and asked to buy it, the town lost its fucking mind. They didn't want two non-locals buying property. They were adamant about it. I frown. I was one of the ones who bitched about non-locals being untrustworthy.

I glance down at Gabby. Not all non-locals are untrustworthy. I hope.

"Hello! You must be Gabrielle," Moon greets from the hostess station.

Gabby's cheeks darken and her head tilts as if to tuck in her chin, but she clears her throat and faces Moon. Strong woman.

"I am. And you are?"

"I'm Moon," she answers before glancing over her shoulder and shouting, "Give me one month!"

"One month?" Gabby steps closer to me to whisper, "What is she talking about?"

"You don't want to know."

Unfortunately, Moon hears her question and has no problem answering her. "Until you two are a couple." She winks.

"We are a couple," Gabby claims. "And we're here on a date."

"Good job, honey. I totally bought it." Moon grabs two menus and motions for us to follow her up the stairs where she leads us to an intimate corner booth.

We sit across from each other, and she slaps the menus on the table. "What can I get you to drink?"

We order a couple of IPAs and she turns to leave, but she swivels on her heel and returns mere seconds later. She leans close and whispers, "I'll try to keep the riffraff away as much as possible, but no promises."

"Riffraff? Does Winter Falls have any riffraff?" Gabby asks as she watches Moon chat with the customers at another table.

I chuckle. "She's not talking about disreputable residents."

Her nose wrinkles in confusion. "What's she talking about?"

I sigh. I might as well tell her. It's not as if she won't figure it out on her own anyway.

"About the nosy residents who want the scoop so they can place their bets."

"This is the second time someone mentioned betting. Does Winter Falls have a secret casino?" Her eyes widen. "Oh, is it a speakeasy? How cool would that be? Do you know the password? How can I become a member?"

I'm kind of disappointed I have to burst her bubble. "There isn't a speakeasy in Winter Falls."

Her shoulders fall. "Bummer."

I chuckle. "You're cuckoo."

She shrugs and the excitement fades from her face. "Well, I do love my Cocoa Puffs."

"Hell, Gabby. I'm sorry. I shouldn't be calling you names after what you've been through."

Her nose scrunches as she stares at me for a long moment before saying, "No."

"No, what?"

"No, I'm not going to let what Patrick did to me ruin me. I will not over-analyze every single thing someone says in the fear they're being cruel to me. I mean, I will over-analyze every single thing people say but only because my DNA is engineered in such a way as to make me into an over-analyzer."

"I made it!" Ashlyn announces as she careens into our table.

I rush to stand to steady her before she hurts herself or the baby. "You need to be more careful," I admonish.

"Ack." She pretends to choke herself. "I'm sick to death of everyone tiptoeing on eggshells around me because I'm pregnant."

"Welcome to my life," Gabby grumbles.

"I came to make you a deal," Ashlyn announces.

Gabby leans close. "What kind of deal? Does it involve me pretending to be you while you escape for a weekend of girl gone wild?"

I groan. Ashlyn has done enough girl gone wild for the rest of her life. I don't know how her husband handles her. On the other hand, Rowan is a former NFL quarterback who regularly got sacked by men weighing upwards of three-hundred and fifty pounds. Dealing with his wife is probably a piece of cake in comparison.

"No. But remind me to hit you up after the baby's born."

Gabby's eyes widen at Ashlyn's pronouncement. "I was joking."

"No take-backs allowed in Winter Falls."

"Really? Is this a town ordinance? No take-backs?"

"Good idea. As the current mayor, I will declare a town ordinance and entitle it Ashlyn's no take-backs rule."

Someone save me. I clear my throat. "What do you need, Ashlyn?"

"I need bigger boobs. Oh wait. My wish came true." She pushes her breasts together. "Awesome, aren't they?"

I squirm in my seat and glance away. Rowan will beat me to a pulp if I remark on his wife's assets.

"I think breasts of every size can be awesome," Gabby responds and my gaze dips to the cleavage created by her dress. I can't help but agree with her assessment. She isn't what anyone would call well-endowed, but her perky breasts make my mouth water something fierce.

"True." Ashlyn agrees. "Anyway, I'm winning this dang bet. I'm tired of the gossip gals winning everything."

Gabby leans closer and whispers, "What bet are we talking about?"

"You know. The one about when you and Farmer Boy here become the real deal."

Gabby's eyes widen to the size of saucers. "What are you talking about? Phoenix and I are the real deal."

Ashlyn waves away her words. "Don't worry. Everyone here knows about the 'deal'."

"The deal? What deal?"

"The one where we're in a fake relationship," I fill in because otherwise the two of them are going to talk around the issue all night long.

Ashlyn slams her hand over my mouth. "Shush. You can't say the f-word in here. You don't know who's listening."

I peel her hand away. "I don't think the secret police are going to care if I drop an f-bomb." Even saying f-bomb makes me sound like a complete wuss.

"Not the f-bomb. The f-word. F-A-K-E."

I chuckle. We're in a brewery. I'm fairly certain every person in the place can spell fake.

Moon arrives with our beers. She pushes Ashlyn out of the way with her hip. "Off you go. I gave you your few minutes."

"Some best friend you are," Ashlyn mutters as she stomps off.

"Sorry. I had to give her a chance to talk to you. She's been my best friend since kindergarten. She knows where all the bodies are buried. But don't worry. I'll fend everyone else off from here on out."

Gabby grins. "If you agree to defend us with your life, we'll forgive you."

Moon bows. "My sword is yours."

"After you put your sword away, can we get an order of hamburgers and fries?" I ask.

"You bet."

Once we're alone again, Gabby leans forward to ask, "Are people seriously betting on us becoming a real couple?"

I don't want to lie to her. "Yes. Does it bother you?"

She taps her chin as she considers her answer. "I guess it's to be expected considering the gossip gals."

My shoulders fall in relief. "This town will bet on anything. When Ellery was pregnant, the betting was rampant. Will the baby be a boy or girl? When will the baby be born? The gossip gals even staked out her house."

She bursts into laughter. "I love Winter Falls," she manages to say between peels of laughter.

If wish I could believe her, then I could keep her. Maybe.

Chapter 15

Goats – troublemakers on four legs

OKAY. I'M READY. I think. I scan my supplies. Google told me I need a shovel, a wheelbarrow, stall freshener, and fresh shavings to muck out the goat stalls. I found all the supplies in the garage next to the goat barn. Huh. Is the term goat barn correct?

Another thing for me to Google. I've lived on the farm for a little over a week now and I've spent almost every evening Googling stuff Phoenix says at dinner. I don't want to sound like an ignoramus, so I nod and hum whenever he talks. Afterwards, I rush to my laptop to research.

Since he smirks whenever I open my computer, I'm pretty sure he has me figured out. He hasn't said anything, though. Thus, our tango continues.

The doors of the barn are open as Phoenix has already let the goats out for the day. They only stay in the barn at night as they're free-range goats. Yeah, I didn't know the term existed either.

I push the wheelbarrow full of supplies toward the barn. By the time I reach the building, sweat is already soaking the back of my t-shirt. Since it's a chilly fifty degrees out this morning, it's safe to say the sweat is the result of my 'exercise is for other people'-philosophy.

I enter the building and my nose wrinkles. Google didn't warn me about the smell. Oh well, I'm here now and I'm not a quitter.

I grab the shovel and make my way to the furthest corner of the barn. I thought I was sweating before. I was wrong. I rub the sweat off of my forehead with the back of my arm. I'm beginning to understand the appeal of wearing a hat. And I hate hats. I don't have the head for them. It sounds impossible, but I look even more dorky in a hat.

When the wheelbarrow is finally full, I prop the shovel against the wall and slowly make my way toward the door. I don't make it more than three steps before a goat jumps in front of the wheelbarrow.

"Come on, kiddo."

Maa!

"Sorry. Sorry. Of course, you aren't a baby. My apologies. Can you please move?"

Maa!

I guess that means no. I angle the wheelbarrow to go around the goat, but she jumps in front of it again.

"Are you serious? Wait. Do you want to play?"

I scan the area for a toy. Naturally, I don't find anything. Phoenix cleaned out the toys yesterday as he was intending to muck the stall yesterday evening but never got around to it, which is why I'm here helping out.

I do the one thing I can think of. I reach into my pocket and pretend to remove a stick before pretending to throw it across the barn. The goat rushes after the non-existent stick and I pick up the handles of the wheelbarrow again.

I'm nearly at the door when another goat arrives. She bleats and prances in a circle around me. She's soon joined by another goat. And another goat.

I drop the handles of the wheelbarrow. Where did all the goats come from? Okay, I'm not an idiot. I realize I'm on a goat farm, but seriously? They were all out in the fields when I arrived to muck out their barn.

"What am I going to do with you guys?"

Maa! Maa! Maa!

I throw up my hands. "I know you're girls. It's just an expression."

Someone chuckles, and I freeze. *Please don't be Phoenix. Please don't be Phoenix.* I glance over and there he is. Defining the word sexy as he leans against the fence with his arms crossed over his chest and chewing on a piece of straw hanging from his mouth.

I groan. Of course, he caught me at my worst. If there was an Olympic competition for catching me at my worst, he'd be a gold medalist. Thankfully, the Olympic committee does not believe there's a need for such a competition.

I wave. "Hi, Phoenix."

Way to make the moment worse, you total dork, you. Maybe I should ask him if he comes here more often. Then, the circle of worst moment ever would be complete, and I could crown myself Dork of the Century.

"What are you up to, Gabby?"

Butterflies in my stomach awaken at his nickname for me. He's the only one I allow to call me Gabby. It makes me believe he just might think I'm special. The butterflies begin to flap their wings. Calm down, you overeager creatures. It doesn't mean anything. He doesn't want a relationship, remember?

I shrug. "Isn't it obvious?"

He pushes off from the barn and prowls toward me. "Playing tag with my goats?"

"Ha! Ha! Hilarious."

He grins. "I thought it was funny."

I do the mature thing. I stick out my tongue at him.

"You, sir, are not funny."

"Sir?" He waggles his eyebrows. "Am I your master now?"

At his question, a vision of him tying my hands to the posts of his bed while he's naked above me pops into my head. My body tingles and I do a full body shiver.

"You okay?"

"I'm peachy." Peachy? Who uses the word peachy? I decide to blather on and hope he misses my dorky vocabulary. "You said last night you didn't get a chance to muck the goat barn yesterday and I thought I'd help out."

"You know you don't need to help out."

"I know, but I want to."

He removes his hat to run a hand through his hair. "I don't know how much more helping out I can handle."

"Hey now. It wasn't my fault a mouse ran past and scared Wendy causing her to kick her legs while I was trying to milk her."

Let's not talk about where all the milk ended up. Let's not. Let me just say wet t-shirt contests could use milk instead of water. The effect is the same.

His body vibrates with silent laughter.

"Whatever. I've got the milking figured out now."

My chest puffs up with pride. It took a disaster – okay more than one disaster, but don't ask me how many – to figure the whole milking thing out and get used to the idea of pinching a goat's teat, but I got there in the end. The goats are milked twice a day and I try to help out at least once.

"Except you scrunch up your nose whenever you help with the milking. It's adorable."

Hold up. Did he say I'm adorable? Or wait. Did he mean my scrunched up nose? I feel my nose scrunching up at the idea. Stop it! We are not adorable.

"Ahem. Do you want help with the stalls?"

He motions to the goats who are now climbing the wheelbarrow and pulling the dirty shavings out. I groan.

"Seriously? You ladies couldn't do me a solid and behave for two minutes? Two whole minutes? 120 seconds was too much for you?"

The goats don't respond to my berating. Of course, they don't. They're goats.

Phoenix is laughing as he shoos the goats out into the pasture where I notice a brand-new scratching post.

"I always put out a new toy of some kind before I begin the mucking. Otherwise …"

I hold up my hand. He doesn't need to continue. I know what happens otherwise.

For the next hour, we work side by side as we clean the stall. We don't talk much. There's no need to talk. We're in synch as we get the job done.

"I'll have to add this to my resume. Able to muck out a goat stall," I say as I collapse on a chair on the porch next to Phoenix.

He hands me a glass of lemonade. "It never hurts to learn new skills."

I hold up my hands where fresh blisters are making their presence known with swollen, red skin. "Define hurt."

He grabs my hands. "Fuck, Gabby. I didn't notice you weren't wearing gloves."

His finger moves over the skin and the butterflies in my stomach shake out their wings. I debate between pulling my hand away because falling for Phoenix is a dead-end road and I've already traveled far enough on that particular road or allowing myself to enjoy the feel of his skin on mine.

The decision is taken out of my hand – pun intended – when Phoenix tugs on my hand until I'm standing.

"Come on. Let's treat these blisters before they get infected."

He leads me into the farmhouse to the small bathroom on the ground floor. He lifts me up and sets me on the vanity before releasing me and digging into the cupboards.

"Aha!" he says when he removes a huge first-aid kit.

"Whoa. Why do you need a supersized first-aid kit?"

"It's a farm," he explains as he lays it on the toilet and opens it up. "You can never be too careful."

He applies petroleum jelly to my blistered hands before covering the wounds with a nonstick gauze bandage. His touch is feather soft and it's all I can do to stop myself from melting into him.

"You'll need to check the area every day for infection," he says as he puts the supplies away.

I lift up my hands. "How am I supposed to work? There's a reason mummies can't type."

He places his hands on my shoulders and steps between my legs. "Don't you deserve a day off every once in a while?"

I bristle. "I take days off."

He raises an eyebrow. "You do? Because you work on your laptop seven days a week."

"There's nothing wrong with working hard," I insist.

"You're not the nice and soft woman I thought you were," he mutters as his gaze lands on my lips.

I hold my breath as I lean ever so slightly forward. *Kiss me. For the love of all things holy, kiss me.* The phone in the kitchen rings and the spell is broken.

His eyes close and he clears his throat. "I better answer that," he says before ambling away without a backward glance.

"Welp. That went well," I tell my image in my mirror. Not embarrassing at all.

Reminder. Phoenix doesn't want a woman. Maybe I should tattoo those words on my forearm because I seem to forget them the second I'm in the man's presence.

Chapter 16

Guessing game – a game played by women throughout the ages where they try to get their partner to figure out why they're mad

PHOENIX

I halt hammering on the fence I'm fixing when I notice a plume of dust in the distance. Someone's coming. And it can't be Juniper since she always rides her bike out to the Wildlife Refuge.

By the time I make it back to the house, Gabby's already standing on the front porch squinting into the distance as she watches the car approach.

"Go inside," I order her. "It could be Patrick."

She grunts. "If it's Patrick, I'm definitely not going inside."

I'm torn. On the one hand, I want to allow her to confront the man who abused her. But, on the other hand, I don't want her in danger. It's the whole reason she's here, to begin with.

Although, I must admit, if only to myself, I enjoy having her here. She doesn't hesitate to help out on the farm. Even if some of the ways she 'helps' cause more harm than good. Plus, she has dinner on the table every night.

And the woman can cook. She doesn't heat up those atrocious ready-made meals from the supermarket. The ones Tina would drive to White Bridge to buy since Winter Falls doesn't believe in ready-made meals. For all the time she spent driving, she could have learned to cook.

I shake my head. I shouldn't compare Tina and Gabby. It's not fair to either one of them. Besides, I'm beginning to learn there's no comparison to be made. Gabby is in another world from Tina.

"I think it's a cop car anyway." Gabby gestures toward the vehicle.

I grunt when I notice she's right. "I guess you can stay outside."

She giggles and pats me on the arm. "I like how you think you had a choice in the matter."

And I like how she's coming out of her shell. She hasn't covered her face with her hair in days. My chest swells with pride. I have no right to be proud of her, but I am.

The patrol car parks in the driveway and Lyric steps out.

Gabby waves at him. "Why didn't you tell us you were stopping by? I would have made some of my homemade lemonade."

Us. Damn, I like the sound of there being an us. Knock it off, Phoenix. She's only here temporarily. She'll flee as soon as she can.

Lyric puts on his hat as he strolls toward the porch. "I'm afraid I'm not here for pleasure."

I feel a whoosh of air before Pan dashes past me, flies off the porch, and rushes to him. She buts his hand until Lyric pets her.

He chuckles. "Does she know she's a goat?"

"What was she doing in the house anyway?"

Gabby crosses her arms over her chest and huffs. "She followed me inside when I finished milking this morning. She's good company."

Assuming you define good company as a pain in the ass. But I'm not having this argument in front of my brother. My brother who's observing our interaction with entirely too much interest as it is.

I narrow my eyes on him. "Don't tell me you placed a bet, too."

He shrugs. "What can I say? Those West sisters and the gossip gals are relentless."

"Tell me about it," I mutter under my breath.

The gossip gals have been trying to pair me up ever since Lyric got back together with his high school sweetheart, Aspen. They think they've gotten me now since I'm playing house with Gabby. But that's just what it is – playing.

Although when she blistered her hands helping me muck out the goat stalls, I was mighty tempted to kiss her. I probably would have if the phone hadn't rung. It appears fate thinks I should keep my hands to myself.

Gabby elbows me. "Don't speak badly of the elderly. They deserve our respect."

"Really? They deserved our respect when they told everyone at the town meeting…" I pause. Damn it. I'm going to embarrass her again. "When they said what they said."

She shoves her palm in my face. She has to stand on tiptoe to reach my face, but she's determined. "Phoenix Apollo Alston, we agreed to never speak of the incident again."

"You middle-named me."

Her hand drops and she places it on her hip. "You deserved it."

Lyric chuckles and draws my attention away from her hips and how much I'd enjoy clenching them with my fingers while driving into her. My cock twitches and I inhale a deep breath before my brain over circuits and follows my body's desires.

"As much fun as this is," he begins, "we should go inside. We've got things to discuss."

"I'll get back to work."

Before Gabby can step in the direction of the office, he stops her. "This concerns you."

"Shootawhoota," she mutters before stomping to the kitchen.

Pan follows her and damn if the stupid goat doesn't keep close to her like she's a pet and not a milking goat from my herd. I can barely get the animal out of the house at the end of the day as it is. If this keeps up, Gabby's going to force me to build an indoor pen for her.

I grasp her elbow and lead her toward the table. "Sit down. Everything will be fine."

"If I have to listen to a police officer seeing as this 'discussion' involves me, I deserve coffee."

"Sit tight. I'll make you one." And then, I continue with my idiocy by kissing her hair.

I nearly freeze when I realize what I've done, but I'm not going to freak out and give my brother any more ammunition to use against me. As it is, news of the hair kiss is going to make the rounds in Winter Falls before the hour is finished.

When I return from the kitchen with coffees for everyone and sit down next to Gabby, I ask, "What's going on?"

Lyric rubs his neck. "It could be nothing."

Gabby snorts. "Which is why you're here."

"Okay. Fine. My gut is telling me it's something." When he pauses, I motion for him to continue. "A stranger has been spotted camping in the woods."

I wait for him to say more, but apparently, he wants me to play the guessing game. "And?"

"I've got a bad feeling."

Crap. Lyric's got great instincts. It's one of the reasons he makes a great cop.

"What is this feeling telling you?"

Gabby raises her hand. "Hold up. We're worried because Lyric has a bad feeling?"

"I trust my gut," he tells her.

"Okey-dokey. I just wanted to make sure I understand what's happening here is all." She sips on her coffee and watches Lyric over the edge of the mug.

"It's too much of a coincidence for us to find someone camping nearby when we're keeping our eyes out for Patrick," he explains.

"I agree."

Gabby sets her coffee cup down on the table before asking, "What are you going to do about it?"

Her voice is no longer the brave Gabby she's been for the past week or two in my presence. No, timid Gabrielle is back. My hands fist in my lap. Damn Patrick to hell. I dare him to come onto my land. I'll handle him.

Winter Falls is non-violent – what do you expect when a town is founded by hippies? – but I have a rifle and shotgun to protect my land and my animals. Coyotes and wolves don't respond to sit-ins and discussions, but they sure as hell respond to buckshot.

"I can't exactly hunt him down and kick him out of town."

"You can't?" Gabby asks softly.

"You want to file for a protection order?" He fires back at her.

Her chin falls forward and her hair covers her face. Damn it. I don't want her retreating into herself again.

I place my hand on her thigh. "Don't worry. He won't get you."

She blows out a breath of air. "I'm not scared of him." Except her softly spoken words don't incite confidence in her words.

"Why don't you step your relationship up?" Lyric suggests. "Go into town and wander around pretending to be a couple a few times. You've only been in town together once. Maybe if you step things up, he'll get the hint and go home."

"I don't know. I don't want him to target Phoenix."

My heart aches at her words. She shouldn't be worried about me, but I can't deny her worry warms my chest.

"Don't worry about me. He won't hurt me," I growl.

"I guess this means I won't come to your wedding this weekend," Gabby says.

"You're coming to the wedding. Aspen will have my ass if one of her sisters doesn't show."

"I'm not her real sister. My brother having a relationship with Aspen's sister doesn't make us related."

Lyric cocks a brow. "You want to tell Aspen that?"

She giggles, and I relax at the sound. There's my Gabby.

"Besides, the whole town will be at the party. There's no way an out-of-towner will slip in."

"Are you sure?"

"As sure as I am my brothers are going to embarrass me during the speeches."

"We won't embarrass you." Lyric doesn't look convinced. Rightfully so. "Much."

He knocks on the table before standing. "I'll let you both get back to work. Keep your eye out for strangers."

"I always do."

When I return to the farmhouse after escorting Lyric to his car, I find Gabby drawing circle eights on the table with her finger.

"What are you thinking?"

Her nose wrinkles. "What if Lyric's wrong? What if my going to their wedding leads Patrick straight there and he causes a commotion and ruins their wedding?"

I lift her out of the chair and wrap my arms around her pulling her flush to me where she belongs. Dammit. These stray, erroneous thoughts need to stop already. I push thoughts of Gabby belonging to me out of my head.

"Their wedding isn't going to be ruined. And none of this is your fault. You are not to blame."

She melts into me, and I hold on tight. Just this once, I promise myself. I won't allow myself to give into the temptation to hold her again after this.

<h1 style="text-align:center">Chapter 17</h1>

Prank – A mischievous act that can actually be super sweet if done correctly

"THIS IS SO EXCITING," Cassandra declares before starting to sing and dance down the street toward the town square.

"Calm down, Ms. What Is Pitch. It's a wedding, not a carnival."

She whirls around to shake her finger at me. "You don't get it. It's a pagan wedding. I've never been to one before."

"How do you know it's a pagan wedding?"

I glance down at my outfit. I'm wearing a summery dress with a fitted bodice and a short skirt. My outfit is typical wedding fair, but am I appropriately dressed for a pagan wedding? I wish Phoenix was here, but he had 'something' to set up before the wedding. I didn't ask what it was. I wanted to be surprised. I'm regretting my choice now, though.

"And here I thought she was excited because weddings are the sacred hunting ground for single men," Elizabeth grumbles.

"Single men such as me?" River jumps in front of us before twirling his hand and doing a bow.

"Who are you supposed to be? Robin Hood?" Elizabeth studies his outfit of khaki pants and white billowing blouse. "You're missing the tights."

He wiggles his eyebrows. "I save the tights for the special ladies."

She giggles as she shoves him. "Poor Maid Marian. She won't know what she's getting into with you, will she?"

"Do you know in some of the early tales of Robin Hood Maid Marian is supposedly a virgin?" He feigns gagging.

"I was wrong. You're not Robin Hood. You're Casanova."

He perks up. "Casanova. Classic. Handsome. Adventurer. I accept." He holds his elbow out to Elizabeth. "Does the lady wish to accompany Casanova to the nuptials?"

She threads her arm through his. "Let's go, Casanova." And off they skip.

"My entire family is bonkers," I mutter.

"I'm not bonkers," Cassandra sings before doing a handless cartwheel on the sidewalk.

"Everyone saw your underwear. Way to prove you're sane."

"Quadrant one is secure."

I squeal and twirl around to find the origin of the squawk. I discover one of the gossip gals standing behind me. I should have known.

"Geez Louise, you scared the daylights out of me." I rub my hand over my chest where my heart is beating like a drum. *Ba-dum. Ba-dum.*

"Who's Louise? I'm Sage."

How could I forget? She doesn't let anyone forget who she is.

"Lovely dress," I say instead. She's wearing a bright pink floor-length dress. Come to think of it I don't think I've seen her in any color besides pink.

She spins around for me. "Thank you, darling."

I nod to her walkie-talkie. "I didn't realize those were all the rage."

"We've all got one," Feather says as she joins us along with the rest of the gossip gals.

They're wearing matching bright pink dresses while holding walkie-talkies. What are they up to now?

"What are the walkie-talkies for?" I ask.

"We're security for the wedding," Sage answers.

My eyes widen. "Security?"

"You're darn tooting! We're not letting Patrick get through our perimeter." Feather shakes her walkie-talkie in the air.

"It's a shame the fabric paint didn't work on these dresses," is Cayenne's bizarre reply. "We were going to have Gossip Gal Security Team written on them."

Is it wrong to be happy the fabric paint didn't work?

"I want to be a member of the Gossip Gal Security Team," Cassandra says.

Sage purses her lips. "You're not wearing a hot pink dress."

"Oh well." Cassandra shrugs and hops away leaving me alone with the gossip gals.

"Shouldn't you be … um… manning the perimeter?" I have no idea what the right terminology is.

"Right you are, my dear Gabrielle." Sage does a salute before starting to boss everyone around. Unlike me, they don't seem to mind being bossed around if their scattering to the winds is any indication.

I find myself alone on the street. I debate turning around and going home. I hate going to events on my own. I might know most of the people attending the wedding but it's still scary entering a party by yourself. Ugh. Why did I insist on coming to this wedding?

Stop it, Gabrielle. You're here to support your friends. You don't have to be a cry baby coward all the time. You can do this. Okay. I got this. Pep talk done.

I walk the final block to the town square, which is absolutely packed with people. No one even notices me when I join them. Huh. Maybe I shouldn't be a scaredy-cat all the time.

I notice Lilac and Beckett standing near the Gazebo. I wave at them, and Lilac beckons for me to join them.

"You should be with us. Family has to stick together," Lilac says.

I don't think she means figuratively stick together as in remain united against one front. No, she's being literal as in the family needs to stand close together.

"I'm not family," I remind her.

"You are not a blood relative, but you are family in the more general sense. Don't ask me to explain. Aspen got quite cross with me when I argued with her over the definition of blood relative."

I cough to hide my giggle at Lilac's explanation. She doesn't mean to be funny, but she's hilarious.

Beckett wraps an arm around my shoulders and kisses my hair. "How are you holding up?"

I elbow him. "Would everyone stop asking me if I'm okay? I'm not going to have a breakdown because my ex-boyfriend went from jerk to supreme asshole of the universe."

At least, I hope not. And, if I do, I hope it's in private. Besides, we don't know for sure it's Patrick who's been camping outside of town.

"What's happening?" I ask when I notice Lilac's mom lighting incense.

"She's blessing the space," Lilac explains. "She'll walk around the area to invite the spirits to gather with us at this blessed time."

"Hey," Phoenix pants as he joins us. His face is red and he's sweating.

I raise an eyebrow at him. "What did you do?" I murmur.

He smirks. "Nothing."

"I don't believe you."

He winks. "Don't worry. It's all in good fun."

"Phoenix Apollo Alston, if you ruin Aspen and Lyric's wedding night, I will make you regret it."

"She middle-named you," Lilac says. "It means she's serious."

Phoenix leans close to whisper in my ear. "We filled the honeymoon suite at *The Inn on Main* with balloons. They're outlawed in Winter Falls, but Aspen secretly loves balloons."

I melt into him. "That's the sweetest prank I've ever heard of."

"Let us gather in our sacred circle," Mrs. West summons us, and everyone moves to stand in a circle around the gazebo where Lyric awaits his bride.

Phoenix elbows me and points to where Aspen is walking toward the gazebo. She looks beautiful sporting a crown of wildflowers and wearing a maxi-length white dress. The dress appears innocent enough until I notice the lace detail around her center showing off a strip of skin. To top it off, she's shoeless.

When she notices Lyric, her pace quickens and she practically runs to him. He chuckles before briefly touching his lips to hers and grasping both of her hands in his. Mrs. West steps forward and gives each of them a ribbon.

"What's going on?"

"It's a handfasting. They'll tie their hands together as they recite their vows before they jump the broom for good luck," Phoenix explains.

"They're going to literally tie the knot?"

He winks down at me. "Now, you're getting it."

As Lyric recites his vows, he wraps the ribbon around their hands. When it's Aspen's turn, she does the same. After they've finished, Mrs. West helps them to tie the knots together before leading them to a broom. Hands lifted in the air, they jump the broom.

"We're married!" Aspen shouts.

"Now for the fun stuff," Phoenix says before strutting to the gazebo and taking center stage.

"What now?"

"Family and friends are invited to tell stories or sing songs about the couple," Lilac explains.

Phoenix clears his throat. He waits until the couple sits on a bench in front of him before he begins.

"I know I'm supposed to tell you loving stories about the couple now, but all of you have been around for the past twenty years of their love story. I think we've had enough of those stories."

"I love love!" Ashlyn yells from the other side of the circle. When she catches me looking at her, she waves.

"Instead, I feel it's my duty as Lyric's brother to tell as many embarrassing stories about the man as possible." He winks at Aspen. "It's not too late to get an annulment."

She sticks her tongue out at him, and Lyric growls, "We're not getting an annulment."

"My first memory of Lyric is playing duck, duck, goose. Except he didn't call it duck, duck, goose. In Lyric's world, the game was penis, penis, vagina." I feel my face flame but the rest of the crowd laughs.

"Of course, this is Winter Falls. No one minds when a five-year-old uses the words penis and vagina. No, the problem was he kept getting the boys and girls mixed up."

He scans the crowd until his gaze falls on Peace, a police officer who works with Lyric.

"Peace was not amused. He told Lyric in no uncertain terms he was a penis and not a vagina. Lyric disagreed, which is how we learned Lyric fights dirty."

"Still does," Peace yells, and laughter erupts from the crowd.

Once quiet falls, Phoenix continues. "And who can forget the time he pointed at Mrs. West when she was pregnant and said, 'I see your belly. I know what you did.'"

"And yet, somehow, he never wants to hear the details," Mrs. West grumbles.

Lyric groans and Phoenix's face turns a shade of green.

"It was me by the way. I was the baby in the belly," Ashlyn says because she has to be the center of attention or her head explodes.

"You're done," Lyric growls before standing.

His hands remain tied to Aspen's, and he ends up dragging her with him as he marches toward Phoenix in the center of the gazebo.

"Enough stories! Let's party!" Aspen shouts before Lyric can speak.

Lyric lunges toward Phoenix who chuckles and waves as he walks off the stage toward me.

"What do you say, Gabby? You want to party?"

I've never been much for parties, but I think this might be one party I want to attend. Pretty much anything Winter Falls has to offer has been fun thus far. And no one makes me feel like I'm the odd one out because of my shyness.

"Yeah." I nod.

He grasps my hand and leads me toward where the tables and chairs are set up. For a moment, I allow myself to pretend we're a real couple. Not two people pretending to be together because of my jerkwad ex-boyfriend.

Sigh. If only pretending could make things come true.

Chapter 18

Kidnapping – doesn't always involve a child

"YOU'RE COMING WITH ME," Juniper announces the second I open the door at the farmhouse to her a week later.

"What's wrong? Did one of your animals get out? Are your dogs loose again? Hold on. Let me get my shoes on." I start to shove my feet into galoshes.

Juniper kicks them away. "No galoshes."

My brow wrinkles and my gaze dips to my fuzzy carpet slippers. "What? You don't expect me to go tromping through the muddy fields in my slippers, do you?"

She grabs my arm and pulls me out of the house. "Who said anything about muddy fields?"

"How else are we going to find your animals?"

"What animals?"

I plant my feet on the porch. "The animals that are missing!"

She huffs. "There are no animals missing."

I rub my forehead. "I don't think I drank enough coffee today."

Phoenix chuckles as he reaches the porch. He takes the three steps in one go and I admire how his muscles flex at the movement.

"Gabby, you always have enough coffee. If we cut you open, your blood wouldn't be red, it'd be brown."

"I don't drink that much coffee."

He snorts. "Sure, you don't." He smiles at Juniper. "What brings you to my side of the fence?"

She waves a hand in my direction. "This one is going with me."

I retreat a step. "W-where are we going?"

"Book club!" she announces it as if book club is a rock concert I've been dying to attend.

"Um, I haven't read any book for book club."

I didn't even know there was a book club in town, to be honest. Although, I shouldn't be surprised. Winter Falls may be small, but it's packed full of community activities. I can totally envision myself settling here forever – preferably with a hot goat farmer dude. I glance at Phoenix from under my lashes. He'll do just fine. More than do.

"You don't need to read the book," Juniper tells me. "The couple meet, they fall in love, they have lots of sex, he does something incredibly stupid, they break up, he realizes he can't live without her and begs for her back, and they live happily ever after."

"Don't be a romance hater."

Her smile is triumphant. "See? You should totally come to book club with me."

"Um…"

I search the outside as if the farm can cough up an excuse for me to stay at home with Phoenix. In the evenings, he lays on the couch and watches sports while I sit near him reading, but I always imagine I'm laying with my head in his lap reading while he plays with my hair and watches the television.

I shake my head and clear those visions right out of it. Phoenix doesn't want me. Yes, there was the 'almost kiss' and the infamous 'hair kiss' but nothing since then. We went to a freaking wedding together and nothing happened. If that doesn't scream 'Unavailable!', I don't know what does.

"Go on." Phoenix pushes. "You don't want to spend every night on the sofa with boring old me, do you?"

Sigh. I wish I could tell him how much I want to spend every evening on the couch with him. I wouldn't need to read any sexy romances anymore if I was spending my nights with him.

"Are you worried about being safe?" Juniper asks. "Because you shouldn't be."

I'm not worried about being safe. Worried about Patrick being a dickhead? Now there's a concern. Worried he's going to embarrass the daylights out of me? Practically a given. But worry about being safe? Nah. He can't hurt me when the entire town is looking out for me.

Why am I hesitating then? Duh. Large group of people. No, thanks. Large groups and I don't mix. Shy, introvert here.

"I haven't read the book," I repeat my excuse.

"You don't even know what this month's book is."

Dang. She got me there.

"What book is it?"

"*Things We Never Got Over*."

Double dang. Of course, I've read it. I've read every single book Lucy Score has written.

"Ha!" Juniper points to my face. "Your expression is screaming you've read it. Let's go."

"One sec," Phoenix says and drags me into the farmhouse closing the door behind him. He whirls me around until we're facing each other before squatting down until we're eye to eye. "If you don't want to go, don't go."

"Easy for you to say," I mumble.

He cocks a brow. "It is? Am I not the grumpy, asocial farmer?"

I purse my lips. "Who said you were? You're neither grumpy nor asocial."

He chuckles. "This isn't about me. This is about you. If you don't want to go, no one's going to make you."

"Are you sure? Juniper looks ready to throw me over the back of her bike and kidnap me."

"I limit my kidnapping to sexy male movie stars who are terrified of cute little animals," Juniper shouts through the door.

Phoenix herds me further into the room.

"She can still hear us here," I say as a test.

"What did you say? I can't hear you."

Phoenix's lips tip up at Juniper's shout before he becomes serious again. "You don't have to go. I'll kick Juniper out myself."

"You would?"

"Of course." He pauses. "But maybe you should go."

I frown. Is he trying to get rid of me? Does he not enjoy our evening ritual as much as I do? Stop being a fool, Gabrielle. Phoenix doesn't want you. This is fake. F. A. K. E. Fake.

"I'm not kicking you out, but I think it would be good for you to make friends in town. If you're planning on staying in Winter Falls that is."

I'm totally planning on staying in this quirky town. Everyone's pushy as all get out, but not once has anyone made fun of me for stuttering or being shy. And since the original fiasco at the town meeting where the gossip gals announced my crush on Phoenix, no one has mentioned a thing about it.

Plus, I need at least two lifetimes to try all the treats at *Bake Me Happy* and all the beers at *Naked Falls Brewing.* It's good to have goals.

"Okay," I breathe out. "But what about dinner?"

"We have wine and snacks," Juniper says through the open door, and I glare at her. "What? I got tired of waiting for you guys to finish your heart-to-heart."

"Of course, you did," I mutter before indicating the kitchen. "I meant I made dinner."

"I can eat. What did you make?" She checks the clock. "Oh shoot. We'll be late if we eat and if we're late, Aspen will be pissed."

"Aspen?"

"Who else? She is the owner of *Fall Into A Good Book.*"

"I thought she'd still be on her honeymoon."

"They only went for a week and got back this morning." She grimaces. "Maybe we should skip book club altogether."

I'm getting whiplash from this conversation. "What? Why? You're the one who's ready to kidnap me."

"I forgot about Aspen and Lyric's honeymoon. She's going to spend the entire evening bragging about the trip. I don't need to hear about how awesome the sex with Lyric is." She feigns gagging.

Phoenix coughs. "Me either."

They're a bunch of prudes, which – considering they live in Winter Falls and the stories Phoenix told at the wedding – surprises me. Then again, I do not want to hear about my brother having sex. Ew. Gross. Okay, I get it now.

"Maybe she won't bring up her sexual escapades?"

"Ha!" Juniper barks. "The gossip gals won't let her not bring up her sexual escapades."

"The gossip gals are in the book club?" I'm beginning to think there's no way to avoid the women in hot pink.

"Who do you think picks the books we read?"

"Aspen?"

She bursts out laughing. "Ha! You're hilarious. As if Aspen has any control over the gossip gals."

"No one has control over those ladies," Phoenix mutters next to me.

"They're going to be overexcited tonight with Aspen returning home a married woman. I imagine we won't talk about the book at all."

"But *Things We Never Got Over* is an awesome book. I want to discuss it."

"Great! Let's go discuss this … office romance?" I shake my head. "Billionaire romance?" I shake my head. "Alien romance?"

I huff. "You didn't read the book, did you?"

"I already said there's no need to read the book."

"Wait outside, Juniper. Gabby will me be out in a minute."

"Gabby? He calls you Gabby? Ooohh." She waggles her eyebrows. "I'll wait outside. I don't need to watch my sister from a different mister make out with my brother from another mother."

"Ashlyn isn't the only crazy sister in the West family," I mutter loud enough for her to hear. She winks as she shuts the door behind him.

"Go have fun," Phoenix tells me once we're alone. "I'll warm up dinner and save the leftovers for lunch tomorrow."

I continue to hesitate. Juniper on her own I can handle. A room full of West sisters and the gossip gals? I'm not sure there's an introvert on this planet who can handle that particular scenario.

Phoenix squeezes my neck. "You'll be fine. If you aren't, send out the bat signal."

"The bat signal. Is there an app for that?"

He winks. "There's an app for everything. He squeezes my neck again before dropping his hand. "Have fun. I'll have your hot chocolate waiting for you when you get home."

Home. Oh, how I do love the sound of Phoenix and his farmhouse being my home.

Chapter 19

Mistake – when you decide to 'borrow' someone's goats for an hour without telling him or, you know, getting his approval

I chew on my bottom lip as I watch my sisters along with Lilac and her sisters and the gossip gals enter the paddock.

"I don't think this is a good idea after all."

"You're the one who suggested it at book club," Cayenne reminds me.

Yeah, well, no one warned me about the copious amounts of wine at book club. They said there'd be snacks! One bowl of pretzels does not constitute snacks in my book. And whose idea was it to make sangria? I usually don't enjoy wine unless it's super sweet but sangria? I dare anyone to tell me they don't enjoy the fruity wine.

"It'll be fine. No, it will be better than fine. It will be a new experience for everyone." I sound like I'm trying to convince myself. Probably because I am.

Lilac purses her lips. "I don't understand why I was ordered to attend this new experience."

"Family activity!" Ashlyn and Juniper shout their response in unison.

Apparently, those are the magic words as Lilac walks off without another word.

I cringe as I watch everyone place their matts on the ground. I spent several hours this morning removing goat berries – cute name aside, it's still poop – but I most certainly didn't manage to get all of them.

Especially since I opened the paddock for the goats ten minutes ago. I quickly learned goats can make a mess – and I do mean mess in all shapes and sizes and stink levels – in sixty seconds flat.

"There are only ten goats. I thought we'd each get our own goat," Ashlyn places her hands on her hips and her pregnant tummy juts out.

Juniper studies her younger sister. "Should you even be doing yoga? You're at least a gazillion months pregnant."

"Yoga can improve sleep and reduce stress and anxiety for pregnant women," Lilac says.

Juniper snorts. "Because this one has an abundance of stress and anxiety."

"Maybe not but I am short on sleep."

Juniper rolls her eyes. "Being short on sleep because you're boning your husband all the time is not the 'improvement of sleep' the research refers to."

Ashlyn grins and bounces on her toes. "I do bone my husband an awful lot. It's not my fault, though, the pregnancy hormones make me horny."

Juniper buries her face in her hands. "I had to start this conversation, didn't I? I should know better."

And I'm done listening to people talk about boning. Especially since I'm not boning anyone. Not when the man I want to bone doesn't want to bone me. Lordie gordie. Listen to me use the word boning in every single sentence. I really shouldn't hang around Ashlyn. Talk about a bad influence.

"Listen up," I say, but no one pays attention to me. Of course, I barely spoke louder than a mouse. I blow out a breath and try again. "Listen up."

Cassandra places her fingers in her mouth and does one of those cool really loud whistles. She's tried to teach me how a million times but the only noise I manage to make is a small squeak.

"Our hostess, Gabrielle, needs a few words."

Quiet falls and everyone's attention rivets on me. Eek! This is worse than being a mouse. Stupid Sangria. I am never drinking it again. I don't care how yummy and fruity it tastes. No more.

I clear my throat. "Um, d–d–don't stick your fingers anywhere near a goat's mouth because they will bite, and their bottom teeth can draw blood."

"Oops!" Ashlyn shouts and yanks her hand away from a goat's mouth. And here I thought the warning was unnecessary. All warnings are necessary when she's around.

"There's a chance a goat might poop or pee on your yoga mat."

Feather makes a face. "I can't be sitting in pee or poop. No one will buy my ice cream if they find out."

"No one's going to be rolling around in goat poop. Geez. Get a grip. I'm certain Gabrielle's equipped for the situation." Elizabeth motions to the spray bottles at my feet.

"Ahem. Yes. I have spray disinfectant should any goat have an accident."

"My goat's having an accident right now." Ashlyn points to a goat relieving itself a few feet from her. "Psst. I don't think it's an accident."

Juniper rubs her hands together as she bounces on her toes. "Let's get started. I've always wanted to try goat yoga. The therapeutic benefit of interacting with animals alone is worth it."

"There's not much definitive research on the benefit of interacting with animals," Lilac says.

Juniper rolls her eyes. "People who hang out with animals often say it makes them feel better. How can you argue with that?"

"I would argue—"

"Of course, you would," Juniper mutters.

"Ahem. I would argue hanging around animals that are your pets is vastly different than a goat climbing on top of you during a yoga class."

"The goats are going to climb on us?" Clove shrieks.

"Cool!" Cassandra promptly runs after a goat while cooing to it about her back being available as a perch.

This was definitely a bad idea.

"Goats love to climb but there's no guarantee they'll climb on you," Juniper answers.

Phew. I'm relieved Juniper is here today. She's a complete animal lover. Duh. She manages the Wildlife Refuge. Of course, she loves animals. Good thing she's also knowledgeable about them. She can handle any questions while I somehow try to stop the goats from dropping berries for the group on their yoga mats.

"Shall we begin?" Cayenne asks and everyone settles down. "We'll begin with the Tadasana."

The tada-whata? Good thing I decided my job today was to herd goats because I've never done yoga before, and I don't think goat yoga is the place to start.

"Stand with your feet together and arms at your side. Ground your feet, making sure to press all four corners down into the ground." Cayenne scans the women to ensure they're following her instructions before continuing.

"Now, let's straighten our legs and tuck our tailbones in as we engage our thigh muscles. As you inhale, elongate through your torso and extend your arms up, then out. Exhale and release your shoulder blades away from your head, toward the back of your waist as you release your arms back to your sides."

Confession. Despite watching Cayenne as she gives the instructions, I don't understand a word of what she's saying. I don't foresee a career in yoga in my future.

"Ah!" Aspen screeches.

I rush to her to find her leaning back with her hair hanging down her back. Unfortunately, a goat thought this was the opportune moment to munch on her locks.

"Bad goat." I swat her with my towel, but the doe isn't releasing her prize.

"Come on, girl. Let go. I'll get you a treat. All you have to do is release Aspen's hair."

"Don't give me a bad haircut, goat. I will not be amused."

"Maybe I can yank on your hair?"

"No! Don't yank my hair. It'll hurt."

"Geez, Aspen. Don't be a scaredy cat. It's just a little goat. She won't harm you."

Aspen spears Juniper with a look that could incite fire. "Easy for you to say. You're not the one whose hair is currently on today's goat breakfast menu."

"What the hell is going on here?"

Oh snap! I didn't hear Phoenix approaching.

"Uh oh. Someone's in trouble," Ashlyn sings, completely oblivious to the anger rolling off Phoenix in waves.

"I thought you were at the auction all morning."

"And I thought I could trust you to be on my farm."

Ouch. I flinch at the scorn in his voice.

"You can. Everything's taken care of. The stalls are mucked. The does are milked. Everything's fine."

"Except one of my goats is eating Aspen's hair."

He marches forward and deftly pulls her hair from the goat's jaws before patting the animal on her behind to move her along.

"Why the hell I ever thought you'd fit in on the farm is beyond me."

My eyes itch and I blink fast to stop the tears from falling at his words. But I refuse to be the weak person I've been for the past year and a half since Patrick got his hands on me. No, I will defend myself no matter how much my knees are knocking.

"I thought it would bring in some revenue since you won't let me pay for anything."

"Because you're a guest! You're not my roommate! You're not here to stay! It's fake!"

I have no chance of stopping those tears from falling now. I refuse to wipe them away in front of him, though. Nope. I will not be a sniveling fool. At least not until I'm safely locked behind the bathroom door with the shower running to disguise the sound of my sobbing.

"I think we're going to have to open up a new round of betting. Someone is more stubborn than I gave him credit for."

I nearly lash out at Sage for her callous remarks. Does she not realize my heart is breaking right now?

"I believe this is not the appropriate moment to mention wagers," Lilac says.

I could give a flying fig about Winter Falls' obsession with betting at the moment. What I care about is how Phoenix is staring down at me as if I betrayed him.

"You weren't supposed to even notice."

He snorts. "And that makes it all right? You're not the woman I thought you were." And with his final arrow to my heart hitting its mark, he marches off.

Elizabeth reaches for me, but I can't handle being comforted now. I sprint into the farmhouse and manage to make it to the bathroom before I collapse in tears.

Idiot. I know Phoenix doesn't want me as a girlfriend, but I thought we were at least friends. Although, considering the way he lashed out at me, friends is pushing it. I'm an obligation and nothing more.

Chapter 20

Apology – better include more than just saying the word sorry but hopefully not a pathetic cake

PHOENIX

Crap. Crap. Crap. I'm an asshole. No, worse than an asshole. What's worse than an asshole? Gabby would know. Of course, I can't ask her because she's not talking to me. She hasn't come out of her bedroom when I'm inside since I decided to use her for a whipping post two days ago.

What am I going to do? I stare down at the chocolate coffee cake I made to bribe her into talking to me. It looks like a giant goat took a massive shit on a plate.

Maybe this is a bad idea. The bedroom door creaks open. Too late now.

Gabby slowly creeps down the stairs. As she makes her way to the kitchen where I'm standing her gaze remains locked on the back door I pretended to leave from not five minutes ago, so she doesn't notice me until she's less than a foot in front of me.

"AH!"

She screams and jumps backward into the kitchen table. Her legs buckle and she starts to fall to the ground. I catch her before she hits the floor.

"Easy now," I murmur as I wrap my arms around her.

Relief pours through me at the feeling of her in my arms again. Her avoiding me for two days has been pure hell. I deserved it. No doubt about it. But it was still hell.

She flails in my arms, and I make sure she's steady on her feet before releasing her.

"What are you doing?"

"Standing in my kitchen?"

"Yes, I'm well aware it's *your* kitchen," she snarls.

Damn it. I'm doing a stand-up job of apologizing to her. I tuck my hands in my pockets and try again.

"I wanted to apologize to you."

"You pretended to go outside and hid in the kitchen because you want to apologize?"

When you say it out loud, it sounds idiotic but what other choice did I have? She's a champion in avoiding me. No grumpy good mornings before she's had her coffee. No bringing me a cold glass of lemonade on a hot afternoon. No smell of something delicious for dinner after a long, hard day of work. No spending the evening on the sofa watching a game with her nearby reading.

"I wouldn't say hide."

She crosses her arms over her chest. "Which is why you're standing in the dark."

"I'm not standing in the dark," I argue. She frowns and I quickly add, "I have a surprise for you."

Delight sparks in her eyes, but she blinks to cover it up. "A surprise? Is it how you planned to scare the daylights out of me? If so, mission accomplished."

"Maybe I should wait until you drink your first coffee before I give you the surprise."

She plants her hands on her hips. "I still haven't seen this supposed surprise."

I probably shouldn't have built the surprise up this much. It's sure to disappoint now. I pick up the cake and bring it to her. "I made you a cake."

She bites her lip, but I can't miss how the corner of her lips tip up. "This is a cake?"

"It's a chocolate coffee cake. You love coffee and chocolate …" I trail off with a shrug of my shoulders.

"Did you find a chocolate coffee cake recipe, or did you add just chocolate to a coffee cake recipe?"

"The later?"

"Erm… You can't exactly add an ingredient to a recipe without changing the measurements of the other ingredients."

Ah, now I understand why the cake resembles a pile of shit.

"Maybe it tastes good?" I hope it's at least edible.

"Let's try it," she says before opening the cabinets and removing two plates.

I make us cups of coffee while she cuts the cake. We sit at the kitchen table, and I wait for her to taste the cake before putting a piece in my mouth. Her eyes widen as she chews.

"It's not half bad."

I stuff a piece in my mouth. Huh. She wasn't lying to be nice. It's edible.

I wait until we've finished our cake and coffee before speaking. "I need to apologize."

She nods and I continue. "I was totally out of line the other day. I shouldn't have yelled at you. You surprised me and I acted like a fucking idiot."

"You won't hear me denying it," she mutters.

"Will you accept my apology?"

She drums her fingers on the table for a minute before responding. "How can I not accept your apology when you made me this delicious and beautiful cake?"

I grunt. "It was my first attempt at baking."

"I'll tell Rowan there's a new baker in town and he should watch out."

"You accept my apology?"

She nods but then she dips her chin and her hair covers her face. My teeth clench at the gesture. I thought we were past this.

"Maybe we should talk about what happened?"

"I said I was an idiot."

"Total idiot," she corrects.

"Yes," I agree.

"Biggest idiot in Winter Falls. No. Colorado."

"Fine. I'm the biggest idiot in America. You happy now?"

She giggles but her chin remains dipped with her gaze aimed at the floor.

I wait for her to speak, but I'm not exactly known for my patience. "What do you want to talk about?"

"You said everything was fake."

I grit my teeth at the reminder. I should have never said those words.

"I thought we were friends."

"We are," I'm quick to reassure her.

She remains quiet and I realize I owe her more of an explanation. Damn. Am I really going to tell her my deepest shame?

"There was a girl." Way to keep it vague. "A girlfriend." I swallow as memories of Tina's betrayal bombard me. "Needless to say, things didn't work out."

"It ended bad?"

"The worst way possible."

She gasps. "She didn't abuse you, did she?"

Way to prove I'm the biggest idiot in the world. Of course, Gabby's mind would immediately think of abuse when I say worst way possible.

"No. She betrayed me."

Her nose scrunches up and she finally meets my gaze. "She cheated on you?"

I swallow past the painful reminder and nod.

"Was she crazy? Or blind?" She motions toward me. "You're easily the hottest guy in Colorado. Did she think she could do better?"

"She didn't want a farmer," I say.

"Did she not know you were a farmer when you met? This supports my blind theory. No, a blind person can hear you're a farmer. Was she blind and deaf?"

Nope. Just too good for a farmer and Winter Falls. But I'm done talking about Tina.

"Are we good?"

Her nose wrinkles as she contemplates her answer. "Um, don't use any ice cubes today."

I'm confused by her bizarre response. "Why?"

"I may have accidentally put poop in them."

I bark out a laugh. "Poop?"

"Not real poop, plastic poop."

"I guess if it's plastic poop, it's okay," I say as if I understand what she's going on about. "What are you talking about?"

She plays with the crumbs on her plate. "I was mad at you."

"I know," I prompt when she doesn't say more.

"I wanted to get revenge for the way you humiliated me in front of everyone I know."

I grasp her hand and squeeze. "I'm sorry."

This is where I should tell her the whole truth. How when I saw her doing yoga with the goats, I had a flashback of Tina. She was always whining about how my being a goat farmer wasn't enough. I needed to 'expand my horizons' and 'explore other business opportunities'. With those memories bombarding me, I saw the yoga mats and the goats and promptly lost my mind.

But I don't confess any of it to Gabby. How can I? She's not on the farm for real. I may have been an asshole when I said our relationship is fake, but I wasn't completely wrong.

Gabby clears her throat. "Anyway, I didn't have any tiny baby dolls, so I went with the fake poop thing."

"Tiny baby dolls?"

She waves a hand at me. "Don't ask."

"Okay." I stand and gather our plates. "And I won't use any ice cubes today either."

"And I promise not to use the tiny baby dolls when they arrive in the mail."

I seriously don't want to know.

"We're good?" She nods. "You won't hide from me in your room anymore?"

"I wasn't hiding." I cock an eyebrow. "Fine. I won't hide anymore."

"Good. Because I need to go into town this afternoon and you're coming with."

"I can stay home. I don't need to go into town."

She sounds sincere and I wish with all my heart I could believe her, but I don't.

"Too bad. I need your help." Plus, we need to work harder on selling this fake relationship. I don't tell her that, though. She's liable to shut down at the word fake.

"I'm happy to help."

She's not indulging me. She helps out at the farm all the time. With her here, my workload has become manageable for the first time in years. I wish – I shake my head – Nope. No wishing for things I can't have. Gabby won't stay on the farm long-term. It's a novelty for her now is all.

Chapter 21

First kiss – can knock you on your ass if you're not careful

PHOENIX POKES HIS HEAD into my office. No, not my office. His office that I'm borrowing, but I'd totally steal it if I could. Unfortunately, after this morning's talk, it's painfully obvious he's not interested in a relationship.

His ex burned him as bad as mine did, and we're both carrying the scars. I'm working my butt off to erase mine, but he revels in his. It's a waste, but there's nothing I can do about it. I'm not the girl who's going to change anyone's mind – especially not his.

"You ready?"

He smiles and those two dimples come out to play and I wish like crazy I could be the girl to change his mind. I'd show him how loyal and devoted a woman can be.

"Earth to Gabby."

Phoenix snaps his fingers in front of my face, and I jump in my chair.

"Sorry. I was thinking."

"What were you thinking about?"

My cheeks warm. "Work," I lie.

He doesn't appear to believe me, but he lets it go. "You ready to go into town?"

I quickly save my work before shutting down my computer. I slam the laptop shut and stand. "All ready."

He motions to the door. "After you."

"You never did say what you need my help with," I say as we drive into town in his truck.

He nods to the bed of the truck. "I have to make a delivery."

I glance behind me but do a doubletake when I realize the truck bed is full to the brim with goat poop.

"What are you going to do with goat poop?"

"The manure can be used as fertilizer." Oh. Right. I should know this. "Eden. Have you met Eden?"

"I don't think I have, but I remember passing a store named *Eden's Garden*."

"*Eden's Garden* is her store. Her mother started it and named it after her. When she passed, Eden took over."

"And she uses the goat poop to help grow her plants?"

He chuckles. "Yes, she uses the goat poop."

My nose wrinkles. "But it stinks."

"Actually, goat poop is practically odorless. It's the goat urine that's offending your delicate sense of smell."

I roll my eyes. "I grew up with three sisters and a brother with one bathroom. I wouldn't say my sense of smell is delicate."

"One bathroom? I thought your family had money?"

"Why would you think my family has money?" I mean, it's true, but how does he know?

"You don't seriously think you can keep a secret in Winter Falls, do you?"

"I guess not." And then, because I'm an idiot who yearns for this man to know everything about me, I spill my secrets to him. "My parents came into an inheritance when I was a baby. Before then, they were just your everyday schoolteacher and accountant. They decided to save the money for us kids, so we continued to live in the house they bought when they got married until they died."

His hand lands on my thigh and squeezes. "I'm sorry you lost them."

I inhale a deep breath and let it out slowly. After all this time, it still hurts to think about them. I miss them every day. Mom's the one who taught me to cook. Whenever I'm in the kitchen mixing up ingredients, I think of her and wish I could call her to discuss whatever I'm making. I wish I could ask her what she thinks of Phoenix.

And my dad was the sweetest man. When he came home from work, the first thing he did was search out Mom. He'd lift her up and whirl her around, excited to see her at the end of the day. I want the type of love they had, but I'm beginning to think their love was the stuff of legends.

"Thank you," I squeak. I clear my throat and continue the story. "When Beckett took over raising us, he used some of the inheritance money to feed and clothe us but left the rest in investments. After he landed the job as CEO of *Clean Mountain Environment*, he asked if he could invest the money in stock of the company. Only Olivia objected – but she always objects."

"You never talk about Olivia."

I stare at the window. "Because it's painful. Olivia doesn't love us."

He squeezes my thigh again. "I don't believe it. How could anyone not love you?"

Um, hello? Who are you to talk? You refuse to even try to have a relationship with me. I keep those thoughts to myself, though. No sense cutting myself open in front of someone who's not willing to do the same.

"In conclusion, my family has money, but we don't *have* money."

"Gotcha." He pulls into a field and stops. "Here we are."

A woman waves as she approaches us.

"You must be Gabrielle."

Two can play at this game. "And you're Eden?" Except my words come out sounding like a question instead of a statement. Way to be strong, Gabrielle.

"I haven't seen you in my store. Of course, if you're living on the farm with Phoenix, you don't have much need for plants." She winks. Yep. No secrets in this town.

Phoenix lowers the tailgate and picks a shovel off of the top of the heap of manure.

"Where do you want the fertilizer? Here? Or somewhere else?"

I join him at the truck. "Where's my shovel?"

"I only brought one."

"But how am I supposed to help?"

"I've got a shovel for you," Eden says before handing me the one she was holding.

I proceed to 'help' Phoenix shovel the manure into a big pile in Eden's garden. Ha! Eden. Garden. I just got it. This town is crazy.

Judging by how quickly Phoenix's half of the truck bed empties compared to mine, I'm not much help. He could have easily done this work by himself. But then I wouldn't get the chance to watch his biceps bulge as he works. Who knew biceps were sexy? Trust me. They are when they belong to Phoenix.

He wipes the back of his hand across his forehead before declaring we're finished. His t-shirt is sticking to his chest with perspiration. Sweaty muscles are sexier than plain old muscles. Yowzah! No wonder I feel flush.

"I think we deserve an ice cream after all our hard work," he says as he slams the tailgate shut.

"I won't say no to ice cream." Ever, I think but don't say. He doesn't need to know my obsession with chocolate extends to chocolate ice cream.

"We'll pick the truck up later," he hollers to Eden before taking my hand and leading me toward Main Street where all the shops are.

"You don't mind strolling around town in your work clothes all sweaty?"

"Are you saying I stink?" He lifts his arm and sniffs his armpit. "Smells peachy clean to me. But maybe you have a different opinion." He shoves his armpit into my face. I fight him off as I giggle.

"Don't be gross."

He wraps an arm around my shoulders and draws me near. "Am I being gross now? With my sweaty body draped over yours?"

Oh boy. He does not want to know how much I want his sweaty, naked body hovering over mine. I'd do just about anything to make it happen.

I roll my eyes and glance away before he realizes what I'm thinking. My gaze lands on a man marching toward us. His face is obscured by a hat, but I'd know that walk anywhere. It's Patrick. He really is here.

I thought all this fake relationship and living at the farm stuff was bull cocky. I was convinced Patrick would never come to Winter Falls to find me. But the error of my thinking is standing directly in front of me. I freeze.

"What's wrong?"

"It's Patrick," I whisper and indicate the man with a tilt of my chin. "What do we do?"

Phoenix's nostrils flare and a muscle in his jaw spasms, but he inhales a deep breath and soothes his features.

"We do exactly what we should be doing."

Should be doing? What is he talking about?

His eyes drop to my lips. Does he mean kiss me? I lick my bottom lip as I imagine his mouth on mine. He groans and then his lips meld with mine.

I thought he'd give me one of those lip touches, but Phoenix isn't slow and he isn't gentle. His tongue demands entrance and I don't hesitate to open to him. Why would I? This is all I've wanted for months.

I groan when the taste of coffee, chocolate, and something unique to Phoenix hits me. His tongue plunders my mouth and I am a willing bystander. I grasp his t-shirt and pull him near until there's not an inch of space between us.

I feel Phoenix's hard length press against my belly and tingles spread from my lips down my body to my core. Yes. I want to feel his hardness pushing into me as he kisses me like he never wants to stop.

"I'm opening a new round of bets!" Sage shouts, and I stumble in Phoenix's arms.

He gentles his kiss before pulling away. He leans his forehead against mine while we both try to catch our breaths. His eyes are full of heat and desire, and I can't look away.

"You, Gabrielle Grace Dempsey, are not what I expected."

He's not what I expected either, but he's exactly what I want. Too bad I'm not brave enough to say those words to him.

Chapter 22

*Denial – when you lie about your feelings to 'protect' yourself.
Often comes back to bite you in the ass.*

PHOENIX

"You promise you won't go running around?"

Gabby rolls her eyes. "I'm not exactly the running type."

Surprisingly true despite those lean, shapely legs of hers. Legs I want to feel wrapped around me as I— I stop those thoughts before my cock makes it abundantly clear how in the gutter my thoughts are.

"Maybe, I should—"

She pushes me toward the door. "Stop it. Patrick won't come to the farmhouse. But if he does, I won't open the door to him. Pan will keep me company."

Maa.

"See?" Gabby's smile is triumphant as she strokes the goat's fur. "I've got the perfect company for a Saturday afternoon."

"I'm going. I'm going."

I'd rather spend the afternoon lazing around the farmhouse with Gabby, but after the kiss we shared, I don't trust myself to be in her presence without my lips finding hers again. Damn. The woman can kiss.

I jump on my bike for the short ride into town. I'm leaving the truck for Gabby since her car is still at her apartment. If Patrick shows up and she needs to make a run for it, my truck will be a much better option than a bike.

Although, I sincerely doubt he has a vehicle. This is Winter Falls. If someone is driving around in town in a vehicle without a dispensation, a resident would have spotted it by now. And everyone would know about it since it's impossible to keep a secret in this town.

When I arrive at Rowan's house to watch the college football game, I sneak in the backdoor. I close the sliding door as slowly as possible behind me to prevent it from squeaking.

"Hey, bro," Lyric greets from where he's waiting for me, and I startle causing me to trip. I grab the counter to stop myself from falling on my face.

"Damn, Lyric. Did you have to try and scare the crap out of me?"

"Hell yeah." He grins.

My oldest brother always did think scaring me and River when we were growing up was a blast. He'd wait in our closets in the morning and when we opened the door, he'd say *boo* softly. I quickly learned to use the bathroom before I opened my closet. Of course, then he'd hide in the bathtub behind the shower curtain. Such a little shit.

"I'm glad marriage hasn't changed you."

He smirks. "I'm still the same man, except now I need to drink more fluids."

"No need to brag. Everyone in town has caught you and Aspen going at it at least once. We know how horny the two of you are."

"Enough about me." He hands me a beer. "Are you ready?"

I play dumb. "Why wouldn't I be ready to watch a football game with my brothers and friends?"

There's a reason I tried sneaking into the house after kick-off. There's no way my friends or family will allow the chance to pass without bothering me about the kiss. It's none of their damn business, but it won't stop them from pestering me.

"Funny," Lyric mutters before strolling into the living room.

As soon as I step into the room, the television cuts off and all eyes focus on me. Fuck.

"What happened? Did you lose power?"

"Yeah, dumbass. I lost power to my television, but my lights are miraculously still on." Rowan indicates the overhead light with his beer.

"Did your television break?"

"How long are we going to let him ask evasive questions?" Cole asks, and I glare at him. "What? I was only asking."

"I vote for as long as he wants," River says.

I won't kid myself and think my younger brother is on my side. Nope. River doesn't want to have a discussion of my 'love' life for his own selfish reasons. Namely, he doesn't believe in love. Which is odd since our parents are still madly in love and, as far as I know, he hasn't had some bad experience with a girlfriend the way I did.

In this room, we're in the minority. Everyone except my baby brother and I are loved up. Lyric has Aspen. Rowan is married to Aspen's baby sister, Ashlyn. Cole is engaged to another West sister, Ellery. Gabby's brother, Beckett, is with Lilac. The final West sister, Juniper, is with Maverick, but the movie star is off somewhere shooting a film.

I sigh and collapse on a spot on the sofa. "Let's get the ribbing over with."

Everyone starts talking at once and Lyric whistles to quiet them down.

"Hold on. First, I want to know where Gabby is. Did you drop her at someone's house?"

"No. She's out at the farm."

"Alone?"

"Yeah. Alone. She'll be fine." Although his questions are making me doubt myself again.

"I'll have Peace do a drive-by." He digs his phone out of his pocket and walks off while dialing.

Rowan rubs his hands together. "I want to hear all about what happened after the kiss."

"Hold up," Cole says. "I want to hear all about the kiss."

"What are we? A bunch of women? Do you want me to braid your hair next?" River stands and marches off. "I'll be in the den watching the football game if any real men care to join me."

"Real men aren't afraid to discuss their feelings!" Beckett shouts after him.

I am not going to discuss my feelings with any of these men. I don't care if they are my closest friends.

"We're missing the game."

Rowan snorts. "It's digital television. I paused the game. As long as no one opens their social media, we'll be fine. We'll catch up at half-time."

"But we'll miss the half-time show." I'm grasping at straws at this point.

"I'm recording the entire game."

"Do you have an answer for every problem?"

He smirks. "My wife would say yes."

Yeah, well, his wife is completely crazy. I scan the area. "Where is Ashlyn anyway?"

"The West sisters are hanging out at Cole's place today."

I cock an eyebrow at Cole. "And you're cool with this?"

"They've got Willow with them. They won't create too much chaos with a baby around."

I chuckle. "You haven't gotten to know the family very well yet, have you?"

He waggles his eyebrows. "I think I've gotten to know Ellery pretty damn well."

"Great," Lyric says when he returns. "Peace and Freedom will do drive-bys at your house and we've made it back to the topic of sex."

Beckett groans. "I don't want to hear about my baby sister having sex."

"Good. Because I wasn't planning on talking about it."

Lyric smirks. "They didn't have sex."

"How can you tell?" Cole asks.

"Phoenix is a braggart. He always wants to discuss his conquests."

I glare at him. How dare he think I would tell him about having sex with Gabby? She's not some tramp.

"I think you have me confused with River. I haven't discussed my sex life with you since high school."

"Right. When you asked me how to improve your oral skills."

Beckett growls. "I don't want to hear about this shit. We're talking about my sister."

"Actually," Lyric points out, "we're not since nothing happened."

"Except the kiss," Rowan corrects. "It was the best kind of foreplay."

Beckett growls again, and I hold up my hands. "Nothing happened when we got home."

"Who had him taking care of himself in the shower?" Lyric asks the room.

"Hold on. I didn't say I rubbed one out in the shower." I did – Gabby had me hard as fucking rock – but they don't need to know. What happens in my shower is my private business.

"Why didn't you use Gabby to help you take care of those needs?"

I growl at Rowan. "You don't use a woman like Gabby."

"Good." Beckett nods. "I don't have to kill you." He points to Rowan. "You, I may still kill."

"You can try." Rowan stands to his full six-foot-five height.

"Don't mind if I do." Beckett gets to his feet. He's five inches shorter and a whole lot of pounds lighter than Rowan, but he doesn't seem to give a crap about the uneven odds.

"If you're going to shed blood, go outside," Lyric commands.

Rowan snorts and backs down. "No way. The gossip gals will be here cheering us on within minutes."

"I thought the entertainment was a football game today. This is much better." Cole stuffs a handful of popcorn in his mouth.

"Don't lie. You know Winter Falls well enough by now to know we were going to grill Phoenix about the kiss."

At Lyric's statement, I've had it.

"Enough! There will be no gossiping about Phoenix kissing Gabby. It was a kiss. Nothing more. We only kissed because we're doing this fake relationship thing and she saw her asshat ex creeping around town."

A gasp sounds before a dish clatters to the floor.

Fucking hell. I know that gasp. I glance over my shoulder for confirmation. Damn. It's Gabby. She's staring at me like I stole her puppy before skinning him alive.

I stand. "Gabby. It's not …"

She holds up a hand. "I don't want to hear it."

"Someone's in trouble," Cole sings. I ignore him as my gaze is glued on Gabby.

She twirls on her heel and runs out the back door. I rush after her.

"Wait!"

"This turned out better than I expected," Lyric says as I pass him. I flip him off but don't stop.

"Gabby!"

Chapter 23

Prove someone wrong – show without any doubt what someone said was complete bull crap

PHOENIX

I chase Gabby out of the house. Despite her head start, I catch her in the driveway. She wasn't lying when she said she isn't a runner.

I shackle her wrist before she can open the door to my truck. "Stop. Let me explain."

"There's…nothing…to…explain." She manages to eke out the words between gasps for breath.

She's obviously not going anywhere. I release her hand and she bends over at the waist as she gulps for air. I rub circles on her back as she fights to get herself back in order. After a while, she stands and steps away from me. Her eyes are blazing fury at me.

"I'm sorry."

I expect her to lash at me, but she doesn't. Instead, she inhales a deep breath, blows it out, and nods.

"It's fine."

I cringe. I know better than to believe a woman when she says everything is fine.

"I didn't mean—"

She holds up a hand to cut me off.

"I'm serious. It's fine. You're correct. We're fake. And we did only kiss because I saw Patrick."

Her words don't calm me any. No, they piss me right the fuck off. I know she's not lying. We did only kiss because she saw Patrick. But hearing her say it was fake makes me want to prove to her how our chemistry is anything but fake.

I step toward her, and she retreats until her back is up against the truck. I plant my hands on each side of her and lean in close.

"There was nothing fake about the kiss."

Her gaze falls to my lips, and she bites her bottom lip. I groan. I should be the one biting her lip.

"If you don't want this, say it now."

Her eyes flare and her lips tip up. She wants this, but I want – no, need – to hear her say the words. I cock an eyebrow and wait.

"I want this," she whispers before she pushes up on her toes and melds her lips to mine.

I allow her exactly one second to think she has control before I take over. I thread my fingers through her hair and tilt her head to gain better access before I plunder. I explore every inch of her mouth until she plasters herself to my front.

"Phwwwwwhht."

I force myself to end the kiss so I can figure out who's whistling. I scan the area and my gaze lands on Lyric who's standing on the porch indicating the front window with a tilt of his chin. Fuck. How could I forget Gabby's brother is in there and probably watching the entire encounter?

I place my forehead against Gabby's. "What do you say we get out of here?"

She nods, and I grab her hand and drag her around the vehicle to the passenger side. I lift her up and place her in the seat. She's sexy as hell with her lips swollen and her hair a mess, but I manage to resist the temptation to kiss her again. The next time I kiss her I have no plans to stop until she's writhing beneath me.

I disobey all of Winter Falls' rules about speed and its effect on the environment as I race down the streets until we reach the farmhouse. Whatever patience I had regarding Gabby is gone. I need her and I need her now. When we arrive, I throw the truck into park and reach across the seat for her. She squeals as I haul her to me.

I swallow her giggles with a kiss while I open the door and climb out with her in my arms. She pushes against my shoulders.

"Let me down. I don't want you to hurt yourself."

"Gabby, girl, you barely weigh more than Pan."

She looks torn as to how to respond. I don't give her a chance to contemplate her answer. I rush inside with her in my arms and run up the stairs where I lay her on the bed and cover her body with mine.

I allow myself a few moments to enjoy the view of her finally in my bed before pinning her hands above her head. I trail kisses from her ear down her neck to her shoulder. When I reach her shoulder, I nibble on her skin, and she moans before arching her back to rub her breasts against me.

I feel her hard nipples between our layers of clothing and thrust my jean covered cock against her center. She wraps her legs around mine before rubbing herself against my hard length. Shy Gabby is apparently not afraid to ask for what she wants in the bedroom. Good. No. Not good. Fucking awesome.

I release her hands. I have better things to do with my hand than keep hers captured. Besides, I want her touching me. I pause with my hand on the hem of her t-shirt.

"I'm going to remove your shirt now. Is that okay?"

She grunts. "Are you going to ask for permission before every single move you make?"

"What if I am?" If this turns her on, I can be an accommodating guy.

"You hereby have permission to do whatever you want to me. But no more asking!" She pounds a fist on the mattress. Her impatience is sexy as hell. I can't wait to test it until she explodes.

I cock a brow. "Anything?"

"All the normal stuff."

"What if what I consider normal is not normal to you?"

She slams a hand over my mouth. "This is not fifty questions. There are other things – more fun things – you can be doing with your mouth than talking."

I nibble on her fingers until she yelps and removes her hand. "I don't know. A bit of dirty talk can be exciting." Her mouth slams closed, but her eyes flare. Time to test the theory. I lean forward to whisper into her ear. "How about this? I want to lick every single inch of your skin until you're begging for my cock."

She squirms and begins rubbing herself against my length again. Oh yeah, someone gets off on dirty talking. My shy girl is anything but shy in bed. And I'm the lucky bastard who has the privilege to witness this side of her.

"Let's see what you're hiding for me underneath this t-shirt." I whip the material off of her to reveal miles and miles of creamy smooth skin. Not a blemish in sight. My mouth waters.

Her tits are encased in a black, lacy bra I would have never imagined Gabby wearing. I've never been more happy for my imagination to be proved wrong. I run a finger over the lacy material and goosebumps break out over her skin.

"Stop torturing me."

I smirk. "Oh darling, the torturing has yet to begin."

I pinch her nipple and her head falls back on a long moan. I need to see what color those nipples are. I pull the cups down to discover they're a dusty pink. Dusty pink just became my new favorite color. I lick a circle around her areola, and she shudders.

I massage the other breast while I play with her nipple until she's practically bucking me off of her with her squirming. She threads her fingers through my hair and tries to push my head further down her body.

I lift my gaze to meet hers. "Is there something you want, darling?"

"I want your mouth," she pants.

I kiss her stomach. "How's this?"

"No," she growls. "You know what I mean."

"Maybe I don't."

"You're a tease."

I smirk. "I still don't know where you want my mouth."

"Down there."

I contemplate teasing her more, but my cock is already leaking and calling me foul names. I don't have long before he demands entrance into Gabby's body.

I push her jeans and panties down her body until they're wrapped around her ankles. She kicks off her shoes and her clothes aren't far behind. Her bra hits me in the head as she attempts to throw it across the room.

I chuckle as I unwrap the bra from my head and toss it on the floor.

"Oops." Gabby shrugs.

I smile down and it hits me. How right it feels to have her naked in my bed, waiting for me to make a move. I don't make her wait. I fit my shoulders between her thighs. I bite into the creamy skin of her thigh, and she widens her legs further. Good girl.

I lick her seam from front to back, and her hands latch onto my head. Her fingernails dig into my skin, and I know it's time to get to work.

I spear my tongue into her to discover her already wet and ready for me. While my tongue imitates what my cock wants to be doing, my finger finds her clit and begins to play.

"Holy shit," Gabby murmurs, and I grin at my good girl swearing before increasing the pressure of my finger and the speed of my tongue.

It isn't long before her thighs are quivering around me and her fingernails are nearly drawing blood. I contemplate teasing her longer, but my cock threatens to revolt if I don't get on with the main show.

"Come for me, Gabby," I order, and she does.

"Phoenix!" she shouts my name as her walls convulse against my tongue.

I wait until she collapses against the bed before kneeling above her. "You ready for round two?"

She widens her eyes and contemplates me. "I don't know. Can it beat round one?"

"Hell yeah, it can."

I kiss her stomach before reaching across her to my nightstand to pull a condom out of the drawer. I push my jeans down and my cock jumps out, eager to get on with the festivities. I give him a tug and Gabby's eyes widen.

She reaches forward and her small hand covers mine. Together we pump my cock until precum leaks out. She wipes her finger over the head and gathers the liquid there before licking her finger. I groan at the vision of her sucking on the digit.

"If you want this to last more than thirty seconds, you need to stop it," I growl.

She bats her eyelashes. "Thirty seconds? Why Phoenix Apollo I expected more of you."

She reaches for me, but I slap her hands away and don the condom. I lift her ass up until her pussy is lined up with my cock and push in.

I grit my teeth and stop before I slam into her. One inch and I'm already clenching my ass cheeks to stop myself from coming. Gabby is going to be the death of me.

"More," she demands.

"Give me a sec."

She obviously isn't good at taking orders as she grasps my forearms and pulls herself close impaling herself on my cock.

I moan when I'm fully embedded and my balls slap against her ass. Her walls quiver around me, and I know I've found heaven. A place I want to visit every single day for the rest of my life. Shit. I push those thoughts out of my mind.

I slowly pull out feeling every inch of her warmth. With just my tip still inside her, I ask, "You ready for this?"

She bites her bottom lip and nods.

I slam into her and her back bows as she moans. I can't resist her offering and lean forward to suck her tit into my mouth. I suckle on her as I thrust into her again and again. Each and every time I suck, her walls shudder around me.

In no time, my balls are heavy and my lower back is tingling letting me know I'm not going to make it much longer, but I need to make sure Gabby comes again before me. I sneak a hand down her body until I reach her clit.

"You gonna come for me, darling?" I ask as I rub the sensitive nub.

She groans and tightens around me. "Yes."

"Now, darling," I order.

Her walls tighten around me until I can barely push into her. Hell, yeah. I increase my thrusts until I join her.

"Fuck," I moan as I finish.

I continue to push in and out of her, enjoying every single drop of pleasure until my orgasm wanes. Only then do I collapse on her before rolling to my side and tucking her chin under me where she belongs. I don't fight the feeling. I'm done fighting it.

Chapter 24

Sisters – not always a welcome addition to the family especially when they're nosier than a gossip gal

I AWAKE FEELING MUSCLE soreness I haven't felt in ages – maybe ever if I'm being completely honest with myself. I smile as I do a full body stretch and roll to my side to discover Phoenix's side of the bed is empty. Phoenix's side? Is it Phoenix's side?

Stop, Gabby. You've been awake for one point two minutes. You can hold off the insecurity talk for at least five minutes.

But seriously, where is he? Did he leave without waking me up? Without saying good-bye? Did he even sleep with me, or did he have sex with me and roll over and leave my bed?

So much for waiting five minutes for the insecurity talk.

The toilet in the adjoining bathroom flushes and relief floods my body. He didn't go anywhere. Phew. Insecurity talk over.

The door opens and Phoenix saunters out already completely dressed. Dang. I was hoping for a round of morning sex. Although, I pat my hair. Yikes. It's sticking up in all directions. The picture of a sexy vixen in the morning I am not.

He startles to a halt. "Hey, you're awake."

"Yeppers." Great. Dork has replaced any attempt at sexy vixen. Yeppers? Cringe.

"I'm off. I'll see you later."

He exits the room and I'm left staring at the empty doorway. What just happened? I've done awkward morning afters before but this one wins the most awkward award by a landslide.

And here I thought he felt our connection yesterday. I was certain I saw it in his eyes. Silly girl making up fantasies once again.

My frustrations overwhelm me, and I cover my face with the blankets and scream and kick my legs until I'm exhausted, which frankly probably doesn't last more than a minute. Stamina and I are not friends.

Temper tantrum done, I force myself out of bed. I am not going to lie in the bed and overanalyze every single thing Phoenix and I said and did yesterday. I'd give myself whiplash with a case of what ifs if I did. I refuse to be the weak girl Patrick claimed I was. I can be strong. But first – coffee.

I'm in the kitchen willing the coffeemaker to work faster when my phone rings. I groan and debate not answering it when I notice who's calling. Cassandra. I can barely handle my brash sister on the best of days. Hint. Today is not the best of days.

"Hello."

"We're on our way."

"What? Why?"

"Duh. The kiss."

She hangs up before I can tell her not to come. I need advice about Phoenix, but my older sister is literally the last person on earth I'd ask for advice on anything relationship related. She breaks out into cold sweats at the mere mention of feelings.

The doorbell rings before I've finished my first coffee. She wasn't kidding about being on her way. I debate hiding under the kitchen table, but Cassandra knocks on the window.

"I can see you in there!"

Sigh. I best get this over with. I open the door and Cassandra nearly bowls me over. Elizabeth follows her inside.

"Sorry. Cassandra couldn't come fast enough when she heard."

"Come? Yes! Exactly what I want to know."

My face heats and I dip my chin. I'm not telling my sisters about having sex with Phoenix.

"Heard what?" I ask Elizabeth as I am not responding to Cassandra's crass comment.

"About hottie Farmer McDonald carrying you off in his truck to bring you home and bang you."

Elizabeth shoves Cassandra. "No one was banging anyone."

Cassandra wiggles her eyebrows. "How do you know?"

"Stop!" I hold my hands up in front of me. "I'm not talking about this with you."

"What about with me?" Ashlyn asks as she strolls inside.

My hands fall. "What are you doing here?"

Uh oh. I spoke to soon. She's followed by Aspen, Juniper, and Ellery.

"What are all of you doing here?"

Cassandra shrugs. "I rang them since we don't know anything about love and they're all loved up." She feigns gagging.

"L-l-love?" Wonderful. My stutter is back. Oh, how I missed it. Not.

"I hope someone brought food. I need something in my mouth," Elizabeth says.

Ashlyn raises a brow. "Something in your mouth?"

Cassandra giggles. "She can't help it. She's the queen of saying awkward things."

Ellery frowns at her. "It's rude to call someone awkward."

Cassandra rolls her eyes. "I was teasing."

"We're getting off topic here," Aspen announces in a loud voice.

And here I was excited when Lilac's sisters declared themselves to be our sisters. Amateur mistake.

"Agreed." Cassandra nods. "I want all the details of the banging session."

"Stop calling it banging," Elizabeth huffs.

"What would you have me say? Fornication? Coitus?"

"How about making love?"

My heart stumbles at the word love. I know what I'm feeling for Phoenix is more than a crush. It's more than my body yearning for his. In fact, I'm half-way in love with the man already. Whoa, Gabby! Slow your roll. Half-way in love? When did this happen?

"Can we—"

Aspen holds up a hand to quiet Cassandra. "Hush. Gabrielle is in the middle of realizing how she feels about Phoenix. Don't interrupt."

My eyes widen. "H-h-how do you know?"

"Girl. We've all been there. Granted I fell in love with Lyric when I was about fourteen years old, but I still remember the panic." She circles a finger in my face. "The panic you're feeling at this very moment."

Elizabeth slaps her hand down. "I thought the gossip gals were the only busybodies in town."

Aspen chuckles. "Much to learn have you my little cricket."

"Are you trying to quote Star Wars? There aren't any crickets in Star Wars," Juniper declares.

Aspen rolls her eyes. "Ms. Animal Lover would know."

"I don't know. Was there not one single cricket in the entire set of movies?" Ellery asks.

"There were a lot of movies," Elizabeth adds before pointing to the door and mouthing *run for your life.*

I tiptoe to the backdoor while Elizabeth and Ellery keep Ashlyn, Cassandra, Aspen, and Juniper busy discussing all things Star Wars. I open the door to find Pan waiting for me.

Maa!

"Aha! You were trying to escape!" Cassandra shouts.

Pan bleats in anger before rushing Cassandra with her head bowed. Cassandra's eyes widen and she sprints toward the front door.

Maa!

Pan isn't letting my sister get away. She reaches her before Cassandra can open the door and butts my sister in her behind. Cassandra yelps before whirling around to confront the animal.

"Why you little shit! I'm going to make goat stew with you."

Pan bleats loudly at her before retreating to my side. I scratch her fur. "Good girl."

"Good girl? She rammed me in the ass."

Elizabeth giggles. "Considering your dry spell, you'd think you'd enjoy a good goat ramming."

Ashlyn raises her hand. "I vote we keep Elizabeth. Who's with me?"

Elizabeth rolls her eyes. "I'm not available for pet play."

Aspen nods. "Good to know. We'll add it to your profile when it's your turn."

Elizabeth's eyes widen. "I don't mean…Did you think I meant…" She huffs. "Whatever. Forget it."

"Getting back to our original agenda."

I raise my hand. "I didn't get a copy of the original agenda."

Aspen's lips purse. "Don't be cute. You know exactly what I'm talking about."

A car door slams, and I glance out the window to find my brother rushing toward the farmhouse. Lilac wraps her arms around his middle to try and slow him down. But he's determined and simply keeps going while dragging her behind him.

Beckett bursts into the farmhouse and demands, "Where is he?"

Lilac soothes a hand down his arm. "See? It's just the girls here having tea."

Having tea? I mouth at her, and she shrugs.

"Don't try to bullshit me. You can't lie for shit."

"She doesn't have the experience," Ashlyn hollers, and Lilac frowns at her. "What? It's the truth. You prefer the truth."

"I know why you're gathered here," Beckett claims.

"Good. Maybe you can tell me," I mutter.

"I told you why I'm here. I want to hear about the S-E-X." If Cassandra is trying to be discrete, she ruins it by beginning to sing about sex while shaking her bootie.

"Sex! You had sex with Phoenix?"

My cheeks warm, but I hold strong. "Geez. Beckett. Maybe you could shout louder. I'm not sure the people in Denver heard you."

Cassandra squeals. "That's an admission. You heard it here first, folks. Gabrielle has dusted off the sexual cobwebs with none other than the sexy goat farmer."

My cheeks are blazing now. I bury my face in my hands to hide my blush. I have reached the top of Mountain Embarrassment.

Phoenix bursts into the room. "What the hell is going on here?"

Beckett growls at him. "You took advantage of my sister. I'm going to kick your ass."

Oh, look over there. It's another peak before the summit of Mountain Embarrassment can be reached. Let me go get my climbing gear.

"If you do the deed, you have to pay the price," Ashlyn proclaims.

And for once in my life, I wish I wasn't the mousy one. I wish I could tell her to shut her hole. I don't, though, because I am the mousy one.

The door bangs open. Oh no! While I was berating myself over my inner mouse tendencies, Beckett got hold of Phoenix's collar and is dragging him outside.

"Wait!"

Chapter 25

Fight – usually two-sided unless one side is distracted by the ʻoneʼ

PHOENIX

I allow Beckett to haul me out of the house since I don't want Gabby watching me kick her brother's ass. Make no doubt about it. I will kick his ass for embarrassing her. Oh, I'll let him get a few licks in since I slept with his sister, but he's not taking me out.

I spin around and slam my fist down on Beckett's arm, and he releases my collar immediately.

"How dare you?" he seethes.

"How dare I? How dare you?"

"She's my sister, asshole!"

"Which means you should understand how you embarrassed her."

"She'll get over it."

I growl. "She shouldn't have to get over it, because you shouldn't have said anything to embarrass her."

He circles around me like we're in a boxing ring. What the hell? Where did he learn to fight? Some pansy gym?

"You need to stop worrying about her embarrassment and start worrying about me kicking your ass."

Cue the clichés. He bounces on his toes and shadowboxes a few times. He obviously didn't grow up with brothers.

"Stop! Stop!" Gabby rushes out of the house. She stands in between us with her arms held out wide. "Don't fight. I'm not worth it."

I growl. "Gabby, you are worth everything."

"If she's worth everything, why'd you use her?"

Gabby's face heats up, but she doesn't drop her arms. They tremble, but she straightens her back and holds her ground. Good girl.

"I didn't use her."

"She's living with you for protection. You took advantage of her."

"I would never take advantage of anyone, especially not Gabby."

"Stop calling her Gabby! She hates that nickname."

My gaze finds Gabby's and she attempts a smile. "Usually," she whispers, and I return her smile.

Bam! Beckett's right fist slams into my jaw and my head rears back. Fuck. I should be paying attention to the man who wants to beat me up instead of the woman who's captured my heart.

Wait. What? She's captured my heart? I'm not ready for a woman to capture my heart. My gaze finds hers again, and I realize I'm dead wrong. I may not have been ready for any woman, but she came and captured my heart anyway.

Bam! This time his fist rams into my stomach and I lose sight of Gabby as I keel over. Damn. Pansy boy can hit. I inhale a deep breath before standing and shaking out my fists.

"Gabby, move out of the way, darling."

She stands still for a minute before nodding. "Don't hurt him too bad."

"Did you not see the two hits I already landed, sis?"

She crosses her arms over her chest. "Please don't talk to me, Beckett. I don't like you right now." Her chest heaves and I know it cost her to say those words. But she said them. Damn. I'm proud of her.

"You hit me twice, which means I get two hits."

"You don't get two hits, asshat. I get as many hits as I want. You took advantage of my sister."

I'm done defending myself. He's in a rage and won't listen anyway. I feign right and when he lifts his hands to defend his left-side, I hit him on his right jaw. The sound of flesh on flesh reverberates through the valley as his head flies backward and blood bursts from his lip.

I let him check his jaw to make sure it isn't broken before I attack again. This time I sweep his feet out from under him and take him to the ground. I use the element of surprise to get him on his back in a chokehold.

"You ready to stop now?"

He slams a fist on my shoulder, and I grunt.

"I won't stop until you stop taking advantage of my sister," he gasps.

A siren blares and seconds later a car screeches to a halt in my driveaway. I don't need to glance over my shoulder to know Lyric has arrived. I should have realized Aspen would call him. She's a Winter Falls native and one thing Winter Falls whole-heartedly believes in is non-violence.

"Hey! This is not how the initiation ceremony works," my brother states.

What the hell is he talking about? "This is not some stupid initiation ceremony," I grumble.

Lyric kneels in front of me and frowns at Beckett whose face is now red. "You never let Phoenix get you on the ground. He's a grappler."

He stands and taps me on the shoulder. "Come on. Let him up."

I glare at my brother for a long moment until he taps his badge. Asshole. You can't use your position of power in the middle of a family dispute. I snarl at him, and he smirks. Like I said – asshole.

I release Beckett and spring to my feet. Lilac stomps over to him and offers her hand.

"I do not understand these masculine rituals," she complains as she helps him to his feet.

He wipes blood from his split lip before pushing her behind him.

"There's no need to protect me. I'm returning to the porch to play the simple woman now." She rolls her eyes at him before marching away.

Lyric stands between the two of us with his hands on his hips. "Anyone want to explain what's going on to me?"

Ashlyn raises her hand. "Not you." He points at her. "You keep your pregnant ass on the porch, or I'll tell Rowan you got in the middle of a fist fight."

She gasps. "You wouldn't!"

"Watch me."

She retreats behind Lilac. "I'm being good."

"Back to dumbass number one and dumbass number two."

"Hey!" I protest. "I'm not a dumbass. This is my land and I'm protecting myself and the virtue of my girlfriend."

Gabby gasps. "Girlfriend?"

"What? Do you prefer woman?" Her nose wrinkles in distaste. "Girlfriend it is."

"But this morning, you left the…erm… house like last night didn't mean a thing to you."

I decide to lay it all on the line. Audience be damned. "I care for you, Gabby." Care is entirely too soft a word, but it's all I'm willing to admit with half of Winter Falls as our audience.

"You do?"

"Yeah, darling, I do. I wouldn't have—" I cut myself off when Beckett growls. "You know what if I didn't."

"You didn't say anything."

"I didn't want to overwhelm you."

She steps close enough to whisper, "I care for you, too."

"What did she say?" Cassandra shouts.

"She said she cares for him, too," Lyric yells back. I growl at him, and he shrugs. "What? You want them to make up what she said?"

I cup Gabby's chin. "I'm sorry I left without making my intentions clear."

She shrugs. "It's okay. You don't have to apologize for my insecurities."

I wink. "Sure, I do."

"This is sweet and all, but can we return to the portion of the agenda where I beat the shit out of Phoenix?" Beckett asks.

Gabby closes her eyes. "Can I trade my brother in for a new model?"

Lyric throws his arm over her shoulders and draws her near. "Lucky for you, you have two brand-new brothers-in-law."

"And don't forget the sisters-in-law," Juniper hollers.

Gabby glances over at the porch where her sisters and the West sisters are standing. "I'm not sure I want more sisters," she mutters. "Three is more than enough."

"I understand your trepidation," Lilac says.

Aspen hip checks her. "You love us and you know it."

"Yes, Mom made it clear to me I must love all of you no matter how irritating you become."

"Sister hug!" Ashlyn shouts before attacking Lilac. Juniper, Aspen, and Ellery join in to smother Lilac whose attempts to push them away are futile.

"I thought we agreed you wouldn't do this any longer," Lilac mutters from underneath the pile.

"That was before you fell in love and revealed you have a heart," Juniper says.

Lyric hands Gabby to me before clearing his throat. "I think at this point we can disperse and all go our separate ways."

"No way!" Cassandra shouts. "I want to watch this play out."

Ashlyn emerges from the group hug. "And I brought snacks."

Gabby moans and drops her head to my chest. "Can you make them leave?"

"I got this, little sis." Lyric whistles to gain everyone's attention. "You are no longer welcome on this property. Disperse or I will have you arrested."

"Ha!" Ashlyn shouts. "You don't have enough handcuffs for all of us."

"Obviously, someone has never heard of flexicuffs."

"What are flexicuffs?"

"Flexicuffs are plastic handcuffs. It's basically a cable tie," Lilac explains.

"Way to make getting arrested sound boring," Ashlyn mutters before making her way to Rowan's golfcart. "I'm driving off in ten seconds if anyone wants a ride."

Ellery waves before jumping onto the golfcart and off they go.

"I'm going back to work since the excitement's over." Juniper hops on her bike and pedals away.

"Time for us to skedaddle." Elizabeth grasps Cassandra by the ear and drags her to their electric car. Cassandra swears up and down, but Elizabeth must have a killer grasp because she ends up with her ass in the car.

In less than two minutes, Lilac, Beckett, and Lyric are the only visitors left.

"I believe you need to tell your sister something." Lilac not so subtly hints to Beckett. Of course, the woman doesn't know the word subtle.

Beckett clears his throat and approaches us. "I'm sorry, Gabby. I didn't mean to embarrass you."

Her lips purse as she studies him. "You forgot to apologize for hitting Phoenix."

He growls. "I'm sorry I hit *your boyfriend*." He resembles a petulant teenager with his whiney words.

"And don't call me Gabby."

"If I don't call you Gabby—"

"Ever again."

"If I don't call you Gabby ever again, will you forgive me?"

"I forgive you. But I still think you're an idiot."

"I second," Lilac agrees.

"And I only forgive you if you promise not to get into a fight with Phoenix again."

"I won't get in a fight with him again." He leans forward and kisses her forehead. "Sorry, Gabrielle Grace."

Once they're gone and we're alone, I look down at her. "You okay?"

"You care for me?"

I nod.

"Then, I'm okay."

Damn. No wonder this woman has captured my heart. After all that transpired this morning, she has every reason to throw a hissy fit. But what does she do? She smiles up at me.

Chapter 26

Parade – an excuse to show off your mankini

"ARE YOU READY FOR this?"

I glance down at my outfit. I'm wearing a pair of boots with a plaid skirt and a red sweater.

"Is there a problem with what I'm wearing?"

Phoenix snags me around the waist and hauls me near. "There's not a damn thing wrong with your sexy little school-girl outfit."

"Then—"

My question is cut off when his mouth finds mine. He teases my bottom lip with his teeth until I grab hold of his cheeks and force him to meet my lips. He chuckles before his tongue slips into my mouth to explore.

Unfortunately, his exploration is cut off early when the doorbell rings. He raises his head to snarl at the door, and I giggle. I've never experienced a man annoyed when forced to stop kissing me before. Normally, a kiss is merely a means to an end.

Not with Phoenix. He enjoys taking his time tasting me and learning every nook and cranny of my mouth. It's spectacular.

"Who could it be?" I ask once my breathing returns to normal.

"Soleil."

Now, I'm more confused. "Why is she here?"

"She's going to look after the animals while we enjoy the Mabon festival."

"She is?" He nods. "You mean we don't have to worry about returning here to milk the goats this evening?"

He frowns but nods again.

I bounce on my toes. "This is wonderful! Thank you!"

I plant kisses all over his face until he chuckles and grasps my chin to stop me. "You're welcome."

I skip to the door and throw it open. "You must be Soleil."

"And you must be the woman who's tamed our Phoenix."

"I don't know about tamed."

She barks out a laugh before waving to Phoenix. "You two go on ahead to the festival and have fun for me."

My nose wrinkles. "Dang it. I didn't realize you wouldn't be able to enjoy the festival if you're here. Maybe we should come back in time to help this evening."

Phoenix shackles my wrist and drags me toward the door. "Soleil will be fine on her own."

"Bye, Soleil. Nice to meet you!" I wave at her as Phoenix leads me to a pair of bikes.

"We're biking?"

He stops. "Do you know how to ride a bike?"

I slap his shoulder. "Of course, I know how to ride a bike. But we've never biked into town before."

"There's a parade today. There won't be anywhere to park the truck."

"A parade?" I love parades. I straddle my bike. "What are you waiting for?"

"Whose bike is this anyway?" I ask as we pedal toward town.

His cheeks darken before he clears his throat. "It's yours."

I slam on my brakes and skid to a stop. "Phoenix Apollo Alston, did you buy me a bike?"

He backs up his bike until he's next to me. "It's not a big deal. It's used."

I throw my arms around him and the bikes crash together. "It's a big deal to me."

I don't mention how Patrick never bought me anything – not even for my birthday – while I bought him little gifts all the time. I don't want to ruin the day by bringing up *his* name.

Phoenix kisses my cheek before stepping away to untangle our bikes. "Shall we get going before we miss the start of the parade?"

We arrive in town fifteen minutes later and park our bikes near city hall.

"Don't we need to lock them up?" I don't want anyone stealing my brand-new bike. It's my first gift from Phoenix who is rocking this boyfriend thing.

"Nope. Winter Falls," he says as if merely saying the name of the town is an explanation. I guess it kind of is.

"Come on," he grasps my hand and leads me through the throng of people.

"Who are all these people?" I ask as we push our way through the crowd. "They can't all be locals."

"The Mabon festival is a big draw for tourists."

We reach the bleachers set up in front of the library. Phoenix finds us places about half-way up and we settle into our seats.

"How are we going to catch any candy if we're sitting here?"

Sage gasps. "Gabrielle Grace Dempsey, you watch your mouth."

"What did I do wrong?" I whisper my question to Phoenix.

Cayenne tuts. "Thinking anyone would throw candy in plastic wrapping."

"Do they have the hearing of bats?" I mumble.

"Actually, the greater wax moth has the best hearing of any animal," Juniper declares as she sits down in the row in front of me with Maverick.

At least, I assume the man is her husband since they're holding hands. I don't recognize him as being Maverick Langston the movie star as he's wearing a blond wig, oversized sunglasses, and a ballcap pulled low over his face.

Phoenix groans. "I thought they'd leave us alone now since we've admitted our relationship is real."

"Ha!" Aspen laughs as she sits next to Juniper. "Did you forget you live in Winter Falls?"

"How can I forget?" he mutters and I elbow him.

"Be good."

"Where's your hubby?" I ask Aspen.

"He's on duty today so I'm playing third wheel to my little sister."

"I'm surprised Ashlyn isn't here." She seems to be in the middle of everything.

Aspen points to the first 'car' of the parade. "She is."

Ashlyn and Rowan are sitting in a decked out golf cart. Ashlyn's smile stretches from ear to ear as she waves at everyone while Rowan's expression practically screams he'd rather be anywhere in the world than in this parade.

"I thought the Mabon King and Queen were supposed to lead the parade," Maverick says.

"And I thought you understood nothing will stop my baby sister from hogging the limelight," Juniper responds.

Music blares and a figure dashes out in front of the car causing Ashlyn's smile to dim. I lean closer to see who it is. My eyes widen when I realize it's the pet store owner, Forest.

"Is he…" I swallow. "Is he wearing a mankini?"

"A bright yellow mankini to be exact," Aspen answers.

"And a cowboy hat," Juniper adds.

"Uh oh. Someone doesn't appreciate the crowd's attention not being on her." Aspen points to Ashlyn who's trying to climb out of the golf cart. Rowan is holding her back with both arms while trying to steer the golfcart.

Meanwhile, Forest is loving the attention being riveted on him. He dances around the golfcart and throws his cowboy hat to the audience who scream and cry for more.

"This is the best parade ever."

"Nope. You're wrong. The best parade ever was last year," Aspen declares.

"Why do you say that?"

"Because Aspen did this whole grand gesture thing to get Lyric back and he proposed in front of the whole town," Juniper explains.

I sigh. "Grand gestures are so romantic."

"Speaking of the Chief of Police." Aspen bites her lip and points to the street in front of us.

Lyric swaggers down the street toward Forest who catches sight of him and decides to make a run for it. He dashes into the crowd, but they push him back into the street practically into Lyric's hands.

Aspen sighs. "You gotta love a man who knows how to use handcuffs."

"Does Lyric tie you up often?" Sage shouts her question.

I feel my face heat at the change of topic, but Aspen rolls with it.

"That's for me to know and you to never find out." She winks at Sage before returning her attention to her husband who's now dragging a handcuffed Forest down the street.

Half of the people are booing him while the other half are shouting encouragement.

"You can handcuff me anytime, Chief."

"I've been a bad girl, Chief."

Lyric holds up his left hand and his wedding band sparkles at the women who sigh in unison.

"No offense, Aspen. But this is seriously the best parade ever."

Phoenix chuckles next to me and places a hand on my thigh. "The parade hasn't started yet."

"Yeah, it has." I motion to Ashlyn and Rowan who are finally moving again.

Behind them are the Mabon King and Queen. "How do you get picked Mabon King and Queen?"

"They're high school kids. It's pretty much the same as Homecoming King and Queen."

"Look!" I squeeze Phoenix's arm. "They're handing out candy apples."

He grunts before standing and walking down the bleachers. He gestures toward me while speaking to the Mabon King who hands him a candy apple.

I clap when he returns and hands me the apple. "Thank you," I say before biting into the apple. I moan as the taste of cinnamon hits my tongue.

Phoenix leans over to whisper in my ear. "If you moan again, I won't be responsible for my actions."

I stare into his eyes as I take another bite and do an exaggerated moan.

"You aren't the timid girl you pretend to be."

I swallow my bite before leaning over and whispering in his ear, "Shy and timid are not the same thing."

I finish my apple while I watch the high school cheerleaders do a routine. Next is the high school marching band. They stop in front of the bleachers and the music changes as they begin playing 'Motown Funk'. Everyone stands and dances to the song.

Well, not everyone. Maverick and Phoenix stand but neither one of them shake their booties. I hip check Phoenix. "Come on. Dance."

He crosses his arms over his chest. "I don't dance."

I stick my tongue out at him, but I don't let him being a fuddy duddy ruin my fun. I raise my hands as I continue to dance in place. When the band moves on, I collapse in my seat.

"Best. Parade. Ever," I repeat because it bears repeating.

Phoenix shrugs. "It's just a parade."

"Just a parade? Do you not see what's happening here?" I motion toward the crowds in the street. "Everyone is having a great time with their friends and family. This doesn't happen in big cities where you have to worry about your safety and getting crushed by the crowd. Winter Falls is awesome."

His brow wrinkles as he studies me for a long moment. "You really believe what you're saying."

It wasn't a question, but I answer anyway. "Yes, I do. I love it here."

And I love you, I think but don't say. Eek! So much for being half-way in love with Phoenix. I've fallen and I can't get up. Heck, I don't want to get up. I hope he'll grow to feel the same way about me because Phoenix is it for me.

Chapter 27

Insecurity — a nasty habit that can derail relationships

Phoenix drags his lips from mine. "Good night."

I frown. Good night? We're just getting to the good portion of the evening. The part where clothes come off and naked body parts are involved. But he's not removing my clothes. He's settling down to sleep.

I open my mouth to ask him what's wrong. Why doesn't he want to have sex with me? We had sex before and it was pretty spectacular. Or, at least, I thought it was. Maybe he doesn't agree?

He positions me until I'm lying on my side with him behind me and his arm thrown over my stomach. I wiggle my ass and notice he's hard. At least I know he's sexually attracted to me, but why isn't he doing anything about it?

His arm around my waist tightens. "Go to sleep, darling."

I wiggle my ass again and he groans. "Sleep."

"But we need to take care of your little problem."

He growls. "Little?"

"Okay. We need to take care of your big problem."

"I'm exhausted. I need sleep."

He kisses my hair and I lay still as I wait for his breaths to even out. It isn't long before he's asleep. Maybe he really is just exhausted? Maybe this has nothing to do with me?

Except the little ball of insecurity that lives in my stomach opens its eyes and starts sprouting all kinds of boloney. *Phoenix isn't tired, it's us. We're not enough for him. How you think we can land a hottie like Phoenix is laughable. In fact, you're a joke.*

My insecurity isn't such a little ball anymore. No, it's a walking, talking pain in my behind. *He wants us,* I remind it.

Ha! He wants a willing woman. Any woman would do.

No! He didn't want a relationship and yet he made an exception for me.

Suddenly, I'm no longer on my side. I'm on my back with Phoenix looming over me.

"I thought you were asleep."

He snorts. "As if I can sleep with the thoughts in your head screaming out loud."

I cringe. "They weren't screaming."

He cocks an eyebrow, but I zip my lips shut. I'm not confessing all my insecurities to this man who emits confidence in everything he does.

He touches his lips to mine. "Sleep," he murmurs.

He tucks me into his side, and I force my insecurity back into the ball and clear my mind. Somehow, it works and I fall asleep.

When I wake, Phoenix is long gone as evidenced by his cold side of the bed. Dang. So much for tackling him and convincing him to have morning sex. I'm thirty-five percent convinced I could have wrangled enough courage to tackle him. Okay, more like five-percent, but with him gone, I have zero percent chance. Time to get to work.

"Hello! Earth to Gabrielle."

I startle and nearly drop my phone. "Sorry. I'm here."

My client, Danielle, chuckles. "You may be here in the physical sense but your mind is not on my social media campaign."

"I'm sorry. I have a lot on my mind."

"I hope whatever's on your mind is some yummy man."

I clear my throat. "Why would you think I'm daydreaming about a man?"

"Honey, in my vast experience, daydreaming is always about a man. The question is – are you daydreaming about killing a man or daydreaming about him cuffing you to a bed and having his wicked way with you?"

The second. Definitely the second. Although, I could strangle Phoenix for his one-sided decision to stop having sex with me.

"Sex it is."

"I didn't say a word."

"I could hear your sigh all the way here in California."

I sigh. Again, apparently. "Men are confusing."

She snorts. "And they say women are confusing."

"I'm sorry. This conversation is completely unprofessional."

"Honey, you've been my social media manager for five years now. You're efficient, answer my emails within minutes, and never miss a deadline. I was beginning to think you were a robot. It's about damn time a man realized how special you are."

I feel my cheeks warm and am grateful we're not doing a video call. Before I have a chance to tell her I'm uncertain about how Phoenix feels, she speaks again.

"And don't go down the slippery slope wondering why this man is doing whatever he's doing to make you re-evaluate every single thing in your life. Men are simple creatures. He's probably worrying about who's going to win the game on Saturday while you've invented an entire scenario about him no longer caring for you."

How does she know?

"I'll phone you tomorrow to discuss the campaign, and I expect to hear all about what a spectacular night you had."

She hangs up before I can get this conversation back on track. We were supposed to be having a business chat. Not a heart-to-heart. My phone beeps with a message before I can set it down.

Go get him, tiger.

Me a tiger? Has she ever met me? Actually, Danielle hasn't. Most of my clients haven't. It's one of the reasons I chose social media marketing as my profession. Online, I have no problem pretending to be someone I'm not. Someone who's outgoing and fun. Boy would my clients be disappointed if they ever met me in person.

The ball of insecurity unravels itself again, but I shove it down. I am not going to be shy, timid Gabrielle any longer. I danced at a parade this weekend. In front of the entire town.

And nothing bad happened. No one made fun of me. As a matter of fact, a bunch of people joined me, and we laughed and joked.

Okay. I stand. I got this.

When Phoenix enters the farmhouse for dinner, he pauses when he notices the table. His gaze roams over the candles and flowers before he smiles at me.

"What's the occasion?"

"No occasion." I shrug. "Wash your hands while I get the frittata out of the oven."

I don't have to tell him twice. He kicks off his boots as he hurries toward the washroom.

I'm placing the frittata on the table when he joins me. "What can I do?" he asks with a squeeze of my hip.

I look around the table. There's fresh bread and garlic butter, a bottle of sweet red wine, and the goat cheese and spinach frittata.

"You can pour the wine," I tell him.

He pulls out a chair for me with a wink. "After you."

He digs into his meal with relish. I, on the other hand, am having a hard time getting any food past my throat.

"This is delicious. Where did you get the fresh spinach?"

"From the garden." He pauses with his fork halfway to his mouth. Oh no. Did I overstep? "Did I do something wrong? Was I not supposed to take anything from the garden?"

He clears his throat. "I didn't think there was anything to take from the garden."

I giggle. "No kidding. It was a complete mess. I've been weeding it little by little."

"You have?"

Doubts slam into me once again. "Shoot. I should have asked. I didn't realize."

He reaches across the table and grasps my hand. "Stop. It's fine. I'm surprised is all. Nothing's been planted in the garden for a long time. I didn't realize there were any vegetables left in there at all."

"Most of the vegetables have been ruined, but the spinach and zucchini are fine. Although, I think the zucchini might be classified as marrows by now. I'll do some research about what I can cook with marrows."

He squeezes my hand before releasing it and reaching for the bread. He breaks off a piece and smoothers it in garlic butter before handing it to me.

"Did you bake this bread, too?"

"If you count using a bread machine."

"It counts."

"Then yes."

We finish the rest of our meal in silence. It's a comfortable silence. I've never experienced a comfortable silence with a man before. Usually, men are pushing me to talk as if they find my shyness a personal obstacle to overcome. Ridiculous. Except with Phoenix, I'm not my usual shy. Which reminds me...

It's time. I gather all my courage and ask, "Why are you holding back?"

He won't look me in the eye when he asks, "Holding back?"

"Don't make me say it," I huff.

He drops his fork to scratch the beard growing in after a long day of working on the farm. "You don't need to say it."

When he doesn't say anything further, I prod, "Can you answer my question?"

"I'm not holding back."

"Liar. Liar. Pants on fire." My eyes widen when I realize I spoke my thoughts out loud. "I—"

He waves away my apology with a chuckle. "I'm not lying. I'm not holding back. I'm taking things slow."

"Slow? At this rate, I'll be a reborn virgin soon."

He barks out a laugh. "You're funny when you forget to be shy."

"I only forget to be shy with you," I admit.

He stands and rounds the table. He reaches his hand out for me and I grasp hold. He pulls me to my feet and draws me near. We sway from side to side.

"I don't want to mess this up," he admits.

My nose scrunches as I gaze up at him. "By having sex?"

"By getting in too deep before you're ready."

"I'm ready. I'm more than ready. I'm super duper ready."

He stares into my eyes, and I let him see everything I'm feeling. I'm not going to tell him I love him. It's way too soon. He may eliminate my shyness, but my insecurity is still a living being inside of me. I won't tell him how I feel until I'm certain he feels the same.

I allow my hands to roam over his back until I reach his butt. I squeeze those perfect globes of muscle and he pushes against me. I feel his hard length and smirk.

"You think you've won."

"Haven't I?"

He's still laughing when his lips meet mine. He picks me up and carries me bridal style up the stairs.

"We'll see who's won when I have you squirming in my bed dying for release."

"Still sounds like I'm still winning."

He winks before throwing me on the bed. Yep, I'm definitely winning.

Chapter 28

Blackmail and negotiate – two horns on the same goat

PHOENIX

My hand trembles as I hold the door for *Electric Vibes* open for Gabby. She probably thinks the hippy bar is stupid or crazy. Out-of-towners often describe the bar as 'fun' or 'eccentric', but it's easy to think a place is fun when you're on vacation. It's different when you live in Winter Falls and the only bar in town is a hippy hangout.

"This place is more awesome than I remember." She bounces on her toes as her gaze roams over the bar.

My shoulders relax. Gabby isn't Tina who thought everything about Winter Falls was stupid. Huh. How could I forget Tina never liked the town? She never wanted to go into town because she didn't want to run into any of the 'crazy locals'. And none of the shops were 'up to standard'. Whatever that meant.

"It's a Beatle invasion," Gabby squeals when her gaze lands on the owner, Lennon.

Lennon smiles. "You're my favorite new customer."

She bellies up to the bar. "How did it feel being reincarnated?"

He barks out a laugh. "What are you drinking, crazy girl?"

"I'm not the crazy girl. I'm the boring, shy girl."

"You don't look boring or shy to me."

I wrap an arm around Gabby's shoulders and pull her flush to me. "Off limits," I growl at him.

He raises his hands. "I've already placed my bets." He winks at Gabby. "I'm betting on you."

"Me?" Her nose scrunches us. "Why would anyone bet on me?"

He points at her. "That's why." Someone calls his name, and he walks off.

"What is he talking about?"

She's genuinely confused. She has no idea why anyone would take her side or fight in her corner. She has no clue how wonderful she truly is. Fuck. She's going to destroy my heart when she moves off the farm. Unlike with Tina, I'll never recover from Gabby leaving me.

"He was flirting with you," I say to avoid explaining all the jumbled thoughts running through my mind.

She rolls her eyes. "Sure. Whatever. John Lennon was flirting with little old me."

"Did you say John Lennon?" Cassandra tries to push us apart, but I refuse to give up my hold on Gabby.

"John Lennon's dead. You do realize there are events which transpired before your birth?" Elizabeth asks as she comes up behind us.

Cassandra rolls her eyes. "Nope. The world didn't exist before I was born."

Elizabeth throws her arms in the air. "I don't know why I bother."

River arrives and drapes his arm around Elizabeth's shoulder. "Don't know why you bother what?"

"Why I bother with the lot of you humans."

She shoves my brother away. He pretends to fall, and she reaches to save him but trips on a chair instead and crashes into him. They fall to the floor in a heap. And Elizabeth's face ends up in my brother's crotch.

"Why am I the one who always ends up in embarrassing positions?" she mutters.

River chuckles. "I could argue my position is more embarrassing."

She lifts up to glare at him. "Why? You have women burying their faces in your crotch all the time."

River bursts out laughing. He isn't offended by her insinuation that he's a player. "I usually prefer to remove my pants first."

He stands and helps Elizabeth to her feet. "Come on. Let's find our table," he says and leads her away.

"We can still escape to the farm," I tease Gabby.

She shrugs. "If you want to go home, we can go home."

I'm joking, but she isn't. She's perfectly happy sitting at home reading a book while I watch a game on television. She has no interest in getting all dolled up for a night on the town every weekend. And she certainly won't beg me to take her away from this 'godforsaken' place.

"No way are you two leaving," Beckett announces as he arrives.

Gabby rolls her eyes. "As if you need me on your team. Between you and Lilac, you can beat anyone in this crowd."

Lilac nods. "This is true." She's not bragging. In her mind, she's merely stating a fact. "But couples quiz night is a family activity, and you are required to attend."

We follow them to our table where River, Elizabeth, and Cassandra are already sitting.

Aspen stands from the table next to ours and points at Lilac. "Traitor!"

"How are the Sisters of Mayhem supposed to win when we're missing a sister?" Ashlyn asks.

"Lyric is substituting for me and you have your partners to help you," Lilac answers.

"All of their brains together aren't as big as yours," Aspen whines.

Lyric shakes his head at his wife. "Thanks, Sunshine."

She shrugs. "I'm only telling the truth."

"All bets are now final," Sage calls from her table near the stage.

"Damn this town and it's betting," I mutter.

River bumps my shoulder. "Not as much fun when you're the target, is it?"

"I'd watch it if I were you. You might be next." I nod toward Elizabeth who glances away.

"Nah." He slings an arm over her shoulder. "Bessie and I are just friends." Judging by the way 'Bessie' is blushing, she has more than friendship on her mind. Poor woman. She's in for heartache since my brother can't be tamed.

"Ahem." Lennon climbs onto the stage. "Usual rules apply. The first person to raise their hand will be called on for the answer. If the answer is correct, we'll move on to the next question. If the answer is incorrect, the second person to have raised their hand will be asked to answer the question. And so on."

Ashlyn places a pitcher of beer on our table. "What's this for?"

"Maybe if we get Ms. Smarty Pants drunk, she'll miss some questions."

Lilac leans back in her chair and crosses her arms over her chest. "Maybe you shouldn't divulge your brilliant plan to the enemy."

"Oops!" Ashlyn shrugs before returning to her table.

"Let's begin." At Lennon's announcement, everyone quiets down. "First question. How many hearts does an octopus have?"

Juniper's hand flies into the air. "Three!" she shouts as soon as Lennon calls on her.

"Aren't you supposed to be our animal expert?" River asks me.

"You think I can compete with Juniper?"

"He knows more about goats than me," Juniper whisper-shouts.

"I'm sure everyone's interested in how to milk a goat properly," I mutter.

"I found it interesting," Gabby says.

Cassandra bursts out laughing. "You? Milk a goat? I have to see it to believe it."

Gabby's cheeks darken but she straightens her back and answers, "I can milk a goat."

I kiss her cheek. "You most certainly can."

"Next question. How much time does the average American social media user spend on social media?"

Gabby squeals. "I know this. I know this."

"Raise your hand, then," Lilac commands her.

She raises her hand. "Me! Me! I know the answer."

Lennon nods toward her. "Go ahead, crazy girl."

"Two point seven hours a day."

"Correct."

She throws her arms in the air. "I'm winning. I'm winning."

Lennon clears his throat, and her cheeks darken. Her chin dips before she shakes her head and mouths *sorry* to him. He chuckles and winks at her.

"Next question. Which out-of-towner fell in love with a Winter Falls native and wants to marry her?"

Beckett stands before getting to his knee in front of Lilac.

"Lilac Bean West—"

She frowns. "Why am I getting the middle name treatment if you're going to propose? You are going to propose, aren't you? You're the only out-of-towner who is dating a Winter Falls native but isn't married to her."

Beckett reaches into his pocket and pulls out a jewelry box. "Yes, Lilac no-middle-name West, I'm trying to propose."

"You may proceed."

He smiles. "Lilac, my love, will you marry me?"

"That's it?" Ashlyn asks. "No profound statements about how much you love her and can't live without her? Worst. Proposal. Ever."

Beckett gazes into Lilac's eyes. "My Lilac doesn't want flowery statements or professions of love. She wants to beam me over the head for proposing in front of her family and nearly all of the residents of Winter falls."

"If you are aware of my adversity to you proposing in public, then why are you doing it?"

Beckett lifts his chin toward her parents. Ruby and Daniel are sitting to the side of the stage. Daniel has an arm around Ruby's middle, probably to keep her from jumping into the fray.

"My mother forced you to propose in public?"

Beckett leans close to whisper, "She promised she wouldn't bother us about having children for at least a year if I proposed in front of her."

"My mother is a master blackmailer."

"I prefer the word negotiator," Ruby hollers from her table where she's now actively trying to escape her husband.

"Say yes, Lilac," Sage yells.

"Why? Have you bet on when the proposal would happen?" Sage whistles and looks away.

Lilac purses her lips. "This town and betting."

"If you say yes, you'll be our sister for realz," Cassandra says.

"I don't think being *your* sister is a selling point in a marriage proposal," Elizabeth grumbles.

"May I see the ring?" Lilac asks Beckett and he opens the box before holding it out to her. She picks it up and studies it for a moment.

"I will not take your last name. You will allow me to help pay the bills. And I want two children. Are these terms acceptable to you?"

"Will you use my last name in a social setting?" Lilac nods. "What about three children?"

"Only in the event I have twins, the likelihood of which is one in 250."

Beckett smirks. "I believe we have a deal, Lilac West."

Gabby sniffs and I draw her near. She buries her head in my chest and I feel wet hit my t-shirt. "Hey, darling." I place a finger under her chin and lift her head. "Why the tears?"

"They're happy tears." She whimpers. "Mostly."

"Which ones are the unhappy tears?" I ask as I wipe the liquid from under her eyes.

"I wish my parents were here," she whispers.

Damn. I didn't think about her parents. Of course, she wishes they were here. I hold her close and rock her back and forth.

If she'll let me, I'll give her a substitute set of parents. Mom always wanted a little girl. I should slow down. Take things easy before my heart is irrevocably tied to this woman. But as I feel the wet soak through my t-shirt to the skin, I realize there will be no slowing down.

This woman holds my happiness in her hands.

Chapter 29

Attention hog – not necessarily a hog or a person for that matter

PHOENIX

I watch as Gabby skips across the field toward the barn. She's almost unrecognizable compared to the girl who moved in with me over a month ago. There's no stuttering and no hiding her face with her hair, although there is blushing. The good kind. And lots of it.

She notices me leaning against the barn and changes her direction of travel. She doesn't slow when she nears. Instead, she quickens her pace and launches herself into the air. I brace my legs and catch her.

"Good morning, babes." She beams a smile at me.

"Babes?" I tease.

Her nose wrinkles. "You don't like it? It felt good to me, but I can work on another pet name for you."

"Pet name?"

"Endearment. Moniker. Nickname. Affectionate name."

I ruffle her hair. "I know what a pet name is."

"I've never used a pet name before. I need to work on my game."

I stiffen at her confession. "You've never used a pet name before?"

She shrugs. "No?"

I tweak her nose. "Why not?"

She frowns and looks away. To her credit, she doesn't shield her face with her hair or duck her chin. "Patrick thought pet names were stupid and before Patrick …" She trails off.

Bloody hell. Don't tell me her asshat ex-boyfriend was her only boyfriend.

"Before Patrick?" I prod.

"My boyfriends never lasted long enough for me to think of a pet name for them."

My shoulders drop in relief. Thank fuck. I can't be someone's first serious boyfriend. I need Gabby to want me for me and not because I'm the first man to show her kindness.

Maa!

Gabby's gaze searches the area for the source of the bleating. She gasps when she finds it. "Oh no! A goat is stuck in the fence."

I sigh and let her down. She rushes off and drops to her knees by the fence. She pets the goat as she coos sweet words to her.

"Don't worry, baby girl. We'll get you out of the fence." Her eyes plead with me. "Help, Phoenix."

"There's no need to help."

"No need to help? This poor goat is stuck in a fence, and you say there's no need to help." She slaps my leg. "What is wrong with you?"

"There's nothing wrong with me, but Brenda can get out of the fence anytime she wants."

"What are you talking about?"

"Meet Brenda." I point to the goat with her head 'stuck' in the fence. "Her hobbies include eating grass, bleating at inappropriate moments, and getting her head stuck in the fence."

"She does this on purpose?"

I hold my hand out to Gabby. When she places her hand in mine and I feel the calloused over blisters, a shot of guilt runs through me. This soft woman shouldn't be milking goats and helping to muck stalls.

"She's an attention hog. Or, I guess, an attention goat as it were."

Gabby snags her hand from mine. Her hip juts out and she places her hand on it. Huh. She doesn't appear very soft at this moment. In fact, her eyes would shoot fire at me now if they could. My cock twitches at her sexy as all get out appearance.

"Are you telling me you're going to leave the poor goat stuck in the fence?"

She's cute when she snarls at me. But I'm not a total idiot so I keep those thoughts to myself.

"I'll make you a deal." I wait for her to motion for me to get on with it before continuing. "We ignore Brenda for fifteen minutes. If within such time, she's still stuck in the fence, I'll help her out. But you have to truly ignore her for fifteen minutes."

"Why?"

"Because she does this for attention. If we don't give her what she wants, she'll get bored eventually."

Gabby sticks her hand out. "You've got a deal."

I use my hold on her hand to draw her near. "Sealed with a kiss?"

I don't give her a chance to answer before my lips are on hers. My tongue prods for entry and she immediately opens to me with a sigh. I taste the coffee she's addicted to as well as cinnamon and apples and something completely Gabby. The taste is addicting.

My hands thread through her hair and I tilt her head so I can deepen the kiss. She moans and her fingernails dig into my shoulders. I press my hard length against her stomach, and she hitches a leg around my waist.

I release her hair to catch her leg and wind it around me until she's opened up for me. I thrust my cock into her jean-clad core and her leg tightens around me.

Maa! Maa! Maa!

I slow my kisses until I can release Gabby's lips and glance over my shoulder. Sure enough, Brenda is sauntering away.

"Hey!" Gabby points to the goat. "She could get herself out of the fence."

"I told you. Attention hog."

"Attention goat is more like it."

She giggles and I feel her body shake against mine. I groan at the friction against my cock. I force myself to unwind her leg from my waist.

"What are you doing?" She waggles her eyebrows. "I was enjoying myself?"

It's the obvious question mark at the end of her sentence that has my resolve hardening. I'm more than happy to lay Gabby on the ground and have my wicked way with her, but I know she's not ready to make love in the great outdoors where anyone could see us.

"To be continued tonight." I kiss her nose. "When we're somewhere with a soft bed."

Her eyes widen and her cheeks brighten. "Okay," she breathes out.

"I need to muck the stalls. Did you come outside to help?"

"No!" She clears her throat. "Um, no. I have news."

She bounces on her toes and claps her hands.

"Tell me this exciting news."

She throws her hands in the air and shouts, "We're going to Hollywood!"

My heart squeezes. Hollywood? We? Here I thought she was settling in on the farm and she's been planning to leave me. What the hell?

"It's so exciting. We've been invited to a Hollywood movie premiere. A movie premiere. With red carpets, paparazzi, and glamorous stars. The whole shebang."

Hold on. Maybe Juniper invited her to a premiere of one of Maverick's movies. Maybe I'm jumping the gun here.

"Did Juniper invite you to a movie premiere?"

She slaps my stomach. "No, silly. A client of mine. She's small potatoes. She's just a make-up artist but guess what?" She doesn't wait for me to guess and continues to prattle on. "She invited me to a premiere of the latest movie she worked on. Well, me and my plus one." She winks at me. "That's you. You're my plus one."

Is this the life Gabby wants? Attending movie premieres in Hollywood. It's not my life. I have no desire to put on a monkey suit and walk down a red carpet while paparazzi snap pictures of me.

My life is here on the farm where I'm content. And in Winter Falls where I know and trust all of my neighbors. I will never move away. Moving away for college taught me all I need to know about the outside world.

"Do you not want to go?" When I don't answer, the smile drops from her face.

"It's okay," she says before I can figure out how to maneuver through the landmine of answering. "I don't fit in there either. I'm just a plain girl. I'm not glamorous the way Juniper is." She sighs. "It was a nice dream while it lasted."

The excitement bleeds from her face and she dips her chin. Damn it. I did this to her. I made her think she is less. I'm a fucking asshole. I can't let my fear of her leaving me affect our relationship.

"I'll have to figure out what to do with the farm. I've never let the goats alone for more than a day."

Surprise flares in her eyes. "You mean you'll go?"

"I mean I'll think about it."

She rolls her eyes. "Anytime Beckett said he'd think about it when I was growing up, it meant no."

I wind an arm around her waist and haul her near to kiss her nose. "When I say I'll think about it, it means I'll think about it. I need to make arrangements for the farm if I'm going to be gone overnight."

She bites her lip and looks up at me from beneath her lashes. "Yeah?"

I kiss her forehead. "Yeah."

"You have plenty of time. The premiere's in a month and a half."

A month and a half? She's assuming we'll still be together then. Good. We will be. If I have anything to say about it, we'll be together until our dying days. Assuming Gabby doesn't get carried away with Hollywood premieres and wants to leave Winter Falls for the big city that is. I frown. I guess I need to get her addicted to living on the farm.

"Why don't I escort you inside and you can show me how much you appreciate me agreeing to leave the farm for you?"

I don't bother to say 'thinking about leaving' since the decision is already made. Of course, I'm going to accompany her to a premiere. I'll be damned if she gets all dolled up and I'm not the man standing next to her.

Her breath hitches and heat sparks in her eyes. "Don't you need to muck the stalls?"

"The stalls can wait."

Chapter 30

Avoidance – doing absolutely everything in your power to circumvent discussing being matched by a group of busybodies

I HUM AS I enter *Bake Me Happy*. I finished my work early for the day. Don't worry. I worked at the library this time instead of *Clove's Coffee Corner*. Lesson learned.

Since I'm done early, I thought I'd grab a treat for Phoenix. I happen to know he loves cinnamon.

A man smiles in my direction. "It's about dang time."

He can't be talking to me. I don't know who this man is. I glance over my shoulder, but there's no one there.

"Yes, I'm talking to you."

I point to myself.

He huffs. "Yes, you. Ms. Gabrielle Dempsey."

How does he know my name? "Um, hello?"

I hate how my greeting comes out sounding like a question, but at least I'm not hiding my face behind my hair. Progress!

"I'm Bryan. I keep this bakery running."

He does? "I thought Ashlyn's husband, Rowan, owned the bakery."

He juts out his hip and places his hand on it. "Pfft. That man cannot live without me."

I scan the bakery for other people before stepping closer. "Are you?" I swallow and try again. "Are you and Rowan and Ashlyn in a throuple?"

He throws his head back and laughs. And he laughs. And he laughs. Geez. I wasn't joking.

"You," he gasps out, "are hilarious. Rowan can't handle all of me."

The door behind him swings open and Rowan saunters out carrying a tray of cookies.

"Please, you want me and you know it."

"I do not," Bryan claims but the biting of his lower lip makes him a liar.

Rowan snorts. "Do to. You hit on me all the time in college."

Bryan tilts his nose into the air and sniffs. "I did not."

"No? Do you not remember the shower incident?"

"We agreed to never speak of the shower incident again. I have it in writing. It's in my contract."

Rowan ignores Bryan and addresses me. "It's not in his contract. I would never sign a non-disclosure agreement if it didn't allow me to tell people about how he sauntered into the communal showers at the dorm wearing—"

"Stop!" Bryan screams.

Rowan grins at me. "He's too easy. What can I get you?"

I kind of want to hear what Bryan was wearing, but I believe people are allowed to keep their secrets. I study the vitrines full of baked goodies. "One of everything?"

He chuckles. "You got it."

"I'm joking!" I rush to say. "I want something cinnamony for Phoenix."

"How about an organic cinnamon roll?"

My mouth waters. "Sounds yummy."

"Have a seat. I'll warm one up for you."

I didn't come in here for a treat for myself.

"I'll make you a cappuccino."

He had me at coffee. "Okay." I nod.

"Sit down. I'll bring it over once it's warmed up."

He doesn't need to tell me twice. I find a table in the corner and dig my computer out of my bag. Today's work may be finished, but there's always tomorrow's work.

"There she is!" Sage shouts as she enters the bakery followed by Feather, Petal, Clove, and Cayenne.

Don't any of these women ever work? I know they all have businesses or, in Sage's case, a job.

I put a smile on my face. "How can I help you?"

"You can stop dilly dallying," Feather demands as she sits down across from me. She doesn't bother asking if the seat is free.

"Dilly dallying?"

"Yes." She nods. "It's been nearly two months."

Do I dare ask? Yes, I do. I'm no longer the scaredy-cat I was when I first came to live in Winter Falls. I'm stronger. I can face off with a group of elderly women. They may be the scariest elderly women in the world, but I can handle this.

"Two months since what?"

"Since you started living with Phoenix," she huffs.

Has it been two months? In some ways, it feels as if it's been years. It usually takes me forever to be as comfortable with a person as I am with Phoenix. But there's something about the goat farmer that puts me at ease and brings me peace.

Shoot. It's been two months. Does Phoenix want me to move out? Am I cramping his style? After all, there's no reason for me to stay. We haven't heard a peep from Patrick in weeks.

No. No. No. I am not scaling Mountain Insecurity again. I've scaled that mountain and I am done with it. There are no new peaks for me to climb.

Phoenix cares for me. He said so himself. Sure, my feelings for him are deeper. I love the man, after all, but it's okay. Caring for me is a good place to start.

"Well?" Petal prods, and I nearly jump in my seat. How did I forget I'm surrounded by the gossip gals, even if they aren't wearing their hot pink t-shirts today?

"I'm uncertain as to what you want."

Rowan elbows his way through the crowd of women. "They want you to admit you love Phoenix so they can win the bet," he says as he sets my coffee and cinnamon roll down on the table.

"Where's ours?" Sage demands.

He cocks a brow. "Your what?"

"Young man!" she sputters.

He chuckles as Bryan arrives with cinnamon rolls and coffees for all of them. Clove sniffs the coffee before taking a sip. Her eyes light up at the flavor but her lips turn down in a frown.

"Your coffee is passable," she says.

Rowan bows. "Thank you." He winks at me before retreating and leaving me alone with them. Shoot. I guess I can't depend on backup from him.

I sip on my coffee as I contemplate how to get out of this situation. I have no intention of admitting my feelings to any of them. I may not be from Winter Falls, but I know better than to tell any of the gossip gals my secrets. They won't be secrets any longer than the time it takes them to post the news on the town's Facebook page.

"Project Farm wasn't supposed to last this long," Cayenne complains.

"What's Project Farm?"

Sage rolls her eyes. "It's Phoenix and you, of course."

Yikes. I don't want to touch her comment. Instead, I ask, "Why the moniker Project Farm?"

She points to Cayenne. "She kept forgetting the portmanteaus."

"Portmanteau?"

"You know when you put two words together to form one word."

"I know what a portmanteau is, but I'm confused as to what it has to do with me."

"They like to make portmanteaus as names for their matchmaking projects. It started with Project Weston – aka Aspen West and Lyric Alston," Bryan explains.

"Project Farm isn't a portmanteau."

Sage huffs. "The name isn't important."

But discussing the name did derail them for a little bit. How else can I derail them? The bell over the door rings and Old Man Mercury steps in.

"Hi, Mercury," I greet and wave.

He grunts at me, but I'm determined.

"How are you?"

He taps his walking stick on the floor. "My bones hurt, and these ladies are ruining my town."

"Your town?" Sage screeches. "I've been here just as long as you."

"I have, too. Arlo and I were as involved in starting up Winter Falls as you and Adhara were," Cayenne adds.

"Who's Adhara?" I whisper.

I must not have whispered softly enough because Mercury hears me and answers, "My wife."

"He's a widower," Feather answers.

I stand and walk to Mercury. "I'm sorry for your loss," I say as I squeeze his forearm.

He scowls at me. "What do you know about loss, young lassie?"

"My parents died when I was eight."

Twenty years have passed and yet saying those words still causes my heart to ache for what I will never have. A mom to discuss falling in love with. A dad to walk me down the aisle. Grandparents to spoil my children.

"You apologize, Mercury." Clove points a finger at him. "You know better than to make assumptions about people."

Mercury's lips purse together, and he glares at her.

I pat his forearm. "It's okay. You don't need to apologize."

He grasps my hand. "Young lady, I think I do."

"Nope," I insist. "I get it. Sometimes I get all caught up in what I lost and forget other people have lost more than me. I'm lucky. I have my sisters and my brother."

"And a young man chasing after you from what I've heard."

My cheeks warm. "I wouldn't say chasing."

"He's caught you then, has he?" Mercury winks, and I about fall flat on my ass in surprise at the gesture. "Now." He squeezes my hand. "You better move along before the talk in this town is all about you flirting with me."

"It's your fault for being so darned handsome," I say.

Mercury smiles before taking his coffee and shuffling out the door.

I step to the counter. "Can I pay for his coffee? And my things as well, please."

Rowan hands me a to-go bag with a shake of his head. "No charge." Before I can protest, he continues, "Anyone who can get Old Man Mercury to smile and wink at her has earned a few pastries."

"I wasn't nice to him to get something for free."

"Which is why you aren't paying."

I don't understand his reasoning, but I smile anyway. "Thank you."

"Now, get out of here while Bryan holds off the gossip gals."

I glance over my shoulder to find his assistant throwing his arms all over the place while telling a story. I'm half-tempted to listen to his story. I only just met Bryan, but I know he's got good stories.

I'm not an idiot, though. The gossip gals are distracted and it's time to skedaddle.

Diapers – not just for babies anymore!

"TA-DA!" CASSANDRA SHOUTS WHEN I open the door to her.

"Why are you ta-daing?"

Elizabeth rolls her eyes. "Because she thinks her mere appearance is worth a ta-da."

Nothing new then. "Why are you here? Did I forget you were dropping by?"

Cassandra pushes her way inside the farmhouse. "Of course, we're here. Tonight is the Halloween festival in town."

"And this means you're here because?"

Cassandra ignores my question to snoop through the kitchen cupboards. "Where's the wine?"

"We don't have any."

Huh. I enjoy the sound of that. *We* don't have any. As in Phoenix and I are a couple living together. I mean we are a couple living together, but for how long? Does he want me to stay once the Patrick-issue is dealt with? Or am I moving back into my apartment I barely spent a week living in?

Elizabeth lifts a bag. "I came prepared."

"Who's a good little girl scout?" Cassandra teases.

"Be nice or I won't let you taste my goodies."

Cassandra chuckles. "Taste your goodies?"

Elizabeth rolls her eyes. "Whatever. You know what I meant. I have Sangria and chips and salsa."

I groan. Sangria. The last time I drank the fruity temptation I decided goat yoga was a great idea. Spoiler alert – it wasn't.

"I'm still confused as to why you're here."

"It's the Halloween pre-party, bitches!" Cassandra screams.

"Do you have to be so loud?"

She shrugs. "Maybe."

Maa! Maa!

Her nose wrinkles. "What's that noise?"

What's that noise? We're on a goat farm. It's a goat, of course.

"Pan."

"The goat Pan?"

She's really not getting the whole goat farm thing, is she?

"Yes. She wants inside."

"She wants inside?"

"Are you going to repeat everything I say today?"

She sticks out her tongue before marching to the door. She opens it and Pan saunters inside like she belongs in the house and not outside on the farm. Her attitude might be my fault. There's a possibility I let her inside a bit too much. But she's good company. Besides, who can handle all the bleating when she doesn't get her way? Not me.

Cassandra stares at the goat wandering around the living room with her mouth gaping open. "You weren't kidding."

"You need to put a diaper on her if she's going to stay inside."

Yes, diaper. I quickly learned cleaning goat berries and goat pee was not an activity I want to perform multiple times a day. I clean enough of the stuff when I help Phoenix muck the stalls. And, okay, I may have accidentally stepped in the icky stuff one too many times.

"You are full of shit. No way do you put a diaper on this goat."

"I am not full of poop, but the house will be if you don't put a diaper on her."

Cassandra places her hands on her hips. "Okay, fine. Show me this supposed diaper."

I open a cabinet in the kitchen and retrieve one of Pan's diapers and throw it at my sister. She lets it fall to the ground instead of catching it.

"Either put the diaper on Pan, let her outside, or you're cleaning up any accidents she has."

"Isn't she potty trained?"

Elizabeth giggles. "She's a goat."

I nod toward Pan. "Your choice."

Cassandra stares at me. "Who are you? My little sister doesn't give me orders."

"You mean you don't listen to orders from anyone except your inner voice who happens to be batshit crazy," Elizabeth says.

"I don't know why you paint me as this timid person. I'm not timid. I'm shy. There's a difference."

Cassandra doesn't agree. Of course, she doesn't. The woman lives to argue. "Sorry, sister dear, but for the past year you've been the personification of timid."

"Well, I'm not timid anymore." I point to where Pan's taking a dump. "And you're picking that up."

Cassandra looks to where I'm pointing, and her eyes bug out while she retreats. "Eek! I'm not picking up shit."

"Yes, you are."

"You can't make me!" She stomps her foot.

"What are you? Twelve?"

"I'm thirty-three and your elder, which means you can't order me to do anything."

Elizabeth sighs as she pours a glass of sangria. "You want one?"

I never have been able to resist temptation. I take a sip and my throat burns. "Geez. Do you think you put enough rum in it?"

"Don't worry. If you don't like it, I'll drink it."

I wag my finger at Cassandra. "Nuh-uh. No drinks for you until you clean up the poop and put Pan outside."

"Or you can put a diaper on a goat." Elizabeth leans forward to mock whisper to me. "I bet a YouTube video of Cassandra putting a diaper on Pan would get a gazillion hits."

"You're supposed to be on my side." Cassandra huffs. "You're supposed to feed her Sangria until she spills all about Phoenix."

I raise my eyebrows at Elizabeth. "Really?"

She shrugs. "Curious minds want to know."

I groan. When Elizabeth and Cassandra join forces, trouble isn't far away. I need a diversion.

"How are you getting home if you're drinking Sangria with me?"

"Rumor has it someone has an apartment in town she's not using."

"Yeah, Gabby," Cassandra taunts.

I raise a finger. "One, you don't call me Gabby."

My sisters teased me by calling me Gabby when I was young because I was not gabby. It was supposed to be ironic. Instead, it was stupid. And hurtful. It's also done. Phoenix calls me Gabby and no one else.

"Two, Pan is now peeing. If she pees on the carpet, you're dealing with Phoenix."

"Ah!" Cassandra screams when she looks down and notices Pan's stream of pee arching toward her. She dances backward until her butt hits the kitchen counter. "She's possessed by the devil!"

"The Bible is prejudiced against goats, don't you think?" I ask Elizabeth calm as can be while Cassandra jumps from foot to foot.

"How much pee does this thing have inside her? Is her bladder the size of a swimming pool?"

"And three, Pan isn't a thing." I have to raise my voice to be heard over Cassandra's screeching.

"I'm not putting a diaper on this thing."

"Pan!" I correct.

Pan hears her name and trots over to me. "How are you, my sweet girl?" I ask as I scratch her chin.

"Are you petting her? Are you crazy?"

"Go outside before I end up killing my sister."

Maa!

"I know it isn't fair."

Maa!

"I know you're here every day and they're the intruders. But they have Sangria."

"And chips and salsa," Elizabeth adds.

Maa!

"No chips and salsa for you, but there's some yummy grass outside."

Maa!

"And those rhubarb leaves you enjoy nibbling on."

Maa!

"Good girl." She turns to the door, and I pat her bottom to get her going. "Open the door for her, will you, Cassandra?"

"Yeah, sure. I'll open the door for the goat," she mutters as she stomps to the door and opens it.

Maa! Pan butts Cassandra in the leg before trotting outside and down the stairs of the porch with her head held high and her long ears perked up as if she owns the world.

Cassandra returns to the kitchen and grabs a chair.

"Nope." I hook my foot under the chair to prevent her from pulling it out. "The cleaning supplies are under the sink."

She grunts. "Are you seriously going to make me clean up after a freaking goat?"

"Who else is going to clean up the mess? Cinderella?"

She trudges to the kitchen and opens the cupboard. "This is complete bullshit," she complains as she pulls out supplies. "Where are your paper towels?"

I giggle. "Did you forget we're in Winter Falls? I'd be burned alive on the stake for having paper towels in my house."

"It is apropos since it's Halloween and you're acting like a witch."

"I think they hanged witches but not on Halloween," Elizabeth points out.

"I can't believe you're making me clean up piss and shit when we're supposed to be grilling you."

"Grilling Gabby about what?" Phoenix asks as he enters the house.

Cassandra screams and the cleaning supplies fall to the floor. "Hells bells, you could warn a person."

Phoenix toes off his boots as he answers. "I didn't think you'd hear me over all the bitching and moaning." He kisses my hair before asking, "What happened?"

Elizabeth answers on my behalf. "Gabrielle's teaching Cassandra a lesson in goat management. There were diapers involved."

He cocks a brow at me. "Diapers?"

I roll my eyes. "Don't pretend you don't know I have diapers for Pan when she's in the house."

He shrugs. "As long as they aren't disposable."

Elizabeth holds up the pitcher. "Can I pour you a glass of sangria, Phoenix?"

"I'll have a beer, thanks."

I start to stand to grab his beer, but he pushes down on my shoulder. "Sit. Relax. Enjoy your company. I'm going to have a shower and we'll go to the festival afterwards."

"Do you need any help with the farm before we leave?"

"Everything's all taken care of."

He winks at me before grabbing a beer and climbing the stairs. I watch him go. I never miss the opportunity to watch him walk away. His behind fills out his jeans entirely too well for me to miss it.

"Phoenix and Gabrielle sitting in a tree. K–I–S–S–I–N–G," Elizabeth sings once he's out of view.

Cassandra snorts. "I hope to hell they're doing more than kissing."

My face flushes as memories of all the 'more' we've been doing hit me.

Elizabeth points to my face. "Proof positive there's more."

I keep my mouth shut. There's no need to tell my sisters what I've been up to with Phoenix. Of course, we're having sex. I love the man. I probably should tell him my feelings at some point, but the timing has never been right. I'll figure it out. Later.

Chapter 32

Pitchfork – never around when you need one

PHOENIX

"I'm so excited. I love Halloween," Gabby says as we cycle into town.

I cringe. "Samhain isn't exactly Halloween. The traditions of Halloween are derived from Samhain, but it's not the same thing."

"Explain more, Master."

I can tell from her voice she's kidding, but the idea of her saying master while kneeling before me causes my cock to twitch. I'm usually not into master/subservient play but apparently, with Gabby, everything goes.

I clear my throat. "Samhain is celebrated to welcome in the harvest and usher in the dark half of the year. It's a time when the barriers between the physical world and the spirit break down allowing interaction between humans and those of the otherworld."

"Those of the otherworld? You mean ghosts?"

I contemplate how to answer. Is this the final straw? Will Gabby decide Winter Falls is too crazy for her? Not quirky but full-on crazy? Will she run away when she discovers what we're going to do this evening?

"This is the most awesome thing I've ever heard!"

Okay. Those are not the words I expected her to say.

"Are we going to commune with the dead? Have a séance?"

I chuckle. "No. There's a dumb supper."

"I don't know what could possibly be dumb about food, but I can't wait."

I decide not to explain since we're nearly to Main Street. We park our bikes and I grasp Gabby's hand and lead her to the town square where tables are set up for the supper.

"Are we having supper with the entire town?"

"And our ancestors."

Ashlyn waves at us. "Over here!"

"Wow! This is a ton of food." Gabby's mouth gapes open as she stares at the piles and piles of dishes on all the tables. "Who made all of this? And why wasn't I told? I could have helped."

"Next year," Ashlyn declares. "Newbies don't help their first year in town."

"Is this a rule?" Gabby asks.

"It is now. I'm the mayor. I make the rules."

I sigh and wonder – not for the first time – why no one protested when Ashlyn volunteered to become mayor.

Gabby reaches for a tortilla chip and Ashlyn slaps her hand. "No!"

Gabby rubs her hand. "Ow. What was that for?"

"No eating until after we've had a chance to speak to the ancestors."

Gabby smiles. "We are doing a séance. This is awesome."

"It's not a séance," Ashlyn says. "Trust me. Those are different."

Juniper snorts as she arrives. "How would you know? Your idea of a séance is wearing an old sheet over your head."

I notice my parents making their way toward us. Crap. I forgot they'd be here. I don't know if Gabby's ready to meet them, but she doesn't have a choice now. I tug on her hand. "Come on. There are some people I want you to meet."

My mom's smile is huge when we stop in front of her and dad. "Mom, Dad, I want you to meet Gabrielle."

Gabrielle gasps and her hand in mine begins to tremble. Shit. I should have warned her my parents would be here. I squeeze her hand.

"Gabrielle, these are my parents."

"I-i-it's nice to meet you." Gabby offers Mom her hand, but Mom scoffs and pulls her into a hug.

"Families don't shake hands. They hug."

"You're squishing the poor girl, Radiance," Dad complains.

"Hush, you. You'll get your chance in a second."

Dad winks at me. "About time you brought home a girl."

I did bring home a girl. Tina lived with me for a year.

Dad claps me on the back. "A girl worthy of you."

A girl worthy of me? He's got things backwards. I'm not worthy of Gabby. I'm not nearly good enough for her.

I don't have a chance to get my thoughts in order before Dad yanks Gabby away from Mom for a bear hug. He lifts her off the ground and she giggles. "Nice to meetcha, Gabrielle."

"You too, Mr. Alston."

"You can call me Ever, unless you prefer to call me Dad."

"D–d–dad?" Gabby gulps. She blinks as her eyes swell with tears. I tuck her close to me.

Mom slaps Dad. "You're making her cry. Stop it!"

"My parents passed away," Gabby whispers.

Mom grasps her hand. "I know, sweet girl. I know."

"How do you… Never mind."

"Winter Falls!" they answer in unison and Gabby's lips tip up in an almost smile.

"I'm sorry you lost them, but you have us now." Mom squeezes Gabby's hand once more before releasing it.

A bell rings to announce it's time to begin the dumb supper. My parents, Gabby, and I join the table where my brothers and the West family are already seated.

"I'm the mayor, so I get to start," Ashlyn announces. She holds out her arms. "Dear ancestors, it's been the best year ever."

"What is she doing?" Gabby whispers her question.

I place my hand on her thigh and squeeze. "She's updating her ancestors on the past year."

"Are we going to go around the table and update our ancestors?"

I snort. "No. Ashlyn's just being an attention hog."

"Nothing new there," she mutters, and I chuckle.

"Boo!"

Gabby startles and her fingernails dig into my hand.

"It's Lady Gwyn," I explain and point to the headless woman dressed in white.

"Who's Lady Gwyn? And is that supposed to be a pig?"

"A black pig to be exact. Lady Gwyn chases night wanderers away."

Her fingernails retract from my skin as she relaxes. "Oh. She scared me."

Lady Gwyn dances around as the black 'pig' follows her. She pretends to scare the kids who laugh at her antics.

"Aspen!" Lyric shouts as he runs toward us clad only in his underwear and socks.

Lady Gwyn halts and looks at him. "You're ruining my act!"

"The black pig," is his strange answer.

"Oh shit. You're not the pig?"

"If he's not the pig, who is?" someone asks, but I'm already moving. I shove Gabby toward my dad. "Keep her safe," I order before rushing toward the pig.

The pig stands his ground. "She's mine!" he shouts. "You can't have her."

Lyric flies at him and tackles him to the ground. The pig fights him off, but he doesn't have a chance against my brother who has his arms pinned behind his back in no time. River slaps a pair of handcuffs in his hands.

Once he's cuffed, Lyric hauls him to his feet and yanks the costume off of his head.

"Patrick Cook, I presume."

Patrick struggles in his hold. "Release me this minute. I haven't done anything wrong, and you haven't read me my rights."

Lyric chuckles. "You didn't steal the costume?"

Patrick sneers in response. "I'll pay for it. How much can a measly costume be worth?"

Uh oh. He's going to regret those words. Sage and the rest of the gossip gals make their way to where Lyric's holding Patrick.

"Measly costume?" Sage slaps him with her purse.

"How dare you?" Petal joins in on the fun and slaps him with her purse, too. Since her purse is always full of candles, he winces as it hits him.

"Are you going to let a bunch of old ladies hit me?" Patrick demands of Lyric.

"Old ladies!" Clove screeches, but before her purse can land a blow her husband, Sirius, arrives to haul her away.

She kicks and screams as he carries her. "Let me down, Sirius! I want my chance." He ignores her and keeps moving. He's going to pay for his actions later.

Feather and Cayenne step closer for their turn, but Lyric takes pity on the idiot and blocks them. "But Sage and Petal got to hit him," Cayenne pouts.

"No one's hitting the prisoner," he commands.

"Prisoner?" Patrick snorts. "Once my lawyers hear about this, I'll be out of here."

If it wasn't already obvious what a giant dickhead this guy is, his statement made it crystal clear.

"And how exactly are your lawyers going to hear about this?" Lyric asks.

"I have a right to one phone call."

"You do." Lyric smirks. "But I get to choose when you make your call." He tugs on Patrick's handcuffs. "I'm arresting you on the charge of larceny and stalking."

"Stalking? I didn't stalk anyone."

Every time I think this guy can't be more of a dick, he proves me wrong.

I cross my arms over my chest. "You've been stalking Gabby ever since you figured out where she was."

His attention rivets on me. "Who the hell are you?"

"He's my boyfriend," Gabby says as she stands next to me.

Fuck. I don't know if I should be proud of her for standing up to him or pissed she didn't stay with my dad out of harm's way.

Patrick laughs. "You can't fool me. I know you two are faking a relationship."

I haul her to my side and kiss her hair. "Nothing fake about the way I feel for her."

His nostrils flare and he growls. "You can't have her. She's mine."

Gabby tries to step toward him, but I tighten my hold to keep her plastered to my side. I'm not letting him breathe the same air as her.

"I am not a thing to be owned. I belong to myself."

"My, my. Little Gabrielle has grown claws. We'll have to work on your behavior when we're back together."

Gabby shrinks against me. Damn Patrick. After all the hard work she's done to open up, he's ruining it all. Footsteps shuffle behind me before Mom and Dad appear. Dad grasps my shoulder and Mom sidles up to Gabby until their sides touch.

Cassandra and Elizabeth stand in front of Gabby and the rest of the West sisters join them until we're cocooned by our friends and family. My heart warms at how everyone is taking my woman's back and showing her she's not alone.

Gabby clears her throat. "We will never get back together."

"What's that, mouse? I don't think I heard you over the sound of air," Patrick taunts.

Gabby grasps hold of my hand and squeezes until it hurts. I don't say a word, though. She can have all of my strength. Whatever she needs, I'll gladly give it to her.

"I will never go back to you, you… you jerk, you!"

"Go get 'em, Gabrielle!" Cassandra cheers.

"You'll come back eventually. You love me."

"I never said I love you." Gabby glances up at me. "I didn't."

I grin. "I believe you."

"Thank you."

"Let's run him out of town!" Sage whoops.

"We really need pitchforks for these occasions," Petal notes.

The gossip gals surround Patrick and begin herding him out of town. "Come on," Cassandra yells as she joins them. "Time to take out the garbage."

"Two choices," Lyric grumbles. "Leave of your own accord or spend the night in jail."

"I'm leaving. I know when I'm not wanted." The current situation would indicate he does not in fact know when he's not wanted.

Lyric uncuffs him. He marches down Main Street with his head held high while the gossip gals and Gabby's sisters chase after him while yelling taunts.

"Go with them," Lyric orders River. "And make sure they don't take things too far."

When everyone has moved off, I pinch Gabby's chin and force her to look at me. "It's over."

She blows out a breath. "It's over."

Chapter 33

*Chicken – when you're too afraid to say what you should say
causing you to make stupid mistakes*

I STARE AT THE suitcase on our bed. No, not *our* bed. This bed
not being ours is the whole reason I'm standing here like a
dweeb trying to figure out what I should do. Patrick's gone,
which means the 'danger' is gone, which means the jig is up. I
think.

Maa.

"I'll miss you, too, Pan."

Maa.

"Because …"

My words cut off. Why am I leaving? I collapse on the bed
and bury my face in my hands. I don't know why. I certainly
don't want to go anywhere, but Phoenix didn't ask me to stay.
Which means I should leave, doesn't it?

Maa.

"I'm not being melodramatic."

Maa.

"No, I'm not!"

Good grief. I'm arguing with a goat.

Maa.

I open my mouth to speak but slam it shut before I continue to argue with a goat like I'm crazy pants. The town of Winter Falls must be rubbing off on me.

I stand. "Time to get this show on the boat. On the road? Whatever." I shake my head and open the top dresser drawer.

I'm zipping up my suitcase. Correction – I'm trying to zip up my suitcase when Phoenix strolls into the bedroom.

"Ready for lunch?" His brow furrows when he notices the suitcase "What are you doing?"

I shrug since I don't have a clue what I'm doing.

"Are you packing?"

"Y-y-yes?" Ugh! Stupid stutter. Go away! "Yes?" My answer still comes out sounding like a question but at least I didn't stutter. Small victories.

"Why?"

"Why?"

"Yes. Why?"

Ask me to stay. Ask me to stay.

We fall into silence as I beg him with my eyes to ask me to stay. He frowns and his gaze drops to the suitcase and his frown deepens. If he's unhappy with my departure, he can ask me to stay.

Maa!

"I didn't forget you existed, Pan." Phoenix tickles her chin, but his gaze remains fixated on the suitcase. Pan butts his hand, and he finally gives her his full attention. "Is she wearing a diaper?"

I roll my eyes. "Don't act surprised. You know I put her in a diaper when she's in the house."

He smiles but it doesn't reach his eyes. "I would have loved to see you learn how to put a diaper on a goat."

I'm glad he wasn't around. I think potty training Pan would have been easier than getting her into a diaper the first time.

"Have you ever put a diaper on a goat?"

He nods. "When a doe dies in childbirth, the kids need to be handfed. It's easier to do when they're inside the house."

"Phoenix Apollo! You bottle-fed goats?"

"Every goat farmer has bottle-fed a kid or two."

I wish I could be around for the next round of kids being born.

"Can I come out to the farm when the baby goats are born?"

He sighs and inches forward until he's in my space. "Gabby, you don't need to ask. You're always welcome on the farm."

But not welcome to live here full-time? I want to ask the question, but I don't dare. If the answer is no, I'll be crushed.

"Thank you," I croak. I clear my throat and motion to the suitcase. "Can you …erm… help me shut it?"

He shakes his head. "What is it with women and shutting suitcases?"

Is he referring to Tina? I don't want to think about the other women he's helped with their luggage. I don't want him helping anyone with their luggage except me.

Jealous much, Gabrielle? Not usually actually. But when I think about Phoenix with another woman, I could burn the world down. Apparently, I'm not only jealous but quite destructive when in a jealous rage.

He zips the suitcase shut and lifts it off the bed. "After you."

I stand still in the bedroom for another moment willing him to ask me to stay, but he lifts a brow and doesn't say a word. I huff and spin around.

I give up. He's not going to ask me to stay. He doesn't want me. The same as every other man I've ever been with. Except Patrick who didn't want me until I walked away from him. He doesn't actually want me. He wants to repair his wounded pride.

I stomp down the stairs and out the door where I stop when confronted with the empty driveway. I forgot I don't have a vehicle since mine's sitting in the parking lot of my apartment building. It's a good thing I wasn't planning to sneak away.

Phoenix reaches for my hand and draws me toward his truck parked next to the barn. I enjoy the feel of his hand in mine as we walk. Who knows when the next time I'll get the chance to touch him will be?

He throws my suitcase in the bed of his truck before leading me to the passenger door. His mouth opens as if he's going to speak, but he shakes his head and opens the door for me. He drops my hand and motions for me to hop in.

We don't speak as we drive to my apartment. It's not the comfortable silence I'm used to with him. His annoyance is practically filling the cab. And me? I'm heartbroken.

I thought he'd ask me to stay. I thought he wanted me to stay. I thought he cared about me.

Maybe I was wrong about everything. I try to swallow the lump that appears in my throat. There's one thing I'm not wrong about. I love this man. Maybe he doesn't love me back, but my heart is set on him and there's nothing I can do about it.

He parks on the street in front of my apartment and jumps out without saying a word. I follow him to the cab where he grabs my suitcase.

I hold out my hand. "I can handle things from here."

He grunts.

"You don't have to escort me to the door. I'm a big girl. Besides, Patrick was run out of town."

Stupid, stupid Patrick. If he hadn't shown up at the Samhain festival, I'd still be living in Phoenix's house. I would stay there until I was so entrenched in the fabric of the farm, Phoenix couldn't bare to let me leave.

He motions to the door. Apparently, he's lost the ability to speak. So much for talking out our problems. Problems I didn't realize we had until today. Silly girl with her lovesick heart stuck on a man who doesn't want her.

I trudge up the stairs to the apartment with Phoenix following. I unlock the door and he pushes past me.

"You don't need to check for the boogeyman. We kicked him out of town."

He grunts as he surveys the room before marching to the bedroom where he places my suitcase on the bed.

"I'll walk you out," I say because I need him out of here before I begin to sob. I can already feel the pressure building behind my eyes.

"What's going on?" Sage asks as she flounces into my apartment. Without knocking, mind you.

"Mind your own business," Phoenix grumbles, and I cringe. Even I know telling a gossip gal to mind her own business is not the best idea.

"Phoenix Apollo, I'll have you know I used to change your diapers," Sage says.

He sighs. "I fail to see what changing my diapers when I was a baby has to do with anything."

The rest of the gossip gals enter the apartment, and he rolls his head back to stare at the ceiling. If he's asking for someone up there to beam him away, he's out of luck. Trust me. I know. I've tried it enough myself.

"Can I help you?" I ask since someone has to be polite in this situation.

"Why are you here?" Feather asks.

"Yeah." Petal nods. "Are you moving your things out to the farm?"

"Why didn't you phone us? We could have started packing for you," Clove adds.

"She's not moving out to the farm," Phoenix says, and I inhale a deep breath through my nose before the tears threatening to fall become reality.

I guess he's answered my question as to why he didn't ask me to stay. He doesn't want me to stay. Son of a biscuit. Was he using me? Was I a convenient body? A good cleaner and cook who helped out on the farm?

With those questions rolling around in my head, I do something I never would have thought I could do.

"Out!" I shout and point to the door. "Everyone get out of my apartment!"

The gossip gals look at one another. They seem to be having a silent conversation. Normally, I'd be fascinated with their ability to converse without opening their mouths but not now. They come to some conclusion and nod in unison before making their way to the door.

"We're here if you need us," Sage proclaims before waving as they leave.

"You, too." I poke Phoenix in his hard chest. I ignore the pain and do it again. "Get out and go back to *your* farm," I sneer.

Pain clouds his eyes and he opens his mouth, but I shake my head. "Out!"

He raises his hands in surrender before backing away and out the door. I slam it shut the second I'm alone and collapse against it. I bury my face in my hands as the first tears begin to fall.

Chapter 34

Ritual – an excuse to annoy the hell out of your sister

I ignore the knock on the door the same way I've ignored my telephone for the past day. I have no desire to see anyone or talk to anyone or be in the presence of anyone. I'm better off alone.

"We know you're in there," Cassandra shouts through the door.

"Go away!"

"We'll huff and we'll puff and we'll blow your door down," Elizabeth shouts.

"What are we? The three little pigs?"

"The pigs are the ones in the house. The wolf is the one that blows it down."

A more gentle knock comes this time. "Gabrielle?" Lilac? What is Lilac doing here? "I'm sorry to bother you, but I'm afraid if you don't open the door, I'll pick the lock."

"Pick the lock? Don't you have a key?" Elizabeth asks.

"I gave Gabrielle my keys when she took over the lease."

"Hold on. I think the question we should be asking is how Lilac knows how to pick a lock." Lilac better not teach Cassandra how to pick locks. Her antics barely stay on this side of legal as it is.

"It's actually quite simple. I watched a YouTube video."

I stomp to the door and fling it open. "There! The door's open. Are you happy now?"

I don't wait for their answer before whirling around and returning to the sofa where I bury myself under my blanket again.

"What's going on? Why are you pretending to be an Eskimo?" Cassandra asks.

"Eskimo is offensive. You may say Native Alaskan or Inuit."

Cassandra bows to Lilac. "Whatever you say, Ms. Know It All."

Elizabeth pushes past both of them. "What happened? Did you break up with Phoenix?"

"I don't know."

I sniff and tears well in my eyes. I thought I'd cried all my tears. Is there not a limit to the amount of tears a person can cry in a day? Why does the phrase 'all cried out' exist if it's impossible to ever use up the well of tears a person has in her body?

Elizabeth gathers me and my blanket in her arms and rocks me from side to side. "I'm sorry."

"Sorry? I want to hear why she doesn't know if she's together with Phoenix or not."

Elizabeth sneers at Cassandra. "Can't you be sympathetic for once in your life?"

Cassandra holds up a bag. "I'm sympathetic. I brought liquor and snacks."

"Why is everyone here?" I ask as I wipe under my eyes. The movement doesn't help. Tears continue to flow.

"This is the family support for a break-up ritual," Lilac explains.

Which still doesn't explain why Lilac's here. "No offense, Lilac, but why are you here?"

"Hello! She's marrying our brother, which makes her our sister-in-law, which makes her family."

I glare at Cassandra. "I know that. I meant why are you not at work? You don't seem like the kind of person to involve herself in break-up rituals."

"As it turns out, break-up rituals can be quite helpful in making a person feel better."

I guess I don't need to wonder any longer if we provided comfort when we stormed Lilac's home – this very apartment as it turns out – when she and Beckett were temporarily broken up.

Cassandra punches her hands in the air. "Let the break-up ritual begin!"

"Can you tone it down? My neighbors don't appreciate crazy people, and I have to live here, remember?"

Elizabeth pats my back. "Thanks for the opening. Why do you have to live here? Why aren't you at the farm with Phoenix?"

I pick at the fuzz on my blanket. "He doesn't want me there."

"Says who?"

"Says him." I sound like a petulant teenager, and I don't care.

"Did he kick you out?" Lilac asks. "This is most unusual." She rummages through her purse. "Let me ring him. This is not normal behavior for a Winter Falls man."

"No!" I screech and jump to my feet to rush to her, but my limbs become tangled in the blanket, and I fall to the floor. I don't let my fall slow me down. I kick my legs until they're free of any entanglements and roll to my feet before flinging myself at Lilac.

"Don't phone him!" I snatch for Lilac's phone, but she lifts it in the air. Since she's a giant, I can't reach. I jump but I don't come close to her elbow, let alone the phone. Being short sucks the majority of the time.

"You better promise not to phone Phoenix, Lilac. Otherwise, Ms. Exercise is for Losers is going to pull a muscle."

Lilac nods at Cassandra and I stop jumping. My legs quiver, but I blame it on my lack of fluids over the past twenty-four hours. Crying buckets of tears and not drinking any water would cause anyone to have shaky legs.

"Did he kick you out?" Lilac repeats her question.

"He didn't exactly kick me out."

I return to my spot on the sofa, and Cassandra plops down on the floor near my feet. "He either kicked you out or he didn't. Which is it?"

"He didn't ask me to stay."

"Which is not the same as kicking you out," Lilac points out because she prefers matters to be cut and dry. Gray doesn't exist in her world whereas I'm living in the gray at the moment.

"He had no problem helping me leave. He even carried my luggage upstairs and put it in my bedroom." I raise my eyebrows at them in a silent plea for them to contradict my conclusion that those actions indicate he didn't want me to stay. They don't. Dang.

"Then, when the gossip gals showed up, he said – and I quote here – 'She's not moving out to the farm'."

"Ouch." Cassandra rubs my leg. "If he can't see how wonderful you are and want you to live with him on the farm, it's his loss."

"Totally." Elizabeth nods in agreement.

"I still think this could be a misunderstanding," Lilac says.

"Nope." Cassandra holds up her hand. "You are not here to give our sister hope when she's down in the dumps."

Wait. She's not? I could use an influx of hope. The hope I've been holding onto is thinning fast considering it's been a day since I left the farm and Phoenix hasn't contacted me once. No calls. No messages. No emails. No bat signals. Nothing. I could use an injection of hope – no matter how thin – to keep me going.

Lilac purses her lips. She doesn't enjoy being told what to do any more than Cassandra does. But to her credit, she doesn't bitch at my sister.

"Okay. Where do we begin?"

Cassandra bounces to her feet. "I brought tequila."

I feign gagging. "Can I veto tequila and vote for a beer?"

"Sorry not sorry. Beer is for watching the game or eating pizza. When you're down in the dumps, you need tequila shots."

She skips to the kitchen. "Where are your shot glasses?"

"Are you at least going to give me food before you get me drunk?"

Elizabeth pats my arm. "Yes, I prefer to feed people before I get them drunk."

My nose wrinkles. "Get people drunk often, do you?"

She blushes and waves a hand in front of her face. "I didn't mean… I meant… Never mind."

Cassandra returns with a handful of filled shot glasses. This is not going to be good. The last time I drank tequila I was in college and ended up sleeping on the floor of the bathroom in the dorms. It wasn't even my dorm. And I have zero idea how I got there. It took me fifteen minutes of wandering around the next day to find my dorm room.

My stomach revolts at the smell of the drink, but Cassandra pushes the shot glass closer to me.

"You'll feel better afterwards. Trust me."

"I've never trusted you before, why begin now?" I mutter but I pinch my nose closed and down the shot. The liquid burns as it passes through my esophagus on the way to my stomach. I nearly gag on it but manage to swallow down the bile.

Lilac grimaces as she sets her empty shot glass down on the coffee table. "I believe food and movies are now in order." She lifts a bag.

Cassandra folds her hands together as if she's praying. "Please tell me Juniper hooked you up."

"Juniper hooked me up."

Cassandra squeals before stealing the bag from Lilac and peeking inside. "None of the movies in here have been released yet."

Lilac clears her throat. "Juniper snuck these movies out of the house. Don't make me regret trusting you."

Cassandra's shoulders slump. "You mean I can't post on social media about watching these movies before their release?"

Lilac snatches the bag back. "I don't know if this was a good idea."

"Come on," Elizabeth pleas, "don't punish us for the deeds of our sister."

"Fine. But don't make me uninvite you to my wedding."

"W-w-wedding?" I take a deep breath and try again. "You're planning it already?"

"Sorry. I was told not to discuss anything related to the wedding today."

"Who's ready to watch a movie?" Elizabeth shouts before I have a chance to ask Lilac who told her not to mention her wedding.

"I'll get the snacks." Cassandra rushes to the kitchen for bowls.

Everyone gathers around me as I start the movie on my laptop. The last thing I expected was to laugh today, but that's exactly what I end up doing. Huh. Maybe there's something to this break-up ritual stuff.

Chapter 35

Skinny dipping – a convenient excuse to call your brother a coward

PHOENIX

"Haven't we grown out of this yet?"

Splat!

I guess not. I pick River's boxers off of my chest and throw them on the ground. I hope they're clean, but honestly, I don't want to think about where his boxers may have been.

"Way to prove you're an adult."

River grins. "Adulting is boring."

I address my oldest brother. "You're supposed to be the Chief of Police."

"I am the Chief of Police. And there's nothing illegal about skinny dipping in the falls in Winter Falls." Lyric drops his boxers. At least he didn't throw them at me.

River dives into the water. "Come on. Don't be a chicken."

Lyric snorts. "I think Phoenix has proven, beyond a shadow of a doubt, what a chicken he is."

He cannonballs into the water close enough to the edge to splash me.

"Bwak. Bwak!" River flaps his arms.

"I'm not a chicken. I just have no desire for Lyric's wife and all her sisters to happen upon us when I'm butt-ass naked."

"Aspen has been ordered to stay away."

"And when has your wife ever listened to anything you say?"

He smirks. "Aspen can follow an order."

I groan. "I don't want to hear it."

"You brought it up!" He splashes me. "Get your chicken ass in here."

"Stop calling me a chicken."

"Chicken! Chicken! Chicken!" Lyric and River chant the word in unison over and over again until I'm sure the people in Winter Falls can hear them.

"Knock it off. I'm coming in. But if your wife and her sisters show up to steal our clothes, I will have my revenge."

I'm not making shit up. Aspen and her sisters have stolen our clothes while we've been skinny dipping too many times to count. You'd think we'd learn our lesson. Apparently not.

I drop my drawers and dive into the water before the cold air makes me think better of my decision. I swim underwater until Lyric's legs come into view. I latch onto them and pull him under the water for a count of twenty before I release him.

He comes to the surface splashing and sputtering. He never could hold his breath underwater for very long. "I'm going to kill you."

I calmly tread water as he attempts to catch his breath. "You shouldn't have called me a chicken."

"What would you prefer?" River asks. "Yellow-bellied coward?"

I splash him and he splashes me back. Lyric teams up with him. Enough of this. I duck under the water and swim underwater until I'm behind them. I break the surface and splash them from behind.

"What are you, a fish?" Lyric complains as he moves further away from me.

"I'll take fish over coward any day."

"I'm just calling it the way I see it," River claims.

My nostrils flare. "Why the hell do you think I'm a coward? I told you I wasn't in the mood to go skinny dipping this morning and yet here I am naked as the day I was born swimming. What about those actions scream coward?"

River grunts. "I'm not talking about this morning, you dipshit. I'm talking about you letting Gabrielle leave."

My heart seizes and I suddenly find it difficult to stay afloat. I swim to the riverbank and haul myself out of the water and onto the rocks.

If I think I'm going to have some peace here, I'm wrong. River and Lyric sit on the rocks next to me.

"I don't want to talk about it," I say before they can begin.

Lyric chuckles. "The same way I didn't want to talk about it when Aspen returned to Winter Falls?"

"Not the same thing at all. You and Aspen had a misunderstanding."

He bumps my shoulder. "What's to say you're not having a misunderstanding with Gabrielle now?"

"Because she left," I growl.

My chest aches and I reach a hand up to rub it. I can't believe she left. She just left. She didn't even entertain the idea of staying. I thought we had a connection. I fucking love the woman and she left me. I sure know how to pick women.

"She's not Tina," River says.

"She left," I repeat because there's nothing else to say.

"Did she break up with you?" Lyric asks.

"No, but she hasn't contacted me since she left either."

Lyric cocks an eyebrow. "And have you contacted her?"

River shakes his head. "I never thought my little brother was such a scaredy-cat."

"And I never thought my brother would use words like scaredy-cat."

Lyric stands. "All I'm saying is you need to ask her why she left."

"Wait." I stop him before he can jump into the water. "Do you have inside information?"

He shrugs before diving into the river. I jump in after him and chase him to the other side.

"You know something," I accuse as we walk out of the water toward our clothes.

"Even if I did, I'm bound by confidentiality not to tell."

"Let's go have breakfast at the diner," River suggests as he joins us.

I need to go milk my goats, but I'm curious what Lyric knows. And he does know something. He wouldn't have brought up confidentiality if he didn't.

Gracious, the owner of the diner, rushes to us when we enter the restaurant. "The Alston brothers as I live and breathe. What have I done good in my life to earn this reward?"

I kiss her cheek and wink. "Good morning."

She blushes and fans a hand in front of her face. "Have a seat. I'll be over in a couple of minutes for your orders."

The restaurant is crowded, which is no surprise as it's the only place in town where you can order a hot breakfast, but we manage to snag a booth at the window near the door.

"Who's that delicious specimen of womanhood?" River asks as he ogles a woman in another booth.

"When are you going to grow up?" Lyric asks.

"Grow up? Trust me. I'm all man."

"You're all manwhore is what you are."

I tune them out and gaze outside. What does Lyric know? Did Gabrielle not want to leave the farm? If not, then, why did she? If I live to be a million years old, I will never understand women.

As if I conjured her with my thoughts, there she is – my Gabby. She's walking down Main Street with her head hung low. Shit. Her head should never hang low. She's a goddess and should walk with her head held high.

I frown when I notice a man do a double take as she passes him. I can't blame him. Gabby is gorgeous after all, but he appears shocked to see her. As if he didn't expect her to be here.

I continue to watch as the man begins to follow her. He's wearing a ballcap with a hoody over it and mirrored sunglasses.

"Patrick."

I'm out the door before I realize I'm moving. As I run toward him, Gabby glances over her shoulder and spots him. Her eyes widen and she quickens her pace. Not fast enough. He reaches for her and shackles her wrist before hauling her to him.

"Gotcha!"

"Leave me alone!" She struggles to free herself from him, but he smiles as if he's enjoying her fight. Bastard.

"I can't wait to get you home and begin our training again."

I put on a burst of speed. My lungs are burning and my legs are aching, but I can't let him take her anywhere. I won't let him take her anywhere. I'll die first.

"There will be no training. And you aren't taking her anyway," I growl as I clamp my hand on his shoulder and tear him away from her.

"I've got Gabrielle." Out of the corner of my eye, I see River wrap an arm around her and pull her away from the altercation.

With Gabby safe, I give Patrick my full attention. "Think it's okay to touch women without their consent, do you? How's this for touching without consent?"

I slam my fist into his jaw, and he rears back before collapsing to the ground.

Lyric kneels next to him and slaps his face. "He's out cold."

I shake out my hand. "That's disappointing."

"Brother," River hollers, and I glance over my shoulder at him. He's holding Gabrielle up but she's as white as a ghost. Shit. I rush to them and River places her in my arms where she belongs.

"It's over, Gabby. Patrick will never bother you again."

She snorts. "I've heard that one before."

If she's being sarcastic, she must not be too upset by what happened.

"You need to get a restraining order."

She sighs. "I guess I don't have a choice now."

"Get off of me," Patrick roars when he revives to discover Lyric hauling him to his feet with his hands cuffed behind his back. "I'm the victim here. That man over there assaulted me."

"Yeah, yeah, tell it to the judge." Lyric tows Patrick off.

"You good, bro?" River asks. I lift my chin and he nods before retreating.

I pinch Gabby's chin and lift her head. "Are you okay?"

Chapter 36

Start over – a chance to begin again, which is only available after you've let your inner rage free

AM I OKAY? I shake out my wrist. It might be sore tomorrow but otherwise physically I'm fine. Mentally, on the other hand …

I can't believe what an idiot I was about Patrick. I'm sure every woman has said this at one time or another, but he didn't start out being a jerk. He slowly brought me into his treacherous web until I was stuck to the silky strains and couldn't get out. Except, I did get out.

Or, at least, I thought I did. I had no idea he would follow me to Colorado. I thought the phone calls and flowers were it. After all, he's lazy with a capital L. I'm the one who cooked and cleaned for him. He wouldn't even empty out the trash for goodness sake.

No way did I ever believe he'd follow me and try to grab me off the street and steal me away. Of course, he doesn't understand Winter Falls. If Phoenix hadn't been here to save me, someone else would have. You can't get away with sneaking around in this town.

Phoenix's hand moves from my chin to caress my cheek. "I'm sorry I wasn't there for you, darling."

Wasn't there for me? Darling? His words cause a switch in my mind to flip. *Snap!* One second, I'm wondering what in the world is wrong with Patrick and the next one I'm madder than Pan the first time I tried to put a diaper on her.

I push him away. "And why weren't you there for me?"

He lifts his ball cap and runs a hand through his hair. "Um…"

"I'll tell you why." I poke his shoulder. "Because you don't want me."

"Don't want you?"

I poke him again. It feels good, so I do it again. "Are you having trouble comprehending? Or have you gone deaf?"

"Go, Gabrielle!" Clove cheers.

"Get him!" Feather shouts.

I whirl around to discover the entire gossip gal gang is gathered on the street behind us. And they're not alone. A whole crowd of locals is watching.

"Bets are closing in two minutes. Two minutes, folks!" Sage calls.

"Are you—"

Before I get a chance to lay into Sage about her infernal betting, Aspen motions to me. "Psst. Over here."

"Not now, Aspen. I'm kind of in the middle of something."

"And I have a back room with a door that locks." She indicates her bookstore, *Fall Into A Good Book,* with a tilt of her head.

I hadn't even noticed we were standing in front of the bookstore. I grab Phoenix's hand and drag him into the store. I follow Aspen as she leads me to the back where she opens a door marked 'personnel only'.

"I'll fend them off for as long as I can," she promises before shutting the door.

I reach forward and snap the lock. I inhale a deep breath and blow it out as I stare at the closed door. It doesn't help. My anger buzzes underneath my skin like it's a living thing. For once in my life, I don't try to suppress my feelings. I whirl around.

"Where were we?" I tap my cheek as if I don't know. Don't worry. I know exactly where we were. "Ah, yes. You don't want me but think you should have been there to save me. What a bunch of bull cocky!"

"Why do you think I don't want you?"

I roll my eyes so hard I'm afraid they'll get stuck in the back of my head. "Duh! You let me leave."

"Let you leave?"

"Are you going to repeat everything I say and drive me completely bonkers?" I scream.

There's a rap on the wall. "You might want to keep it down," Aspen hollers through the door.

"What are you doing, Aspen Cloud? How are we supposed to eavesdrop if we can't hear them?"

I groan at Feather's question.

"This town." I shake my head.

"And that right there is why I let you leave."

What in the world is he talking about? "What right where?"

"You getting annoyed with this town. You're going to leave and then where will I be?"

He can't be serious. My head falls back, and I stare at the ceiling. I study it but there are no answers there. I guess I have to maneuver my way out of this situation all on my own.

"Are you comparing me to her again?"

He shrugs. "When the shoe fits."

Whatever anger had ebbed roars back to life with a vengeance. "Phoenix Apollo Alston, don't you ever compare me to your ex-girlfriend again! Do you hear me!"

"We all hear you," Sage answers.

I stomp toward him. "Did what's her face help milk the goats?"

"No."

"Did she help muck the stalls?"

"No."

"Did she learn how to put a diaper on a goat?"

"Did she say diaper on a goat?" Clove asks.

Phoenix's lips tip up in an almost there smile. "No, Tina did none of those things." His lips flatten out. "But she did leave. The same way you did."

I throw my hands in the air. "Because you didn't ask me to stay!"

"Boo!" Cayenne yells. "You should have asked her, Phoenix. I need to revise my bet now."

Silence falls as Phoenix studies me. "Would you have said yes?"

"What did he say? I didn't hear." Sage knocks on the door. "Speak up."

"Did you not hear what I just said?" I ask Phoenix.

He rubs a hand over his forehead. "I heard everything you said, but I don't know what you mean."

I sigh. "I learned how to milk the goats, muck the stalls, and diaper a goat. What do you think my answer would be if you had asked me to stay?"

His nose wrinkles. "Yes?"

"You don't get it, do you?" And dang him for looking so adorably confused as he tries to puzzle out in his head what I'm telling him. "I love you, you blockhead."

His gaze finds mine as a smile slowly forms and his dimples peek out.

"You love me?"

The hope in his eyes gives me all the courage I need to answer. "Yes, I love you. Even if you repeat every single thing I have to say, which is super annoying by the way, I love you."

It's such a relief to finally say the words. I feel as if a weight has been lifted from my chest and I'm finally free. Maybe Phoenix doesn't love me. He may not even care for me. It doesn't matter. I put those words out in the universe.

I'm a total liar. Of course, it matters if Phoenix doesn't care for me. I'll be thoroughly crushed. Two days in my pajamas while recovering from a night of tequila shots with crazy Cassandra will seem easy peasy compared to the funk I'd fall into.

But I'm not ready to give up defeat. There will be no waving of a white flag. Not yet. I'm holding onto the last thread of hope with all my might.

Phoenix cradles my face with his hands. "I love you, too, Gabby."

My heart stalls before it resumes beating with a vengeance. But I don't have time to worry about whether I'm having a heart attack. Not with the lips of the man I love on mine. He licks the seam until I open up for him and his tongue dives in to explore.

I grasp his shoulders and pull him near until his body is flush with mine. I moan when I feel his hard length press against my belly. I hitch my leg around his waist, and he grabs my thigh to hold me there. He thrusts his length into my center, and I groan. *Yes.*

"Aha!" My fussy brain barely registers the sound of metal scraping against metal. "I found my extra key!"

"Why do you have an extra key to my storeroom, Sage?" Aspen screeches, and I startle.

My eyes widen as I stare up at Phoenix. "They're going to break in here."

He lowers my leg and grasps my hand. "Come on. There's a back door. We can take the rear alley to the square where my truck's parked."

"Will we make it there before the mob catches us?"

"You worried about keeping up?" He doesn't give me a chance to answer before he throws me over his shoulder like I'm a sack of goat feed. "Open the door."

I reach down to open the door and he rushes out with me bouncing on his back.

I giggle. "I guess you can say you caught the girl."

He pats my behind. "I certainly did."

"Looks like I was wrong. I don't need a grand gesture."

"Women. What about me carrying you away isn't a grand gesture?"

"Men. They never understand."

He tickles my sides until I forget all about wanting a grand gesture for him to prove his love after he let me leave. Who needs a grand gesture? I got the guy.

Chapter 37

Grand gesture – An elaborate action designed to win the girl and embarrass the boy

PHOENIX

I wake to a warm, naked body sprawled on top of me. I tighten my arms around Gabby and open my eyes to discover she's already awake and studying me.

I run a finger down her back. I can't stop touching her silky-smooth skin. "Like what you see?"

She taps her chin. "Looks aren't everything. I might need a demonstration of capabilities."

I flip us over until I'm looming above her. "You need a demonstration, do you?"

She bites her bottom lip. "Yes, please."

I lick a line from her shoulder to her ear. She groans and tilts her head to give me better access. Hell, yeah. Gabby is anything but shy when she's in our bed.

My alarm goes off and I grunt before laying my forehead against hers. "Time to get up."

Her nose wrinkles. "I thought Soleil was coming to milk the goats this morning."

"I'm certain she's already come and gone since it's 10 a.m."

She gasps. "What? We slept until ten?"

"Yep." I don't remind her it's her fault we slept late since I woke up in the middle of the night to her hand fisting my cock.

"Wait. Why is your alarm going off if Soleil already milked the goats?"

I tap her nose. "Maybe because I have a surprise for you."

She wraps her legs around my waist and rubs herself against my cock. "I think I know what the surprise is, and I approve."

My cock decides to play heat-seeking missile and aims for her wet warmth. I lift up on my elbows before he can complete his mission. We don't have time for sex, no matter how quick we are. Plans have been made. Rehearsals have been done.

I get to my knees before jumping off the bed. "You have thirty minutes to get ready."

"How am I supposed to get ready if I don't know what to wear?"

Lucky for me, her sisters warned me about this question. "Jeans and a sweater are fine."

She sits up in bed. Her tits bounce and I have to fist my hands before I decide to climb back into bed with her. To hell with this grand gesture.

"Are we going to the falls? I've wanted to have a picnic there since I learned someone and his brothers enjoy skinny dipping in the water." She waggles her eyebrows at me.

"It's entirely too cold for skinny dipping."

"We could always have a picnic."

I know what game she's playing, and I know better than to engage. "I'm not revealing the surprise."

She juts her bottom lip out in a pout and bats her eyelashes at me. "You're not?"

I chuckle. "Nope, but nice try."

She pounds her fist against the mattress. "What if I hate surprises?"

I point to the clock. "Every minute you sit there arguing is a minute less you have to get ready."

She squeals and climbs out of bed. "I get the bathroom first," she yells and slams the door behind her.

Forty minutes later she's finally ready and we can leave. "How do I look?" she asks as she twirls around showing off her sweater and jeans – both of which are skintight.

"Like you think it's fun to tease me all day," I say before adjusting myself. "Are you going to be able to bike in those clothes?"

"No problem." She does a squat. "It's stretch."

Her tits bounce as she comes out of her squat. My cock twitches at the view. It's a total sucker for a good pair of breasts. It's going to be a long ass day. I grasp her hand and lead her to the bikes before I'm tempted to throw her over my shoulder and return to bed.

"I hope this 'surprise' isn't some kind of outrageous proposal," she says as she climbs on the bike.

My heart spasms and I freeze with my leg lifted in the air. "You don't want to marry me?"

"Of course, I want to marry you." My heart resumes its regularly scheduled beating program. "But you have a lot – a ton! – of groveling to do first."

I step away from the bike and close in on her until I'm crowding her. "I didn't do enough groveling last night?" The flush on her cheeks stretches down her neck. I know from experience it will travel all the way down her chest to her navel. "When I kissed every single inch of your body."

Her breath hitches and her eyes fall close, and I contemplate skipping her surprise for the millionth time this morning. My phone beeps with a message and I remember I can't skip. Her sisters, my family, and the gossip gals would kill me if we didn't show up.

"You...," she gasps before swallowing and trying again. "You did physical groveling. You haven't done emotional groveling yet."

What the hell is emotional groveling? I check my watch. I don't have time to find out.

We cycle into Winter Falls and prop our bikes against city hall.

"I don't think I'll ever get used to not locking up my bike. Don't get me wrong. I love it, but it feels weird."

I grip her hand and lead her down Main Street toward *Bake Me Happy*. "First stop. Coffee."

"Yeah!" She skips to the entrance and flings the door open.

Rowan is waiting for us with two coffees and some treats. "Here you go."

She sticks her nose in the bag and sniffs. "Yum. Cinnamon."

I'm partial to cinnamon myself. The scent reminds me of the taste of Gabby's skin.

"Next stop. *Fall Into A Good Book*. You can pick out any book in the store."

"Is this a favorite things day?" She bounces on her toes and claps. "What's after the bookstore? Is it lunch at the brewery? Or maybe a tasting of beer at the brewery?"

"Slow your roll. It's supposed to be a surprise." I hand her one of the coffee cups. "Drink your coffee and relax. Enjoy the day for what it is."

As we walk down Main Street toward the bookstore, people begin to gather behind us. Lucky for me, Gabby doesn't notice. She's too busy loving her coffee and treat to pay attention to her surroundings. I need to have a talk with her about situational awareness but not today.

I drop her hand – ostensibly to reach for my treat – but I drop behind her and make my way to the middle of the street instead. Once I'm in place, I nod to Ashlyn who's holding the speaker. She presses play and music blares through the quiet street.

"Eek!" Gabby shrieks and bobbles her coffee and treat in her hand. "What's going on?"

Instead of explaining, I begin to dance to *The Way You Make Me Feel*. I feel like a fool, dancing on Main Street with her friends and family in a flash mob to a Michael Jackson song, but she wanted a grand gesture, so she's getting a grand gesture. She can have whatever her heart desires.

She sets her things on the ground as she claps and dances along with the music. My parents join her, and she smiles up at them. Her smile and happiness make any embarrassment worthwhile.

The gossip gals arrive wearing those hot pink t-shirts they love. This time they say *Gossip Gal Dance Team.* They're also carrying pink and silver pompoms. They shake the pompoms in time to the music as I finish up the choreographed dance with my brothers, Gabby's sisters, and the West family.

The second the music cuts off, Gabby's on the move. She runs at me and throws herself into my arms.

"That was awesome!"

"Grand gesture enough for you?"

"It was perfect! Absolutely perfect. And who knew you could dance? Maybe you should do a private dance for me later." She waggles her eyes.

River groans. "Help! My ears are burning. I don't want to know what my brother and sister-in-law get up to in the bedroom."

Elizabeth hip checks him. "Oh please. You're not an innocent."

He places his hand over his chest. "I'm wounded. How can you think I'm not innocent?"

She snorts. "I have literally witnessed you score a woman in less than five seconds."

"You don't know. Maybe I took her home, tucked her into bed, and then left."

She bursts out laughing. "Do you even know what it means to tuck a woman in bed?"

I carry Gabby away from our bickering siblings. "I have another surprise for you."

"Please be a stripper pole for our bedroom."

I tweak her nose. "What happened to my shy girl?"

"She took a hike when the man she loves swallowed his embarrassment to dance in a flash mob for her."

My lips meet hers, but I keep the kiss brief. The entire town is milling around Main Street. They don't need to witness us making out.

"Grab the envelope in my back pocket."

Gabby reaches around me, but she doesn't grab the envelope. She squeezes and kneads my ass instead. "I can't find it."

"Stop messing around." She pouts, and I bite her bottom lip. "You can have all the time you want to play with my ass later."

"Promise?"

I nod and she takes out the envelope. When she tries to hand it to me, I shake my head. "Open it."

She tears it open and pulls out the sheaf of papers. "What's this?" I don't answer her question as she's already reading what it is. "Tickets to Los Angeles. But you don't like the big city."

"But you do and you want to go to that premiere for your client."

"You remembered."

"Gabby, I remember everything."

"We're going to LA?"

"We're going to LA."

"Yeah. LA or bust!" She waves the papers around in the air. She has the biggest smile on her face. It stretches from ear to ear and her happiness radiates from her. I've never seen anything more beautiful in my life.

I was wrong to ever compare her to Tina, but I learned my lesson. Gabby is incomparable. She's unique and she's all mine.

"And here I thought our meet-cute was a disaster."

I have no idea what she's talking about. "Nothing about you is a disaster. I love you, Gabrielle Grace Dempsey."

Although her last name will be Alston as soon as I can manage it. I'm not letting her get away. I want my ring on my finger, my last name on her driver's license, and her in my bed every night. I won't settle for anything less.

"And I love you, Phoenix Apollo Alston."

Chapter 38

Friend – the other nasty F-word

ELIZABETH

River groans. "Help! My ears are burning. I don't want to know what my brother and sister-in-law get up to in the bedroom."

I hip check him. "Oh please. You're not an innocent."

He places his hand over his chest. "I'm wounded. How can you think I'm not innocent?"

I snort. "I have literally witnessed you score a woman in less than five seconds."

"You don't know. Maybe I took her home, tucked her into bed, and then left."

I burst out laughing. "Do you even know what it means to tuck a woman in bed?"

He grabs my hand and tingles erupt from my fingers through my arm and down my body. Ugh! Why does the mere touch of this player cause my body to go up in flames? Nothing can ever happen, I remind my body.

"Naked Falls Brewing set up a stand outside the brewery this morning. Let's grab some beers."

It's not an unusual request. Since his brother and my sister got together, River and I have become good friends.

"Why do they have a stand set up this morning?" I ask as he leads me down Main Street toward the brewery.

He nods toward *Clove's Coffee Corner* and *Nature Coop*, both of which have stands set up in front of their stores.

"Winter Falls will use any excuse to have a party."

"I can't wait to move here."

He screeches to a halt. "You're moving to Winter Falls?"

Judging by his wrinkled brow, he doesn't think much of the idea. What the hell? Does he not want me living in the same town as him? I thought we were friends.

"What? Am I not good enough for the town?" I tease to hide how his initial response hurt my feelings.

He coughs and smooths out the wrinkles on his forehead. "Of course, you're good enough. Maybe too good. But I thought you enjoyed living in White Bridge?"

I bite my lip as I contemplate how much to reveal to him. Unbeknownst to everyone, I've been in negotiations for a piece of property across the street from *The Inn on Main* where I want to begin my own beauty salon. I have a job as a hairdresser in a salon in White Bridge, but I've always wanted to own my own business.

If I have my own business, I can decorate it however I want, have the kind of extra spa services I want, and I can treat my employees the way they should be treated.

"Never mind." I shrug. "It was only an idea."

He lets the subject drop and now I'm butt hurt. Stupid girl. Thinking you can be friends with a player. I tug on his hand for him to let me go but he holds tight.

He drags me down Main Street past the library, *Eden's Garden,* and *Bertie's Recording Studio* until we're at the brewery. Instead of stopping at the booth in front of the brewery, he pulls me into the alleyway between the recording studio and the brewery.

I look around the alleyway, but it's a simple alley. And it's empty.

"What are we doing here?"

"I need to apologize."

My nose wrinkles. "What for?"

"I hurt your feelings."

"No, you didn't," I immediately deny, because I'm not talking about feelings with the man I have a huge crush on who will never reciprocate said crush.

River is not only a player but as far as I can tell, he doesn't do 'feelings'. He keeps things light and airy. Lucky for him, Winter Falls is a tourist town and enough female tourists throw themselves at him to keep him embedded in his player ways without entangling himself with a local.

He maneuvers me until my back is against the wall and he's looming over me. My heart gallops at his close proximity and my hands itch to touch him.

River is sexy with a capital S. I never thought I'd find a redhead sexy, especially since I'm a redhead, but he works it. The sides of his head are shaved with the hair on the top kept long. It's a hairstyle I've cut a gazillion times for hipsters back in Saint Louis.

But River is anything but a hipster. He doesn't follow the latest trend and he certainly doesn't give a shit about fashion. He does his own thing. It's entirely too appealing to me.

"Bessie." River is the only person in the world I let get away with calling me Bessie. Bessie is the name of a horse or a woman from the eighteenth century. Usually, I hate the nickname. But coming from River's lips, I don't seem to mind it.

When I don't respond to his plea, he frames my face with his hands. "Tell me what I did wrong."

The feel of his hands on my face is not helping me to hide my crush from him. Not when I want to close my eyes and lean into his caress.

"You didn't do anything wrong," I argue.

"I don't want you mad at me. You're one of my best friends."

I flinch at the word friend. Friend is all I'll ever be to River. I've made my peace with it. Kind of. Friends is my only choice. I know it sounds as if I'm settling for breadcrumbs, but I'm not settling. I'm being a grown-up and accepting the situation for what it is.

"What's wrong?"

Of course, River didn't miss my flinch. He's standing mere inches from me. He'd be an idiot to miss it and if there's one thing River is not – it's an idiot.

I blow out a sigh and decide on a half-truth. "You don't want me living in Winter Falls." There. I don't sound like a love-sick teenager.

He frowns and glances away. "It's not that."

"I hear a but at the end of your sentence."

He returns his gaze to mine and grins. "I can never fool you, can I, Bessie?"

"I grew up with three sisters and a brother," I say as if the number of siblings I have explains everything. It kind of does when one of your siblings is Cassandra the crazy and another one is Olivia the police magnet.

"I do want you to live here," he claims now.

He's not telling me the entire truth, but I decide to drop my further questions. I don't need to know every deep, dark secret he has. I want to. Oh boy do I want to, but it'll never happen.

I smile up at him. "Your wish may be granted."

"You're not going to tell me more, are you?"

"Nope," I answer making sure to pop the P.

I don't want to jinx things. Plus, I haven't told my family yet. Cassandra would lose her shit if someone knew about my moving before her. And my sister is zero fun when she loses her shit.

River tucks a strand of my hair behind my ear. "You certain you don't want to tell me?"

I shove at his shoulders, but he doesn't budge. "Don't try your seduction tricks with me. I'm immune." I'm also a big, fat liar whose pants will burst into flames any second now.

His gaze dips to my lips and my tongue peeks out to lick my bottom lip without me telling it to. His head dips and I hold my breath. This is the worst idea ever, but the knowledge doesn't stop me from chanting *kiss me, kiss me* in my head anyway. What can I say? The heart wants what the heart wants.

At long last, his lips meet mine. I sigh and his tongue pushes into my mouth. The taste of coffee, mint, and just plain River hits me and I moan. His hands cradle my face as he devours my mouth. And devour is the only word to describe what's happening. And I'm happy to let it. More than happy.

My hands on his shoulders switch from pushing him away to pulling him near. His hard length hits my belly and tingles explode in my stomach before traveling south to my core.

"Well, well, well, what do we have here?"

At Cassandra's question, River tears his mouth from mine. He stares down at me with confusion plain to see in his eyes. Hey, he's the one who kissed me! I didn't assault him.

"I need to… I should …"

He doesn't manage to finish a sentence before rushing off down the alley in the opposite direction of Cassandra.

"I can't wait to hear about this."

I hold up my hand to my sister and follow River down the alley. I'm not chasing after him, but I'm definitely not discussing the kiss with my sister. Not when I have no clue what the kiss meant.

Does River want me? Judging by the bulge in his pants the answer is yes. But does he want me for more than a roll in the hay? I'm not a one-night stand kind of girl.

Shit. This is going to screw with our friendship, isn't it?

D. E. Haggerty
Love and Laughter in Every Chapter

About the Author

D.E. Haggerty is an American who has spent the majority of her adult life abroad. She has lived in Istanbul, various places throughout Germany, and currently finds herself in The Hague. She has been a military policewoman, a lawyer, a B&B owner/operator and now a writer.

www.ingramcontent.com/pod-product-compliance
Lightning Source LLC
Chambersburg PA
CBHW071243300726

48975CB00002B/535